RIP CHORD

ALSO BY JEANNE GLIDEWELL

A Lexie Starr Mystery Series

Leave No Stone Unturned

The Extinguished Guest

Haunted

With This Ring

Just Ducky

Cozy Camping

Marriage and Mayhem

The Spirit of the Season

A Ripple Effect Cozy Mystery Series

A Rip Roaring Good Time

Rip Tide

Ripped To Shreds

Rip Your Heart Out

Ripped Apart

Ripped Off

No Big Rip

The Grim Ripper

Rip Chord

RIP CHORD

A RIPPLE EFFECT COZY MYSTERY
BOOK 9

JEANNE GLIDEWELL

ePublishing Works!
644 Shrewsbury Commons Ave
Ste 249
Shrewsbury PA 17361
United States of America

www.epublishingworks.com
Phone: 866-846-5123

Released: May 2024
ISBN: 978-1-64457-629-8 (Paperback)
ISBN: 978-1-64457-630-4 (Hard Cover)

FROM THE DESK OF JEANNE GLIDEWELL

As always, I appreciate everyone who has chosen to read *Rip Chord*. I hope it sounds like I've been to the area where I've set this story, even though I've never been to northern California. I hope *Rip Chord* evokes fond memories if, unlike me, you've visited the Redwood National Forest and its surrounding area.

Traveling has brought much joy to my life. I've traveled to over seventy countries on six continents and been to every state in America except for North Dakota. Recently, my husband Bob and I visited Ecuador and the Galápagos Islands. As an avid wildlife photographer, I was in hog heaven—the vast variety of wildlife there is unbelievable. Many of the amazing species we saw are found nowhere else on Earth. It's a trip I'd recommend everyone take at least once.

My favorite adventure was our 2013 African safari at Kenya's Masai Mara National Reserve. It brings to mind a favorite quote of mine by St. Augustine. *The world is a book and those who do not travel read only one page.* Get out into the world and read, my friends!

Lexie Starr is mentioned numerous times in this story. If you've yet to read one of my Lexie Starr cozy mysteries, I hope you will check one out soon.

Due to serious health issues, *Rip Chord* will be my final novel. I appreciate you for welcoming one or more of my cozy mysteries onto your reading list and I wish you a long, rewarding life filled with great books!

Farewell and Happy Reading,

Jeanne

Rip Chord is dedicated to Bob, my husband of forty years this August, who is my soul mate and the love of my life. He's always been my rock when I needed someone to lean on and I will forever be his. He never complains when I disappear into my office to write for hours at a time. But he gets nervous when I ask him questions like, "Do you know how much arsenic it'd take to kill a man about your size?" Or, "Do you have any ideas on how to kill someone without leaving behind any evidence?" He claims to sleep with one eye open now. He warned me if he ever died in a suspicious manner, the homicide detectives would scour through my internet cache where I'd researched dozens of potential ways to kill a person. I'd be lucky if I wasn't arrested on the spot. I love you Bob and your wonderful sense of humor. I pray we share many more years of marital bliss together.

ACKNOWLEDGMENTS

I want to thank my editor, Hannah Phillips, for her exceptional editing skills, and my proofreaders: Sarah Goodman, of Olathe, Kansas; Sheila Davis of Fairway, Kansas; and Cindy Travis, of Overland Park, Kansas, for their much-appreciated advice, time and efforts. I am forever indebted to these remarkable ladies.

I also want to thank Brian Paules, Anna Paules, and the rest of the eBook Prep and ePublishing Works team. They have been supportive, patient, professional, and encouraging while allowing me to be me, and for that, I am eternally grateful.

CHARACTER LIST

Rapella Ripple—Rapella is a seventy-two-year-old full-time RVer who has a tendency to find herself knee-deep in murder cases no matter where she and her husband travel.

Clyde "Rip" Ripple—Rip is Rapella's husband of over fifty years. Also a seventy-two-year-old full-time RVer, he gets upset with his wife when her interference in murder cases lands her in life-or-death situations.

Jack and Janet Wright—Jack and Janet are RVers from Kansas whom the Ripples meet in the Mystic River RV Park. Jack buddies up with Rip while Janet becomes Rapella's partner-in-crime-solving.

Charlie Short—Charlie is a forty-year-old baritone singer in the Del Norte County barbershop quartet.

Ferdinand "Fern" Short—Fern is Charlie's forty-year-old wife with whom he shares a nine-year-old son named Jacob. Jacob is about to celebrate his tenth birthday.

Henry Harpodingle—Henry is a thirty-eight-year-old family law attorney who is killed when he falls from a thirteenth-story balcony. He was the tenor in the Del Norte County barbershop quartet before his death.

Stanley "Stan" Ledge—Stan is an extremely thin bass singer in the Del Norte County barbershop quartet.

Marvin "Buster" Boeing—Buster is a hefty lead singer in the Del Norte County barbershop quartet and the owner of a towing company.

Clara Boeing—Clara is Buster's ex-wife, who works as a massage therapist. Their recent divorce was the result of an affair she had gotten involved in.

Moose Crossing—Moose is the handsome owner of the Moose Crossing Winery that's across the road from the Mystic Forest RV Park where the Ripples are camping for much of the spring season.

Devin Tubbs—Devin is a thirty-six-year-old security guard at the Crescent City Wal-Mart.

Wilson Harpodingle—Wilson is Henry's forty-two-year-old brother who sings baritone for the Siskiyou County barbershop quartet.

Amanda Castonova—Amanda is a waitress at the Annie Creek Café in Crater Lake National Forest and a cousin of Henry and Wilson Harpodingle.

Amie Harpodingle—Amie is the mother of the Harpodingle brothers and works as a cashier at the Wal-Mart in Crescent City, California.

ONE

"**B**ringing in the sheaves, bringing in the sheaves.
    We will come rejoicing, bringing in the sheaves."

I listened to my husband, Clyde "Rip" Ripple's beautiful tenor tone as he sang along to the classic gospel hymn. It was mid-March and we were sitting near the back of the sanctuary at the Pacific Light Church in Klamath, California. I was merely mouthing the words because the sound of me singing could make an owl purposely fly headfirst into a bridge abutment. Or so I've been told.

As full-time RVers for the last decade, we'd recently towed our brand-new thirty-six-foot fifth wheel trailer to the West Coast. Visiting the Redwood National Park had been on my bucket list for years. With no other plans in our immediate future, we'd decided to spend much of the spring season in the Mystic Forest RV Park on Highway 101 in Klamath. The peaceful park, surrounded by gorgeous trees, was well-maintained, run by a delightful couple, and just half a mile from the historic Trees of Mystery nature attraction. It seemed the perfect place to spend a couple of months enjoying the added space the longer trailer with three slide-outs provided.

The thirty-foot travel trailer I'd affectionately nicknamed the Chartreuse Caboose that we'd traveled in for nearly a decade had begun to feel cramped and outdated. We'd traded it off for the new, nicely equipped fifth wheel in Denver, Colorado, on our way to California. I'm not good with numbers, but I'm pretty sure that when all was said and done, the Colorado RV dealership had allotted us a grand total of three-hundred-dollars as a trade-in value for the Caboose. Rip had done all the negotiating, however, and I'm convinced he would've paid them that much to take it off our hands. When Rip showed a whiff of resistance to the lowball trade-in value of the Caboose, the sales manager offered to throw in a set of locking lug nuts. I could've ordered the lug nuts from Amazon for less than fifty bucks, but Rip caved in like a bounce house with a huge gash in it and agreed to the offer.

We then bought a new Dodge Ram 3500 truck to tow the new fifth wheel. The two major purchases nearly wiped out our emergency fund and we'd have to cut back for a while until we could build it back up. Fortunately, we had saved most of what we'd received for our house in Rockport when we sold it to become full-time RVers.

Pacific Light, a nearby non-denominational church, had been a good choice and we were both enjoying the sermon and hymns. I was no longer even pretending to be singing. Instead, I soaked in Rip's soothing voice as he sang along with the choir and most of the congregation.

"Sowing in the sunshine, sowing in the shadows
Fearing neither clouds nor winter's chilling breeze
By and by, the harvest and the labor ended

We shall come rejoicing, bringing in the sheaves."

When the final chorus ended, a gentleman sitting in the row in front of us turned around and whispered softly. "Greetings, folks. I'm Charlie Short, and this is my wife, Ferdinand, and our son, Jacob. Welcome to our fold here at Pacific Light."

"We're happy to be here," I responded. Short was an ironic last name for the couple because Charlie was so tall he nearly had to duck to enter the nave and his wife was so petite she was on eye level with her husband's navel. Jacob, who looked to be about ten or eleven, appeared to be of normal height for a kid his age. Fortunately for him, it had all averaged out to his benefit. "It's nice to meet you all. We are Rip and Rapella Ripple."

"It's nice to meet you two, as well," Charlie said. "My wife goes by Fern, by the way. We couldn't help admiring your lovely voice, Rip. The melodious nature of that last stanza you sang was incredible."

"Thank you," Rip said. By his expression, I could tell he wasn't sure what "melodious" meant but knew it was complimentary. "I sang in our church choir growing up and have always loved gospel music."

"I'm not surprised. It seems a little forward of me to ask you, having just met, but will you meet us in the kitchen area when the services conclude? The Bible Study ladies always serve coffee and doughnuts afterward so we can all mingle and mix with the rest of the flock."

Rip looked mystified. He'd undoubtedly heard nothing after the word "doughnuts," and it had little to do with the fact that, as usual, he wasn't wearing his expensive hearing aids. Curious as to why the Shorts wanted to converse further with us, I automatically replied to Charlie, "Of course."

"So you see, with Henry gone, we are in dire need of a fourth member of our group if we are to three-peat our championship in the upcoming Northern California Barbershop Quartet competition. Over a dozen counties will be represented in the contest. Henry Harpodingle was a tenor with a very similar tone as yours," Charlie Short explained before adding, "When he was sober, that is. And with the sudden loss of our tenor, it's going to be nearly impossible to win the competition for a third year in a row."

"When is this competition?" Rip asked, around a mouthful of chocolate long john. Doughnuts were not on the heart-healthy diet the STAT Cardiac Clinic in Rochester, Minnesota, had put him on following his recent coronary stent placement procedure. But I remained silent rather than chastise him in front of the Shorts. Rip had stated on more than one occasion that he'd rather be dead than be forced to give up every single pleasure in his life, so I decided one long john on occasion was not apt to kill him. I thought of the old adage, "death by a thousand cuts." In Rip's case, it would be more of a "death by a thousand pastries" kind of thing.

"The competition will be held on Saturday, May fourteenth, which gives us almost exactly six weeks to prepare. We practice on Tuesday and Thursday evenings from seven to nine here in the church, where the acoustics are ideal. Occasionally, we practice at our house when the church is unavailable."

"Well, I'm not sure if—"

"Listen," Charlie interrupted, sensing Rip's reluctance, "I sing baritone, Buster Boeing sings lead, and Stanley Ledge sings bass. With you singing tenor, Rip, the chords the four of us could create together would be magical. At least come to our practice this Tuesday to check it out before you make your decision. It will be held at our house because the Ladies Club meets at the church that night."

"Well, I don't know—"

"Rip!" This time, I cut him off. As I spoke, I wiped a dusting of powdered sugar off Rip's upper lip. "Why not at least go to one practice before you turn down the opportunity? You love to sing and your lovely voice is one of your greatest attributes. Besides, what have you got to lose?"

"You actually have a lot to gain." As he spoke, Charlie replaced the first doughnut he'd snarfed down in record time with a second one.

"I suppose it couldn't hurt me to give it a shot," Rip consented without asking Charlie to clarify his last remark. Looking at Fern, he added, "Give Rapella your address and I'll be there at seven o'clock Tuesday night."

"Thank you." Charlie appeared to be greatly relieved. It was obvious winning the competition was important to him. "Rapella, why don't you come along with your husband? You can visit with Fern while we practice."

"I might just do that." I was fairly certain I'd accompany Rip but didn't want to make a firm commitment in case something more appealing presented itself in the meantime.

"Please do." Charlie smiled at me and then stuck his right hand out to shake Rip's. "I'm looking forward to harmonizing with you."

"Likewise," Rip replied. "I'm sorry about the loss of your former tenor."

"What happened to Henry Harpodingle?" I wanted to remark about the deceased man's unusual surname. I'd have had it changed to Harper the moment I was of age to legally do so. Instead I asked, "Has he moved or fallen ill?"

"No," Charlie replied as Fern's eyes misted over. "He accidentally fell off a thirteenth-floor balcony last Sunday, March 6th. It was devastating to see such a healthy young man's life end so tragically. Especially so soon after Henry sang a moving solo for the congregation at church the previous Sunday. He sang *I'll Fly Away* by Albert E. Brumley."

"That is such a beautiful song," I said. *But it is an ironic tune to have been the last one Mr. Harpodingle sang,* I could've added.

Rip and I stood in silence as Charlie began to chant in a deep baritone voice.

"I'll fly away, oh, Glory
I'll fly away
When I die, Hallelujah, by and by
I'll fly away."

As Charlie sang, I pictured a young man in his prime flying off of a thirteenth-story balcony and wondered how one could topple over a balcony's railing accidentally. *Is it possible Mr. Harpodingle flung himself off the balcony intentionally?* I thought. *Or, worse yet, could someone else have been anxious for Henry to meet his maker?*

It was never a good omen when my thoughts drifted in that direction. I'd soon find out this time was no exception.

TWO

W hen we arrived Tuesday evening at seven, Fern was in the kitchen with her and Charlie's nine-year-old son, Jacob. Jacob had been assigned the task of bringing four dozen chocolate chip cookies to school the following day to share with his fellow fifth-graders. They'd be celebrating his upcoming tenth birthday on Saturday. As was the custom, the child celebrating a birthday was the one responsible for bringing snacks for his own birthday party.

After greeting us warmly, Rip and I conversed with the rest of the quartet and met Stanley Ledge, who went by Stan, and Marvin Bridges, who was nicknamed Buster. We snacked on pastries Fern had offered before the men left to warm up in the Shorts' living room. I stayed behind to chat with Fern. We made small talk for a few minutes. At one point, Fern turned to place a cookie sheet into her oven while Jacob was busily stirring up more dough. I took the opportunity to leave the kitchen and join the men. I was anxious to see how Rip fit into the singing group.

"What was that horrific sound I just heard?" Charlie Short looked puzzled and slightly alarmed. "It sounded like a cat hung up in a barbwire fence."

Everyone in the room fell silent, looking around as if to locate the source of the irritating noise. I did the same, even though I had a sneaking suspicion from where it had originated. Rip caught my eye just then. His eyebrows were arched.

"Rapella, honey," he began, "you weren't just singing along with the four of us, were you?"

Embarrassed, my eyes focused on my shoestrings as I replied. "Yeah, well, maybe just a little."

"Why don't you go into the kitchen and help Fern and Jacob with the cookies he needs to take to school tomorrow for his birthday party? I'm sure you'd enjoy that more than listening to us practice."

"Yes, I think I'll do that." I was grateful Rip was trying to keep the situation from being even more humiliating for me. A "cat hung up in a barbwire fence" was hardly a flattering analogy of my singing prowess, but I've heard squalling cats more in tune than I could ever hope to be. I was born with a few admirable talents. Singing wasn't one of them.

I'd been reluctant to butt into the mother/son bonding moment taking place in the kitchen, but I now felt as out of place in the living room as Sam Walton would've felt in a Target Store. Having been banished from the living room, I joined the pair in the kitchen. They seemed pleased to have me join them and I greatly enjoyed the playful bantering the two exchanged. Jacob had an engaging personality and Fern encouraged him to express himself. Their repartee kept me laughing throughout the next two hours. At one point, I decided to ask Fern about the death of Henry Harpodingle. I wondered if she found Henry's cause of death as curious as I did.

"Were you close with Mr. Harpodingle, Fern?" I asked. "His

death must have been a real shock to all of you, not to mention to
his family."

"Yes, it came as quite a shock to all of us. Henry was only
thirty-eight, two years younger than my husband and me. Henry
was single and had no children, which was sad to Charlie and me
as we were childhood sweethearts."

"Oh, my! What a shame." Fern looked puzzled by my
response, so I felt compelled to explain. "And by that, I mean
Henry's death, not the fact you and Charlie were childhood sweethearts. Rip and I were too, only thirty-some-odd years earlier than
you and Charlie."

"It's inspiring how you and Rip have managed to keep your
marriage so strong for over fifty years," Fern said. "Sometimes I
fear Charlie and I…"

Fern looked up to see Jacob eyeing her with interest and
clammed up instantly. I sensed she was about to admit to something she didn't want her son to hear. I quickly reverted back to the
subject of Henry's death to spare her any discomfort. "Thirty-eight
is way too young to die. What was Henry like?"

Fern flashed me a grateful smile. "He was a kind man and well-
liked. He was of average weight and height and had brown hair
and brown eyes."

"He sounds very unremarkable," I said, even though she'd told
me little about what he was like as a person and more about his
physical attributes than I needed to know.

"Yes. If you look up the word 'unremarkable,' there should be a
photo of Henry. But that only accurately describes his looks.
Personality-wise, there was nothing unremarkable or average about
him."

"Interesting," I replied. "Did Henry have an extended family?
Parents? Siblings?"

"He's never been married but was engaged for a while. His
mother is still alive and he has an older brother named Wilson who

looks as if he could've been Henry's twin. Wilson lives in Somes Bar."

"Somes Bar? What an unusual name for a town."

"It's an unincorporated community on the Salmon River with maybe two hundred residents," Fern explained. "Ironically, Wilson is on the Siskiyou County barbershop quartet. He sings baritone, whereas Henry was a tenor. Both brothers are lawyers, as well. Or, at least, Henry *was* a lawyer, prior to his death."

"The brothers are lawyers and yet neither one of them thought to have their last name changed to something less . . ." I paused as I tried to conjure up the word I was looking for.

"Yucky?"

"I guess that describes it as good as any word."

"I think it had something to do with honoring their father. Some men might not be wild about having Short as their surname, but I know Charlie would be hurt if Jacob were to legally change his last name when he turned eighteen."

"I suppose you're right. What kind of law did the brothers practice?"

"Henry practiced family law, mostly divorces, and Wilson is a personal injury lawyer, or ambulance chaser, as I call him. He's the type who'll encourage you to sue your mother for everything she's got if you stupidly drop a banana peel on her kitchen floor and then slip on it and break your little toe."

"Oh, my goodness! Did he actually sue his own mother after breaking a little toe in her house?"

Fern laughed. "I was being facetious. But I'll bet his mom has never kept bananas in her house. The similarities between the Harpodinger brothers end there. Personality-wise, the brothers were as polar opposite as they could be. Henry was a player who'd look more at home throwing cocktails together behind a bar than he would presenting a case in front of a jury. I doubt he would've ever settled down with a wife and family. Wilson, on the other hand, is a no-nonsense type of guy. He has a fiancée, but the future of that union remains to be seen."

"Do you know if Henry and Wilson got along?"

"Got along?" Fern's eyebrows arched so much they resembled a drawbridge. "Ha! Not hardly. I heard it was all their parents could do to keep them from killing each other when they were younger."

Maybe they couldn't *keep one of them from killing the other*, I thought. "That's too bad. My four brothers were my best, and only, friends growing up. I was very much a tomboy. I did have a female friend named Marla, but after she got head lice for the third time, my mom wouldn't let me hang around with her any longer. Ma said with five kids to raise, and enough chores that needed done to choke a horse, she didn't have time to be scrubbing my head with lye soap."

"I was shocked when Wilson asked Henry to be his best man and then was surprised again when Henry arranged such an elaborate bachelor's party for his brother." Fern continued as though she hadn't even heard my head lice story. She was in a zone now, so I let her go on. "And now the wedding's been put off indefinitely. I'm beginning to think it'll never happen because Wilson has suddenly developed cold feet. It's a shame, because I really like his fiancée."

"It may still work out." I was more intrigued by Henry's death than Wilson's bachelor's party. "The thing that stymies me is how in the world could Henry accidentally fall off a thirteen-story balcony? Did the railing give way? Or was it just not high enough? It seems very uncanny."

"To be honest, Rapella, it seems extremely odd to me too." Fern had whispered her remark, making me wonder if she didn't want Jacob to hear her. I decided to whisper back just in case that was her concern.

"Did the authorities look into his death as a possible suicide, or worse yet, a murder?"

"Not enough, in my opinion." Fern looked around. I noticed

her glance into the living room through the open door. I realized then that it might be Charlie, rather than Jacob, who she didn't want to overhear her remarks. "But I can't say anything because Charlie gets upset if I even mention the possibility it wasn't merely an unfortunate mishap. He just can't stomach the notion anyone would intentionally kill his best friend."

"Charlie and Henry were best friends, huh?" I mused. "No wonder he doesn't want to even think about the possibility of murder or suicide. I'm so sorry such a tragedy happened to someone so dear to your family. I can only imagine how tough this has been for all of you."

"Well, once again, to be honest, I wasn't as fond of Henry as Charlie was." Fern glanced at the clock above the kitchen sink and donned an oven mitt. She pulled the tray of smoldering cookies out of the oven and placed it on a hot pad in front of Jacob. "Give them a few minutes to cool, son, before you remove them from the tray."

"Yes, ma'am." I was caught off guard when Jacob replied as if he was responding to the Mother Superior at a Catholic school. But then, he followed it up with, "How stupid do you think I am? My mama didn't raise no fool, you know."

We all laughed as Jacob pretended to grasp the cookie sheet at both ends along with donning a facial expression of pure agony.

Fern picked the spatula up off the table and smacked her son on the head with it. With a forced admonishing tone, she scolded Jacob. "Don't be cheeky, you little wisecracker! You hear me?"

"Yes, ma'am," Jacob repeated as we all chuckled again at his antics.

After we'd stopped laughing, she looked at her son and said, "Jacob, why don't you go work on that math assignment that's due tomorrow while Rapella and I finish up the cookies?"

Jacob nodded in agreement. He walked over to Fern and kissed her cheek. Before exiting the kitchen to attend to his homework, he turned to me and said, "It was nice to meet you, Mrs. Ripple."

What a delightful boy, I thought. It was obvious Fern and Charlie had raised him well. I admired the mother/son relationship that Fern and Jacob shared. It was clear the love between them was intense and unconditional. My daughter Regina and I had shared a similar rapport when she was about Jacob's age. Regina had grown a bit more distant as she'd aged, but we were still very close. She was a daddy's girl. I didn't even try to compete with Rip for Regina's affection.

I watched as Fern spooned another dozen dollops on a fresh cookie sheet. I was afraid she'd gotten distracted and wouldn't finish her commentary about her apparent dislike for her husband's unlucky best friend. So I prompted her with a fabrication.

"Going back to your previous comments, I never cared much for Rip's best friend either. He was just kind of a dick, if you know what I mean. He was pompous and overbearing, and worse yet, his word was worth about as much as a hairbrush to an eel."

Fern looked at me in puzzlement. I guess she'd never thought about an eel's lack of need for a hairbrush. *Unlike me*, I thought, *her mind must not wonder in wonky directions when she gets bored.*

Finally, she responded. "It really wasn't like that. Henry was a decent enough guy, but I felt like he had a bad influence on Charlie. Charlie was always hoping Henry would find a soul mate so the four of us could attend more couple-appropriate events together. Most of his relationships were short-lived flings, but Henry *was* engaged for a short while. Charlie was actually relieved when their engagement fell through. He never really liked Henry's fiancée. Charlie thought she was more interested in living the good life as a well-to-do lawyer's wife than she was in Henry himself. I didn't trust her either."

"That's too bad. Unfortunately, there are women out there with agendas that have nothing to do with love," I said in agreement. "I can see why you had issues with Henry's fiancée, but why did you feel Henry was a bad influence on Charlie?"

"He just had a tendency to monopolize too much of Charlie's time. He was needy in that way. He acted as though Charlie was single too. He'd drag my husband to strip clubs, bars, bachelor parties, and things like that, which I didn't appreciate. Charlie wasn't thrilled about it, but he didn't want to hurt his friend's feelings, he'd say. So he'd go along with it for Henry's sake."

Sure, I thought. *I'm sure Charlie hated every minute he was forced to sit in strip clubs watching nude women twirl tassels attached to their nipples with pasties. I wonder how many of Charlie's dollar bills disappeared into their garter belts while he was ruing the fact he had to be there. Against his will, of course.*

I couldn't say something like that out loud though, so instead, I said, "I can understand how hard that was for both you and Charlie. At least, you'll probably be seeing a lot more of your husband now that Henry's gone."

"Yeah." She leaned over then to whisper in my ear. This time, it was very apparent she didn't want Charlie to hear because I could barely make out her words. "I'm not sure if that's a good thing or not."

On our way back to Mystic Forest RV Park, I reiterated some of my conversation with Fern to Rip. I was particularly mystified by Fern's implication that spending more time with Charlie now that his time-monopolizing friend, Henry Harpodingle, was deceased, might not be such a good thing. I hadn't promised to keep the exchange confidential. That would've been similar to telling a hungry Rottweiler he was not to mess with the raw T-bone on the kitchen counter.

"I know that sounds foreign to you and me," Rip responded.

"But there are marriages that can become toxic when there is too much togetherness between the pair. What begins as a close connection gradually morphs into an all-encompassing possessiveness that ends up with one or the other partner trying to control everything about the marriage. A few examples are how the finances are handled, how the kids are raised, where they live and work, down to even simple decisions like what television shows they watch. The transformation is often so gradual that neither partner even realizes it's happening until one of them is completely dominated by the other. I witnessed that phenomenon multiple times throughout my career."

Rip had been a lifelong law enforcement officer; first as a beat cop, and finally as the sheriff of Aransas County, Texas, during the final decade of his career. I wanted to tease Rip by reminding him I hadn't been allowed to touch the TV's remote control since before I'd promised to love him until death did us part. There have been a couple of instances where I'd have liked to kill him just to get out from under that often very challenging clause in our marriage vows. But instead of potentially stirring up a nest of fire ants, I continued to listen to him speak.

"Do you remember Abe and Stella Morrison?" He asked.

"Of course. They lived across the street from us in Rockport." Rockport, a small Texas community on the Gulf Coast, was our hometown. We had lived there our entire lives until about fourteen years ago. At that point, Rip had retired and we'd sold our home and nearly everything we owned. We then bought the Chartreuse Caboose and hit the road as full-time RVers. We'd never looked back nor ever regretted our decision. We were, however, greatly enjoying the new, fancier fifth wheel we'd traded the Caboose in on. "What about Abe and Stella?"

"One night, about a year before I retired, Officer Randle and I responded to a domestic dispute call at their house. Stella had verbally threatened to kill Abe with a smoldering fireplace poker

29

unless he changed the channel from an old western movie he'd been watching to the season finale of *The Bachelorette*."

Oh, yeah, I thought. *Been there, done that. Same addictive television series, no less.* I remembered that night well. It was August 1, 2011. That evening, I couldn't get Rip to turn the television off the MLB game between the Cleveland Indians and the Boston Red Sox. The game aired at exactly the same time as the season finale of *The Bachelorette*. I was so angry. I threatened to strangle Rip with the electrical cord of my curling iron. But, unlike Stella, apparently, I didn't threaten to kill him out loud. Rather than resort to violence, I'd decided to tell Rip I needed to go visit a sick friend of mine, who lived about two blocks away from us. I'd spent the next couple of hours at Sharon's house, watching who Ashley would bestow her final rose upon: J.P., the construction manager from New York, or Ben, the winemaker from California. The only violence that evening occurred when Sharon, a devoted wine connoisseur, smashed her wine glass into her brick fireplace in discontent. She'd been praying Ashley would choose Ben. But, alas, she chose J.P., and the last I heard the pair had divorced in 2020 after two children and eight years of marriage. Ben, on the other hand, is still single and writing children's books. *Did he never get over Ashley?* I have to wonder.

I decided not to go down a rabbit hole and mention the night Rip barely survived without ever knowing he was in the slightest bit of danger. Instead I asked him what he thought about singing with the barbershop quartet now that he'd practiced with them.

"It was actually very enjoyable," he replied. "Do you mind if I join the group, just until after the upcoming competition has been completed?"

"No, I don't mind. I think it'd be a lot of fun for both of us."

"Good. I didn't realize how much I'd missed singing until tonight." Rip flipped on his blinker to turn into the campground, which was only a few miles from the Shorts' house. "Charlie, Stan, and Buster all seem like good guys. We didn't spend a lot of time chatting about personal things, though. These guys are dead serious about winning the singing contest. They are determined to be the champions for the third year in a row."

"Did they seem satisfied with what you brought to the table?"

"I think so," Rip said. "At least they all appeared to be very anxious to have me join their team. Stan, who's a CPA at a local accounting firm, told me I was exactly the fourth wheel the quartet needed to have a legitimate shot at rolling smoothly on to a 'three-peat,' as he called it."

"What a nice thing for Stan to say. I have to agree with him. The four of you harmonized beautifully together, at least when I wasn't chirping along with you." I laughed at my admission of being a dreadful singer.

"Chirping?" Rip asked with a snort.

"Okay," I said, backhanding him on his shoulder with my left hand as he pulled the new Dodge truck into our campsite. "Squealing, then. 'Like a cat hung up in a barbwire fence,' I believe Charlie described it."

Rip reached over and clasped the hand I'd just swatted him with, and said, "You may not be Whitney Houston or Celine Dion, but you are the entire world to me."

"As you are to me too, sweetheart. I love you, Rip."

"I love you more," he habitually responded. He laughed and added, "Now get inside and whip me up something to snack on. I'm so hungry I could eat a handful of Dolly's tuna-flavored dental treats."

"You do know you'd first have to pry them out of her cold, dead paws, don't you?" I asked with a laugh. "She'd never give them up willingly while she was still breathing. Not even for you, her favorite servant."

"Yeah, I guess you're right," Rip conceded. "Maybe it'd be easier to just settle for a bowl of popcorn."

"I have a better idea. Fern sent me home with a bag of chocolate chip cookies since they ended up making way more than Jacob needs to take to school tomorrow." I held up the paper bag and shook it as I climbed up the stairs of the fifth wheel. "I believe there are a dozen of them in here, and they're still warm."

"Perfect!" Rip sounded delighted. "So what are you gonna eat?"

THREE

"Rapella," Rip said quietly as I sat up in bed the next morning. "You're going to have to come look at something."

Curious about what Rip could possibly want me to jump out of bed to see had me quickly getting to my feet and donning my robe. I followed Rip to the living room.

"Oh, my!" I exclaimed. "What could possibly have pissed off Her Majesty this much?"

Dolly, our tubby grey and white tabby, was sitting in the middle of the end table next to the sofa with her back to us. Her spine was as straight and rigid as a pool cue and she refused to turn her head to look at us. This was always a sure sign she was extremely displeased with her two servants.

"I don't know," Rip admitted. "I thought she'd finally gotten over us trading in the Caboose."

"I thought she had too."

Like most felines, Dolly did not handle change well. It had quickly become apparent exchanging the older model travel trailer for a brand new, larger fifth wheel was a personal affront to her.

She'd neither been consulted, nor given a heads up, and that was an unforgivable offense on our part. Instead, she'd been unceremoniously snatched up from her cozy napping place above the Caboose's sofa and dumped into the middle of the fancy new rig with no pomp and circumstances whatsoever. Gone were all three of her favorite napping spots, the recliner she shared with her papa, and her private privy. Replacing all that was a shiny vinyl floor that irritated Dolly purely by its cleanliness and shiny patina.

She was obviously opposed to using the litter box in full view of Rip and me because she had waited to do her business until we were both outside the new rig ever since we'd bought it. The personal privy had been Rip's clever idea and he planned to do the same thing with the new RV. He'd cut a square hole in the floor behind the recliner, trimmed the opening nicely, and installed a ramp down into one of the storage areas in the trailer's undercarriage. Even though it's said cats can see in the dark, Rip had put a motion-sensing light in Dolly's latrine so she "wouldn't have to squint." As you can tell, Dolly was one pampered pussy. Rip treated her like visiting royalty. The basement bathroom was beneficial to us, as well. We only had to open the storage compartment from outside to clean out the litter box, which kept it out of sight and out of mind. More importantly, it didn't stink up our living quarters.

Just then, Dolly turned around and glared at the two of us. She marched over to the plastic placemat where her food and water bowls were usually located. Regina had given us the placemat with a photo of Dolly on it for Christmas. She'd said she'd ordered the cute gift from a printing company called *Shutterfly*. Rip and I had received matching placements so we could admire our fur baby while we ate, which is just one of the many things Her Majesty expects of us.

"Aha!" Rip said as he turned to me. "It's your fault she's ticked off. Her food and water bowls are not where they're supposed to be."

I laughed at our persnickety kitty's disgusted expression. Before going to bed the previous night, I'd placed both bowls into the sink. I'd planned to wash them before filling them with Dolly's breakfast this morning. Rip and I had both overslept. When Dolly found no sign of breakfast or even her bowls at her official feeding time of seven o'clock, she was madder than a rabid raccoon. Clearly, that kind of oversight would not be tolerated.

"I'm so sorry, Your Majesty," I pleaded with our indignant pet. "Will you forgive me if I promise never to do it again?"

I locked eyes with Dolly, who did not appear to be in a forgiving mood.

"It's gonna take more than an apology," Rip informed me.

"Dolly, how about if I give you half a can of tuna fish straight out of the *Chicken of the Sea* can?"

The tuna did the trick. After filling her belly, Dolly settled down into her new favorite napping place and began to purr loudly. Rip and I indulged in a rare treat, as well. We enjoyed a breakfast of bacon, egg, and cheese omelets. We then got dressed and left the campground for a day of sightseeing. I'd wanted to visit the Redwood National Forest since my daddy had told me about it when I was a child. Seeing the mammoth sequoia trees with my own eyes would be a dream come true. It promised to be a fun day for us as tourists.

We were headed up US-97 North on our way from Klamath Falls to Crater Lake National Park in southern Oregon, about a forty-five minute drive. Crater Lake is the deepest lake in the United States and we wanted to drive the thirty-three-mile scenic loop around it called Rim Drive. It would be the first thing on our busy day's schedule.

"Rip?" I asked.

"Yes, dear."

"Did Charlie happen to mention anything at practice last night about Henry Harpodingle's death? Fern told me Henry was Charlie's best friend."

"Really?" Rip looked surprised. "You wouldn't have known they were best buds by the way Charlie spoke about him."

"Why? What'd Charlie say?"

"He said Henry was a loose cannon and he wasn't a bit surprised when he heard about his death. He was impulsive and reckless, Charlie said. He thought it'd only been a matter of time before something tragic occurred to Henry."

"So," I began, "did it seem to you as though Charlie was convinced his friend's death was an accident?"

"That was the impression I got. He said Henry had a tendency to drink too much and too often. He thinks his friend fell off the balcony in a drunken stupor."

"That's not easy to do, even if the individual is totally tanked. It may even be more difficult to do if a person's intoxicated. The balcony surely had a substantial railing around it. Did the railing give way or something?"

"Charlie didn't say, but I'd assume it stayed intact. Apparently, there were several college-aged kids walking along the road in front of the fourteen-story five-star hotel. They spotted what looked like a mannequin from the lobby falling from a higher-up floor of the building. Henry's body hit the pavement no more than fifty feet from them. They all immediately looked up and saw nothing or no one on any of the balconies facing them. But they did say Henry didn't holler, scream, or even flail about as he fell. 'It was if he had intentionally leaped from the balcony and was resolved to his fate,' one of the boys told the policemen who'd responded to the scene."

"That's interesting," I said. "You'd think the eyewitness accounts would've convinced the detectives he'd likely taken his own life. What did the witnesses do after Henry's body hit the ground?"

"As you'd expect, they raced to where he lay, hoping to be able to save him, but instantly realized Henry was beyond help. One of the threesome checked for a pulse and found none while another one called 9-1-1. The police were immediately dispatched. According to Charlie, Henry's blood alcohol level was several times the legal limit and no sign of foul play was evident. They interviewed the hotel manager and a number of hotel guests, both on his floor and on the floors above and below him. None of them heard or witnessed anything, but several said he was acting very oddly just prior to his death."

Rip's last comment got my attention. "Did any of those guests describe his behavior?"

"To the detectives, yes, but Charlie didn't know any of the details."

"Hmm," I mused. "I just find the entire incident curious. Don't you?"

"Yes, I do," Rip admitted. He studied my face for a moment before speaking again. "But, to be clear, I have no intention or desire to get involved in the man's death, and I hope you don't either. I just want to enjoy our time here on the West Coast and also my involvement in the barbershop quartet."

"Yes, of course. So do I."

Rip looked skeptical at my response. But I was being totally truthful. I didn't particularly want to get involved in the death of a complete stranger. I'd ended up in too many life-or-death situations to even consider getting involved in yet another case. I was looking forward to some rest and relaxation and was anxious to see the beautiful sights this part of the country had to offer. "After Crater Lake, should we take in Redwood National Park?"

"Absolutely, my dear. As per usual, I'll just go wherever I'm told."

We had a wonderful day of sightseeing. It began with a two-and-a-half-hour drive to Crater Lake National Park in southern Oregon. It is the fifth oldest national park in the country and the only one in Oregon. The caldera of Crater Lake is a remnant of a destroyed volcano called Mount Mazama that collapsed into itself around 5700 BC.

We hadn't anticipated how much snow would still cover the lake. The woman at the entrance informed us that only Rim Drive was open to drive that day, and it was only drivable due to a milder-than-normal winter season. Traveling Rim Drive, which is a thirty-three-mile loop around the rim of the caldera, was slow-going but beautiful. We stopped at several scenic viewpoints: Discovery Point, Sinnott Memorial, and Watchman Overlooks. We then marveled at the Pinnacles, which were spires that consisted of ash and pumice that had slowly melded together from many years of hot gas that had moved to the surface.

We stopped for a bowl of delicious chili at Annie Creek Café and Gift Shop before heading back to Klamath. I ordered water with two lemon wedges and Rip ordered unsweetened ice tea, unadorned. The kind waitress, named Amanda Castonova, who'd recommended the chili, brought us our meal and was very talkative. She was lamenting the fact it had been an extremely slow day at the eatery. "On days like today, I get so bored I want to slice my wrists open with one of the knives we give customers who order the eight-ounce rib eye. I have to remind myself that one of these days, I'm going to quit working and build my dream home overlooking Mad River."

"*Mad* River?" I asked.

"Yes, that's its real name," she replied. "And I'm just *mad* for it. It's absolutely gorgeous and one of the best steelhead trout rivers in the country. There's lots of king and Coho salmon caught in the river, too. I've been fishing on Mad River ever since I was knee-high to a Coors can. My daddy took me out fishing with him when I was about five and I've been 'hooked' ever since."

"I love your play on words. Was it your daddy who told you that you were knee-high to a Coors can?" I asked.

Amanda smiled wistfully. "Yes. Daddy drank a case of beer every day. I think that's who my cousin got it from."

Rather than comment on her alcoholic relatives, I said, "The word 'grasshopper' is usually used with that analogy, but I remember my dad telling me I was knee-high to a shotgun shell."

"Did he shoot a gun a lot?" Amanda asked.

"No, but he threatened to about once a day." It crossed my mind that I was hardly the person to tell someone how an actual analogy should be spoken. I screwed up analogies on a regular basis, and normally just made up my own. "He threatened to use it twice as much when I started dating Rip."

"Oh, my daddy threatened people with a gun a lot too." Amanda went on to elaborate. "The last time, he actually did shoot it. The county sheriff sustained a gunshot wound to the abdomen and Daddy got twenty years in the pen for attempted murder. He ain't touched a gun since. Or a beer, either, since he was drunk when he shot the sheriff."

We assumed Amanda was being serious even though she was laughing. We chuckled along with her and continued to chat even though our chili was growing cold. As an avid but not very successful fisherman, Rip replied, "You're speaking my language now, dear. I love to fish. Now I, too, want to build a dream home on the Mad River. Do you really believe you'll one day be able to build that dream home?"

"On a waitress's salary" was the unspoken end of that question by Rip. But Amanda was not discouraged. I thought her optimistic outlook was inspiring when she replied, "Where there's a will, there's a way. I put twenty percent of every paycheck in a savings account and am gradually building up quite a respectable nest egg."

"Good for you. It's nice to have goals and to work at reaching them one day," Rip said. "My dream was to find the love of my life, have a family, and spend the rest of my days in marital bliss. And look at me now!"

Rip's sentiment was so lovingly expressed that both Amanda's and my eyes misted over.

"Thank you, honey," I replied. "I love you more!"

"Ahh, you two lovebirds are so sweet." Amanda gushed. "I hope I find a true love like yours one day."

"Be patient and you will find your soul mate, sweetheart," I assured her. "I guarantee it will be worth the wait."

"How old were you when you got married?" Amanda asked.

"Eighteen." I could feel my face flush at my admission.

"What part of 'patience' didn't I understand?" Amanda snorted in amusement. Not too many women can carry off a snort as adorably as she could.

"I was pregnant. We had plenty of patience. It was my daddy and his deer-hunting rifle that had none."

We all laughed, and Rip said, "Being threatened at gunpoint to marry someone's daughter was terrifying at the time, but it didn't take long for me to realize it was the best thing that ever happened to me. In the years that followed, Rapella's daddy and I became close."

"They had so much fun together I often felt like a third wheel," I added.

"That's awesome." Amanda smiled at both of us as I leaned over and kissed Rip on the cheek. The waitress looked around to make sure no one needed any service and then continued to chat with us. The subject of Rip joining a barbershop quartet came up when Amanda said she was looking forward to choir practice that evening. She told us singing ran in her family and she sang soprano in her church choir.

When I mentioned that Rip had been asked to join the quartet after their former tenor was killed in a fatal fall from a fancy hotel balcony, Amanda paled dramatically. She was nearly as white as the dusting of snow that covered the large propane tank right outside our window.

"Are you all right, dear?" I asked.

"Not really," Amanda replied. "Henry was my cousin. He's the guy I said probably inherited his alcoholism from my daddy."

"Are you kidding?" I didn't mean to indicate I thought the waitress would joke about a man's tragic death, but she took me literally.

"No, of course not!"

"I'm sorry," I said. "I was only shocked to hear you knew Henry Harpodingle. It's such an incredible coincidence. What a tremendously small world we live in."

"Yes, it truly is." Amanda stopped to wipe a tear off her cheek. "Henry was my Aunt Amie's youngest son. Henry's brother, Wilson, was her oldest, and he lives in Somes Bar, California. Aunt Amie is my mother's youngest sister and lives in a town called Crescent City."

"Oh, yes," Rip chimed in. "We're staying in a campground in Klamath, California, and I recall passing through Crescent City on Highway 101 on our way here this morning."

"Crescent City is in the same county of Del Norte as Klamath. Aunt Amie's been trying to get the county sheriff to further investigate Henry's death. Neither she nor I believe Henry fell or jumped off the balcony of the hotel room he was staying in. Yes, he had a tendency to drink too much and party too hard on occasion, but he was hardly suicidal. And he never got so smashed he'd climb over the railing and accidentally fall off his balcony."

"Just out of curiosity, what is your aunt's last name?" Rip shot me a look after I asked the waitress the question. I deciphered that look as a warning that we were **not** getting involved in Amanda's cousin's death, no matter what transpired in the future that might persuade us to intervene. I brushed the unspoken caveat off as if it was a fly that had landed on the rim of my chili bowl.

"Her name is Amie. Amie Harpodingle, of course. She lives right by the Wal-Mart on East Washington Boulevard in Crescent City and works as a cashier there. It's the nearest Wal-Mart to your location in Klamath."

"If she works at the closest Wal-Mart to us, I can almost guarantee you we will run into her there someday." My response was met with a repeat of the admonishing look Rip had just given me a few seconds earlier. "We make a weekly pilgrimage to Wal-Mart whether we need anything there or not."

"You can't miss her if you're there. She's thin, an inch or so taller than you, Rapella, at about five-feet-ten. She has the prettiest green eyes you've ever seen and usually wears a cap on her head. She's been working in the self-checkout area the last few months. She once told me that it seems to her that some people steal more items than they pay for when they are ringing up their own purchases. She questioned a nun, dressed in a full habit, whose four reusable bags worth of products added up to four dollars and thirty cents. The item on top of one of the bags was a five-pound roast."

"Oh. My. God," I said in shock. "What did the nun say when she was questioned?"

"She said, 'The Lord giveth and the Lord taketh away.'"

I chuckled for a moment and asked, "What happened afterward?"

"It turns out that police officers have the same power as the

Lord. They giveth the nun her Miranda rights and taketh her away in their squad car." Now we were all laughing heartily.

"It sounds as if the nun got what she had coming to her," I said. "Having vowed to live a life of poverty, chastity, and obedience does not give her the right to shoplift groceries. But I have mixed emotions about self-checkout stands. For one, I hate the idea that they are encouraging people to be thieves if what your Aunt Amie said is accurate. I also think they can be handy if you are in a hurry, but they can also be a scourge on society by taking jobs away from people. Before long, human beings will be obsolete and robots will run the world. That's why I rarely choose the self-checkout option."

"Oh, geez. I hope robots don't take over the world," she replied with a grim expression. She wisely looked directly at Rip when she asked, "How could a robot be nearly as charming of a waitress as I am?"

"That would be impossible. I don't even know another human who could be as charming as you are, much less a robot," Rip explained to the waitress, clearly amused by her question. I knew his response was going to cost us in the form of a whopping big tip. "Pay no attention to my wife's bleak predictions, dear. She's a glass totally empty type of person. If you're not careful, her uncheerfulness can become downright infectious."

Amanda laughed and asked, "Uncheerfulness? Is that even a word?"

I shook my head. "No, it's not. I'm sorry to sound like a Debbie Downer. I'm usually more optimistic than that. It's just that the state of the world right now has me feeling more anxious than usual."

Amanda laughed again. "No worries. I understand completely. Uncheerfulness or not, I really like you both. I work the breakfast and lunch shifts, Wednesdays through Sundays, and if you two get a chance, come back in one day soon and try the pulled brisket basket. The brisket in the sandwich is so tender it melts in your mouth. Fun fact: Annie Creek's French fries were recently voted the best French fries in Klamath County and once hit the top ten list in all of Oregon."

"That's amazing. Congratulations!" Afraid my *uncheerfulness* would shine like a beacon in the night, I didn't want to tell Amanda that, like doughnuts, French fries were no longer on Rip's heart-healthy diet. "We will make a point to come back and try them, sweetie."

"Most definitely," Rip added. I could tell he already had visions of greasy French fries dancing in his head. I didn't want to burst his artery-clogging bubble by telling him a nice side salad would be substituted for the fries if he ordered the brisket sandwich. I'd save that to ruin his mood on that "one day soon" when we returned to the café.

"Great! I'll hold you to it," Amanda said. "And look for Aunt Amie the next time you're at Wal-Mart."

"We will. And we'll make sure to say hello to her if we see her. I'll tell her what a charming waitress you are and how much we enjoyed chatting with you." I made a concerted effort not to look at Rip as I added, "We will keep your family in our prayers. I sincerely hope you can get the Del Norte County Sheriff's Department to delve further into your cousin's death. Henry deserves justice if his death was a result of foul play, and his family deserves closure. Closure will only come with the undeniable proof his death was accidental and not at the hands of someone else."

Amanda nodded before adding, "Or the cops apprehend his killer. I think I'd prefer to think his death was accidental. It would eat me up to know his life was intentionally taken from him."

"I'd feel the same way, sweetie," I said.

Amanda left with tears in her eyes to wait on a family of four who'd just entered the cozy café and we finished up our meal before paying our tab and adding an exorbitant tip. We then returned to our bright red, fancy new truck to head back to the Mystic Forest RV Park. The drive around Crater Lake had taken more time than we'd anticipated. We decided to leave the giant sequoias in Calaveras Big Trees State Park for another day. We vowed to see for ourselves how tender the brisket was that same day.

It had begun to rain while we were inside the café. On the way home, Rip reminded me in no uncertain terms that no matter how much we liked Amanda, we were not getting involved in Mr. Harpodingle's death, come hell or high water.

Ironically, it turned out to be high water that turned the tide and landed me smack dab in the middle of the man's murder case. As was his wish, Rip would remain removed from the case and oblivious to my involvement in it.

FOUR

"I was afraid of that," Rip said as he eased down on the brakes and pulled the truck off the road. One hundred yards back, we'd passed a sign that read, "Low water bridge ahead. Impassable when flooded."

We were now staring at a flooded bridge. It had begun to rain Persians and Poodles soon after we'd left the café. Between that and the snow melt that occurred every spring, there was at least a foot of water running over the bridge, possibly more.

"We're going to have to turn back and find a detour around this bridge," Rip said.

"Turn around, don't drown," I recited the popular adage. Rip glanced in his side-view mirror and said, "What the heck? What part of 'impassable' didn't this idiot understand?"

Just then, a black Mercedes Benz sports car went around us and approached the edge of the water. Rip quickly released his seat belt and opened his door. Alarmed, I asked, "What are you doing?"

"This numbskull must have more money than sense. I can't let him get swept away by the force of the water without at least trying to talk some sense into him. Maybe I'll repeat the proverb you just quoted."

"Okay, honey, but be careful."

"I will be."

I watched as Rip knocked on the driver's side of the sports car, motioning for the occupant to lower his window. Water was running off Rip's bald head. In his quest to save the "idiot" from his own stupidity, Rip seemed unfazed by the drenching rain. I was praying he wouldn't lose his footing. The water he was standing in was now ankle-deep. It was his career in law enforcement leaching out of him that made him put others' safety ahead of his own.

What looked like a lively debate ensued. I could tell the driver of the Mercedes convertible was a man, most likely in his forties. He had lowered his window about an inch and was conversing through the tiny gap with my husband, who was soaked to the bone. It took more than ten minutes of persuasion, but eventually, Rip's persistence paid off, and the man backed his car up, turned it around, and put the gearshift in park. He and I followed Rip's return to the truck with our eyes. Rip was shaking his head in disbelief.

"What's up?" I asked as he crawled into the driver's seat, dripping water like an air-conditioner's drain hose on a scorching hot day.

"The dude's name is Wilson," Rip explained. "He said he's trying to get home to Somes Bar because he's scheduled to take a deposition from an expert witness in an hour. It's about an upcoming case, he said. His client broke his neck diving into the shallow end of the city's pool."

"So, he's an attorney?" It was essentially a rhetorical statement. Fern had told me the late tenor had an older brother named Wilson who lived in Somes Bar. Amanda told Rip and me pretty much the same thing.

"Apparently," Rip mumbled. "But he's not the first lawyer I've met who didn't have the sense to come in out of the rain."

I wanted to respond so badly I nearly bit my tongue in half. The man Rip was referring to was bone dry and Rip was as soaked as a kitten that'd just been fished out of a roaring river—like the one a few yards from where we were parked. Fortunately, before I could make a sarcastic remark, Rip continued. "He said he just purchased the car this morning with proceeds from an insurance policy. I asked him why he was in such a hellfire hurry to destroy his brand new Mercedes and possibly die in it when it got swept away by the flood waters. It took a while, but he eventually realized being on time for the deposition was not worth risking his life for. It could always be rescheduled. So he agreed to turn around and take a detour he knows about. He invited us to follow him."

"Doesn't that seem weird to you?" I asked.

"Huh?" Rip looked at me skeptically. "He lives in the area. I don't find it odd at all that he knows another route that'll get us around this low water bridge."

"That's not what I was talking about. Remember Amanda telling us that Henry Harpodingle, the former tenor in the barber-shop quartet, had an older brother named Wilson?"

"If you say so," he replied. Rip could not have remembered Henry's brother's name if his life depended on it. He'd undoubt-edly forgotten the name Wilson before Amanda had finished her sentence. He pulled up behind the sports car and began to follow it. "What about it?"

"Amanda said her cousin Wilson, like Henry, was a lawyer. This man in front of us named Wilson is a lawyer. Amanda said her Uncle Wilson lived in Somes Bar." As I spoke, I was tapping out a question on my phone. "This says Somes Bar is a town of about two hundred people."

"So?" Rip looked both irritated and impatient. Meanwhile, I was trying to figure out who was denser, him or the attorney in front of us who thought he could drive a pint-sized sports car across a flooded bridge. The uprooted sycamore tree racing downstream on top of the water just yards from his car should have been a clue to this attorney, who, without a doubt, was Wilson Harpodingle.

"With a population of a couple of hundred citizens, it's hard to imagine there are more than one personal injury lawyer named Wilson among their ranks."

"That is a lot of coincidences, isn't it?" Rip asked.

"Too many to be just coincidences," I replied. "Obviously, this guy is Henry Harpodingle's brother Wilson. It looks as if the world just got even smaller."

When Rip shrugged as if he had lost interest in the conversation, I tapped the model of the car in front of us into my phone. I then asked, "I also don't find it merely coincidental that Wilson just fell into a pot of insurance money large enough to afford that Mercedes Benz SL Roadster that lists at nearly $138,000. That's about the same amount we just paid for our new fifth wheel. My guess is the money was from a life insurance policy he carried on his recently deceased younger brother."

Rip didn't respond, but I could sense he was listening, so I continued. "How many men in their early forties get life insurance policies on a healthy younger brother?"

"You mean other than men in their forties who have a reason to believe they might cash in on that policy in the near future?" Rip asked. Bingo!

"Exactly!" I exclaimed.

"Whatever," Rip said dryly. "It's none of our business where this man got the money to buy his fancy convertible. And, like I've said before, we are not getting involved in Harry's death."

"Henry," I corrected.

"Whoever."

Rip's response brought a definitive and resounding end to our exchange about the man leading us to the detour around the flooded bridge. However, by Rip's uncharacteristic silence, I knew he was brooding about the situation. We followed the sports car for several miles along a winding road that eventually led us to the other side of the flooded bridge and back on our path to the RV park.

"How does bacon and eggs sound for breakfast?" I asked Rip the next morning as he sat on the side of the bed, putting his socks on.

"Bacon and eggs?" He clearly thought he had misunderstood my question because, as usual, he wasn't wearing his expensive hearing aids.

"Yes."

"Bacon and eggs?" he repeated. "Instead of oatmeal and cantaloupe?"

"Yes."

"Absolutely! You are my new best friend, Rapella."

"I was already your best friend, dear. But I just thought you should be allowed a treat once in a while for doing such a good job with your new diet and exercise regimen. You have only complained a hundred times about both things, and that is way less than I'd anticipated."

"I'll complain even less if you'll make bacon and eggs more often." Rip knew he was pushing his luck but thought it was worth the effort. "Is it a deal?"

"Hardly," I replied, beginning to feel guilty about the ruse I was pulling on the poor guy. "It doesn't work that way."

"Well, it was worth a shot." Rip reached for his blue jeans, a sparkle in his eyes I hadn't seen in a while. Now I felt so bad I slipped into the kitchen and removed a package of frozen sausage links from the freezer.

"Oh, darn!" I exclaimed.

"What?" Rip's voice emanated from behind the closed door of the bathroom. He asked warily, "What do you mean by 'oh, darn?'"

"We don't have any bacon. I was just positive we had a pack in the crisper. But we do have some maple-flavored sausage links I can defrost and fry up."

"That'll suffice," Rip said. "It's not as good as bacon, but it's definitely better than oatmeal. And whoever decided pork sausage should taste like a maple tree has a screw loose."

"You like the maple flavoring, and you know it!" I chastised him. Then, as nonchalantly as I could, I added, "I think I will go to Wal-Mart today to pick up some bacon and a few other things we are out of. We need a loaf of—"

"Ra. Pel. La." Rip dragged my name out like it was twenty-seven letters long. "Don't tell me you are going to go to Wal-Mart so you can hunt down that waitress's aunt and interrogate her about her son's death."

"The woman's name is Amie Harpodingle," I replied. "And, no, that thought had never even crossed my mind."

Liar, liar, jammies on fire. That thought had crossed my mind so many times throughout the previous night it had left tracks on my cerebrum, like that of a badger pacing around on a muddy street. I hadn't got more than a couple of hours of sleep all night.

"Yeah," Rip said dryly. "Of course, it hadn't crossed your mind. I know you tossed and turned because you kept me from getting a good night's sleep too. The poor woman is in mourning from the loss of her son. Not to mention how much stress Doctor Moretti's murder case caused both of us in Minnesota. We need to chill out while we're here in California. We certainly don't need to get involved in another mystifying death. We never even met Harry."

"His name was Henry Harpodingle," I said sharply. Rip had

hit the proverbial nail on the head. It was the mystifying part of the man's demise that haunted me. "And I don't plan to get involved in his death, Rip. I do think the local detectives should delve into it a bit more, but that's for them to do, not us."

"Good. I'm glad we agree on that."

"However—"

"Ra. Pel. La." This time, my name sounded as though he'd tacked on another nine letters.

"I was just going to say if I happened to run into Amie Harpodingle at the store, I would introduce myself and tell her how impressed we were with her niece, Amanda, yesterday when she waited on us at Annie Creek Café."

"And that's all?" Rip asked. "Not a word about her son's horrific death?"

"Of course not," I said. "Like you said, she's in mourning right now." *If Amie happens to bring up the subject, how can I not respond to her? Not responding would be plum rude of me,* I thought. *And being rude to the grieving mother is the last thing I wanted to do.*

"Okay, then," Rip said in a relieved tone. "I'll take my eggs sunny-side-up, as always, and an extra dollop of gravy on my biscuits."

"Who said anything about biscuits and gravy? I wanted to offer you a treat, not clog up another artery."

"Once again, it was worth a shot."

After breakfast, I had the pleasure of doing a small load of laundry in the RV's stacked washer and dryer. "Small" because that's the only size load the appliances could hold. "Pleasure" because I didn't have to lug the dirty clothes up to the park's laundry facilities. Later, as I sifted through the items inside my small pantry to find something to fix for lunch, I said, "Oh, darn. We're out of raisins. I reckon I ought to go ahead and make that trip to Wal-Mart to replenish our groceries before it looks like Mother Hubbard owns this fifth wheel."

"Good idea, dear," Rip said. "We surely don't want to have to suffer through another day without any raisins."

I sensed he had seen through my ploy. He made it even clearer with his next remark.

"You know what, dear?" Rip spoke with a deadpan expression. "I think I'll go with you to the store this afternoon."

"Go with me? Why? Whatever for?" My startled reaction was more suitable to him having told me he wanted to have his finger-nails painted lavender to match his skivvies. "You hate shopping!"

"I know, but I'd like to have a look at their sock selection."

"You want to have a look at their sock selection?" I repeated the query in case I'd misheard. And then I repeated it a second time. "You want to look at their sock selection?"

"Yes."

"When have you ever given a rat's behind about socks? In fact, right now, you have on a pair that doesn't even match."

"Exactly!" he exclaimed. "I've always let you buy my socks for me and that's how I ended up with this pair of one brown sock and one black one."

"But—"

"And you screwed up twice, Rapella."

"How's that?" I regretted the question even as I asked it.

"I have another pair just like this one in my drawer," Rip had the audacity to say.

"Of course you do!" I spat out. "That's because—"

"Now, now, dear." Rip tried to keep a straight face, but failed miserably. "I'm not blaming you, but I think if I were to pick out my own socks, this kind of mistake wouldn't be so apt to happen. For a third time, I might add."

I didn't respond verbally. Instead, I threw a package of jumbo marshmallows at him, which bounced off his bald head harmlessly. I had bought the marshmallows, along with graham crackers and Hershey's chocolate bars, to make s'mores over the fire pit at our RV site one chilly evening.

Rip said, "Seriously, dear, I just want to get out of the fifth wheel for a little while. And I might look for a warmer jacket at Wal-Mart. I hadn't realized it'd be so cold here in April."

"That's a good idea," I replied. "I might do the same."

"Now it's your turn."

"My turn to do what?" I asked.

"Your turn to explain why *you* really want to go to Wal-Mart." Rip sounded skeptical. "Or is an explanation even necessary?"

"We have been making a weekly shopping trip to Wal-Mart ever since Sam Walton opened their doors. Just because I want to go there today doesn't mean I want to discuss Henry Harpodingle's death with his mother." I knew exactly what Rip had been implying.

"No, of course not." Now his skepticism had turned into down-right sarcasm. "And if you think I believe that, then you probably also believe I could give a flying fig what color my socks are."

"Even if I did happen to run into Amie, the only thing I'd do is offer my condolences for her loss."

"Of course, that's all you'd do."

This time, I threw a box of baking soda at him. If Rip hadn't ducked when he did, it might've left a mark. Instead, it bounced off the couch just below our sprawled-out tabby. Dolly leaped six feet in the air and let out a blood-curdling screech.

"Peel Her Majesty off the ceiling and let's go," Rip instructed as he grabbed his key fob off the kitchen table and headed out the door.

FIVE

Our basket contained all six of the items on my grocery list and seventeen more, so Rip and I headed to the opposite side of the large discount store in Crescent City. Rip peeled off at the men's clothing section and I proceeded on to the women's. I had barely parked my basket out of the way so as not to block the path of other shoppers when he walked up and threw a jacket into the basket.

"Seriously?" I asked. "You've selected a jacket already? Was that the one and only jacket you looked at?"

"Yes." Rip looked confused. "It's an extra large and looks warm, which checks off both of the prerequisite boxes. Why would I have gone to the trouble to look at a second coat?"

"Was being a drab shade of beige a prerequisite, too?"

"Nope. I didn't care what color it was as long as it fit and kept me from being cold."

"Then I guess there was absolutely no reason for you to look any further for a more attractive jacket." I thought the sarcasm in my tone was unmistakable. I was wrong.

"Precisely my point," he replied. He pointed at a purple parka and said, "That one looks especially warm, and it appears as if it'd fit you adequately."

"I don't like it."

"Why not? What's wrong with it? I suppose you could try it on if you're concerned it might be too snug."

"It's not too small, Rip!" I nearly spat at him. "If anything it's too big. It's a large and I wear a medium."

"Oh, look!" Rip exclaimed as if he'd just discovered a one-hundred-dollar bill lying on the pavement in the parking lot. He grabbed a smaller purple parka off the rack and tossed it in the basket on top of the dreadful beige coat he'd chosen for himself. Looking decidedly pleased with himself, he added, "It's a medium. Are you ready to roll?"

"No, Rip, I am not ready to roll! I don't like that god-awful jacket!"

"Why? What's wrong with it? It looks warm and it's a med—"

"I don't care, Rip! It's purple!"

"So?"

"You only see purple coats on old ladies!" Before he could muster up the guts to remind me of my age, I angrily slipped the purple coat on, did a 360-degree turn, and yelled, "This parka would be perfect if I was going to spend a week petting penguins in Antarctica. Otherwise, I'd soon morph into a puddle of sweat. Not to mention, this parka is butt ugly!"

I shouted so loud that I startled a younger couple two racks away. The man turned away and laughed and the woman shook her head and gave me a thumbs-down gesture. I turned back to Rip. "See? That young lady agrees with me."

"That lady is young," he replied. "While you, on the other hand, are a little long in the—"

"If you dare say the word 'tooth' right now, you won't have a single one left in your head by the time you leave this store," I warned, lifting up my overstuffed handbag as if to wield it like a nunchuck. "Unless you want the pleasure of wearing a full set of dentures like I do, you better head on out to the truck and wait for me there. It might take a while because I plan to try on every single jacket Wal-Mart has to offer."

"Yes, dear," Rip responded with a sheepish grin. As he walked toward the exit door, he said, "Take your time. I wouldn't want you to be seen in a jacket that makes people think you're over thirty."

I could see Rip's shoulders twitching, which was a sign he was laughing. I wasn't amused. Then he stopped suddenly and stood face-to-face with a slim lady wearing a cap who was several inches taller than him. I stared as Rip and the Wal-Mart employee I knew to be Amie Harpodingle begin to converse. Moments later, the pair turned in unison and headed out the door to the parking lot, still chatting. Leaving my basket behind, I raced for the exit.

"Bong! Bong! Bong!" I heard as I sprinted out toward the parking lot. I got no more than six steps before I was grabbed from behind by a young man who didn't appear old enough to own a driver's license. He had a mullet reminiscent of my nephew Bennie's senior picture in 1980 and adolescent acne that covered his cheeks but left his forehead and chin relatively unscathed.

"You need to come with me, ma'am," he said politely.

"I will **not** come with you, young man!" I exclaimed. I pointed to Rip and Amie, who were getting further and further away. "I am joining my husband, so get your hands off me!"

Before I knew it, there were two other men standing in front of me. They were both in their thirties, I'd estimate. The young man who had grabbed me as I ran out the door whispered to the stockier of the two older security guards. "How dare you men manhandle me this way? I have every right to leave the store whenever I want to."

"Not in a jacket you didn't pay for, you don't," said the heavier man wearing a jacket that said "Security" on the back. The stitched-on name tag on the front of the jacket read "Devin Tubbs."

"Oh, crap!" I said. "I forgot I still had this jacket on."

"How could you forget you had it on?" The second security guard asked. His name tag read Weston Wortal. "It's got to be 120 degrees inside that thing."

"It is!" I replied loudly. "And that's not even the main reason I had no intention of buying it. I was side-tracked by seeing my husband exit the store with one of your check-out ladies and bolted after him without realizing I still had it on."

"And you thought your husband was leaving you for a younger woman he met here at the store?" Weston Wortal asked with a snarky guffaw!

"Of course not, you buffoon! Does your boss know how discourteous you are to paying customers?"

"Oh, I'm very courteous to *paying* customers," Weston replied cheekily. "But shoplifters are another thing altogether."

Devin Tubbs shot Weston Wortal a warning glance, as if to advise him to lay off me. I appreciated it, but he wasn't so kind as to let me go on about my way. I tried again to explain how I'd accidentally left the store still wearing the jacket.

"I explained to you two I wasn't going to steal this jacket. I only wanted to see what my husband and the cashier were discussing."

I could tell by their expressions that I might as well have been reciting my recipe for Mississippi Mud cake, because neither of the two looked convinced by my explanation. "Listen, I have never shoplifted anything in my entire life and I'm sure not going to start by stealing this putrid purple parka. Shouldn't you be watching out for nuns stuffing roasts and other items into their bags without ringing them up instead of harassing me when my oversight was purely an accident?"

It soon became clear the security guards were unfamiliar with the 'shoplifting nun' story that Amie had related to her niece,

Amanda, who had then repeated it to Rip and me. For all I knew, Amanda had made up the story to amuse us. It was funny then, but I was not laughing now.

I was allowed to call Rip, and then forced to wait in Wal-Mart Jail while I waited for him to return to the store and help me explain to the thirty-something-year-old security guards why I had left the store without paying for the jacket. Just FYI, the Wal-Mart Jail in the Crescent City Wal-Mart doubled as a storage/break room. The guards referred to it as the containment room.

The room was dark, dank, and cramped. Worse yet, it smelled of a pastrami sandwich that had expired four or five days earlier. I sat in a rickety plastic chair next to a metal shelving unit with janitorial supplies, individually wrapped toilet tissue rolls, and a case of urinal cakes stored haphazardly on the shelves. I had to snicker when I studied a warning sticker on the cardboard box containing two dozen blue urinal cakes. "Not for human consumption." *Perhaps*, I thought, *if they'd named the urinal deodorizer blocks something that sounded less tasty, they wouldn't have had to warn buyers not to eat them.*

Just then, the heavyset security guard, Devin Tubbs, walked in and caught me laughing as I eyed the case of urinal cakes. He said, "You are not allowed to mess with the products in this room."

"Were you afraid I'd stuff a few urinal cakes in my bra?"

Taking the high road, Devin refused to respond to my snide remark and said, "This room is only intended to contain you while we wait for the police officers to arrive."

The police officers to arrive? I thought. *Who does this big galoot think he is?*

"Do you have a license to carry, Mr. Tubbs?"

"Yes," he replied after a moment of contemplation. "But I can't have a gun in my possession while I'm on Wal-Mart property."

"I wasn't talking about a gun. I was referring to that chip on your shoulder. I wasn't 'messing' with anything in here when you walked in. Do you truly think I'm going to try and filch a roll of cheap, one-ply toilet paper I wouldn't wipe my cat's ass with, or worse yet, nibble on one of those urinal cakes? I'd no more do something like that than I'd try to make off with that horrible purple parka!"

I noticed then that Rip was standing behind Devin, who was large enough to totally obscure my husband. That should've been enough to shut me up, but I was on a roll and couldn't stop my tirade. I stepped outside the room and continued. "It's utterly appalling how much authority you seem to think that mall-cop badge gives you. According to California state law, I cannot openly carry a weapon in this Wal-Mart, but I *can* conceal and carry a handgun. You, on the other hand, are forbidden to have a gun in your possession on the store's premises. What's that tell you?"

"Rapella," Rip suddenly stepped between me and the security guard. *For my protection*, I wondered, *or the guard's?* The answer to that question soon became apparent. Rip's stern tone was a warning that I'd likely end up in police custody rather than Wal-Mart's if I didn't immediately stow my irritation with the guard, who was merely doing his job. I could read his expression as easily as I'd read the warning on the urinal deodorizer box that inferred the cakes were not to be served with a candle in the center of them at a child's birthday party. I glared at Rip as he said, "I'd imagine Wal-Mart frowns on having their security personnel shoot someone for trying to steal a coat. In this day and age a lot of companies won't even let them apprehend shoplifters."

"I am not a shoplifter, Rip!" I was livid. "Nor did I consciously try to steal that dreadful parka! Whose side are you on anyway?"

"I'm not on anyone's side. You made it clear when I handed you the coat that you thought it was hideous. I know you wouldn't steal a nickel from anyone. Just let me take care of this, honey. Wait in there," he added as he nodded at the door of the so-called "containment room."

Reluctantly, I opened the door and stepped back inside the

claustrophobic room. I was seething at Wortal and Tubbs' treatment of me while simultaneously beating myself up for not thinking to take the stupid jacket off before sprinting out of the store. I was beyond humiliated.

As an outlet for my frustration, I decided if I was going to be accused of messing with the products in the room, I was going to have fun messing with them. I dug the black Sharpie I always carried out of my handbag and wrote "No shit?" on the urinal cake box just below the "Not for human consumption" warning. The simple act of rebellion helped soften my temperament. But not near enough. So I tore open a roll of thin, tacky toilet tissue and TP'ed the room while I waited to be exonerated and released from Wal-Mart's custody.

Then, I took a blank card from the rack next to the employee time clock, which was mounted on the wall next to the door. I wrote "Englebert Humperdinck" across the top of the card and said, "Reporting for duty," as I clocked him in. I then placed Mr. Humperdinck's time card in the slot beneath Paul Hopper's so as not to interfere with the rack's alphabetical order. I was surprised how many people were employed by this Wal-Mart that served a town of no more than six thousand residents. But then, we were in this Wal-Mart, and we were staying in Klamath, which was over half an hour away. It clearly serves a lot more people than just those who live in Crescent City. As I sat back down in the rickety chair, I wondered how long it would take for someone to realize the eighty-seven-year-old British pop singer was not an employee of the discount store.

Just then one of the legs of the chair made an eerie creaking sound. I knew it was just a matter of time before I, or the next detainee who sat in it, went tumbling to the ground. *A felon like me could break a hip. Maybe I should ensure that doesn't happen and cost Sam Walton's heirs a bundle in a personal injury lawsuit. I'd bet Wilson Harpodingle would salivate over a lawsuit like that.* I stood up, and with what required alarmingly little effort, I ripped all four legs off the chair and placed them on top of a box of rubber gloves on the shelving unit. With my permanent marker, I wrote "You're welcome" on the seat of the legless chair.

Minutes later, I put my ear up against the door, hoping to find out what was taking so long. I was beginning to worry I might be in more trouble than I'd anticipated. I even second-guessed my wisdom in vandalizing the containment room. Then I heard Rip's voice conversing with one of the guards on the other side of the door. I recognized the voice as the larger of the two guards. Then I heard the two men laugh, which both relieved me and pissed me off. It relieved me because I didn't believe Rip would be laughing if he knew we were waiting for one of Crescent City's finest to come cuff and stuff me in the back of a squad car. But it royally ticked me off because I didn't find the situation one bit humorous. I'd been publicly disgraced and was now concerned the story would get back to Amanda via her Aunt Amie. I didn't relish the notion I'd be further embarrassed when we returned to Annie Creek Café to try out their brisket sandwich and fries.

Before leaving the room, I withdrew both Devin Tubbs and Weston Wortal's time cards from the rack and clocked them out. As far I was concerned, they'd stopped doing anything worth getting compensated for the moment they drug me back into the store and "incarcerated me" in their Wal-Mart Jail.

I was allowed to leave with Rip about five minutes later. I don't know if he'd utilized his Aransas County Sheriff's badge as a "get out of jail free" card or not, and I didn't want to ask. Rip still carried the badge even though it was woefully outdated and he'd retired from that position well over a decade earlier. What is typically referred to as "professional courtesy" between law enforcement officers had gotten him out of two speeding tickets and a failure to yield charge in the fourteen years we'd been traveling the country as full-time RVers. I was glad he'd hung on to it all of these years in the event he had to "outmuscle" a couple of young security guards who weren't even allowed to carry a weapon.

It took me a few minutes to simmer down as we headed toward the campground. The entire "shoplifting" incident at Wal-Mart had taken the wind out of my sails. It was only when we were nearly back to the RV park that I realized I hadn't asked Rip about his conversation with Amie Harpodingle.

"So, what did you learn from visiting with Amie?" I asked, as excited as an eight-year-old who'd just been told by a department store Santa Claus she was getting a puppy for Christmas. My ensuing disappointment was just as poignant as when I'd tugged on that Santa's beard only to discover the imposter was clean-shaven. My mother had stormed back into the store to chastise the man for promising me a puppy when all I was really getting was a Chatty Cathy. The new doll was all the rage when it was released in 1959, so my mom thought I'd be over the moon about the present, despite the fact I was a tomboy. Instead, I ripped the boring doll's head off as punishment to it for not being a boisterous beagle. That was the year I stopped believing in Santa Claus. I now listened to Rip, whose response was just one more disillusionment in my life.

"Well, I learned that she got off work three hours early today because she had a dental appointment. She told me she religiously goes in to have them cleaned every six months. Apparently, gingivitis runs in her family. This morning, however, she woke up with a bad toothache and was afraid the molar might be abscessed." Rip glanced at me and noticed I was unmoved by the news she was diligent about her dental hygiene. He added, "She also said the store was unusually quiet today."

"Go on." I was already aware the store was quiet today. My outburst for the security guards to take their grimy hands off me had seemed to echo from the produce section all the way to the door leading out to the lawn and garden department.

'Um, well," Rip was obviously struggling to remember what all he and the Wal-Mart cashier had discussed. "Oh, yeah. She also told me that the self-checkout stands were all shut down for over two hours early this morning because of a computer glitch."

"Oh really? How fascinating!" I spoke in a sickeningly sweet voice before my tone did a one-eighty and I snapped at him. "Who cares if the shoppers actually had to go through a regular check-out stand, Rip? Get to the interesting part of your exchange with Amie."

"I thought that was the interesting part."

"Didn't you mention that we met her niece, Amanda, yesterday at the café in Crater Lake National Park?" I asked.

"Um, no."

"Why not?" I was getting impatient. "Was it because you couldn't remember her niece's name?"

"No," he stated in indignation. "I remembered Amber's name, but—"

"Amanda. Her name is Amanda!"

"Amanda, I meant," Rip responded, "but I couldn't remember the name of the café."

"What difference does the name of the café make, which incidentally is Annie Creek Café?"

"Listen, Rapella," Rip began, "I know you well enough to know you were hoping I had asked her about Henry and if she believed her other son had taken out a life insurance policy on his brother. I may be as curious about the situation now as you are, Rapella. But I was not going to walk up to a complete stranger and begin grilling her about the death of one son and the integrity of the other. Don't you think she's been under enough stress as it is?"

"That's true," I admitted. "Doing so would've been highly insensitive at this point."

"At this point?"

"Yes," I said. "You only just met."

Rip appeared dubious. He stared at me as if waiting for me to continue. So, unfortunately, I did.

"I applaud you for opening up a line of communication with Amie. The next time we run into her at Wal-Mart, you can chat her up a little more now that you're no longer strangers. After a few more interactions at the store with her, you can begin questioning her about the death of her son."

"I have no intention of ever questioning the grieving mother about the death of her son, Rapella. I may be intrigued by the man's death, but as I've said multiple times before, we are not getting involved in it. No doubt more about the case will come to light as the local detectives delve further into his death."

"That's just it, Rip," I countered. "It looks as if they've declared his death an accident. I doubt they'll look any deeper into the uncanny, and in my opinion, improbable, tragedy."

"If they don't, they don't." Rip was adamant. "It's not our call to make. We are here to enjoy the sights and have a good time, and that's exactly what I plan to do."

"Okay, okay," I agreed. "I can't help being curious about the situation."

"As I said, I'm intrigued by it too. But that doesn't mean I think we ought to butt into what might be another murder case."

"Did you happen to point me out and tell her I was your wife before the pimply-faced kid stopped me and accused me of shoplifting?"

"Tell her you were my wife?" Rip repeated in astonishment. He looked as if I'd asked him if he'd like me to go back inside the store and pilfer that beige jacket he'd picked out. "Oh, hell no, I didn't tell her you were my wife!"

I didn't know whether to wallop him with my purse or kiss him. At least Amie wouldn't be calling her niece that evening to tell her the funny story about the senior citizen who tried to steal the most repulsive jacket the discount store offered.

Having just realized I truly had abandoned the basket full of stuff we'd picked out in the women's clothing department, I asked, "Should I go back inside and purchase the groceries and—"

Rip didn't even let me finish. "How bad do we need raisins tonight?"

"Good point."

I decided it was in my best interest to change the subject at that stage. "So what are we going to do for fun this afternoon?"

"This morning wasn't enough fun for you?"

We decided to visit a park called Trees of Mystery because it was so close to the RV park we were camping at. It was already nearly one o'clock and we were both hungry. We planned to grab lunch at a restaurant inside the park called Forest Café before exploring the other attractions.

To give lunch time to settle in our stomachs, the first activity we chose to do was journey through the forest treetops aboard a SkyTrail tram. Each car held six people. The two couples riding along with us were very friendly. The husband and wife in their sixties from Ayer, Massachusetts, were very quiet, and the two women from Billings, Montana, never stopped talking. But they were humorous and amicable, so we laughed along with their light-hearted jabbering.

The SkyTrail tram soared through the top of the forest at a relaxing pace as we observed the redwoods from a downward perspective. It was an incredible experience. After about ten minutes, we came to a stop at Ted's Ridge, where there was a large observation deck. Spectacular views of the Klamath backcountry were to the east, and Hidden Beach and the Pacific Ocean were to the west. From there, we had to hike back down the mountain on a path called Wilderness Trail. Rip was less than thrilled when he realized the tram did not return us to the point at which we'd boarded it.

About three-quarters of a mile into the hike, Rip's grumbling began to border on being obnoxious. Granted, he'd recently had the arterial stent procedure in Minnesota, and he'd had hip replacement surgery several years prior. But even before those two operations, he wasn't the fittest person in the world, or even the fittest person in our marriage. Although it wasn't advisable, I could do jumping jacks and squat thrusts in circles around him if I wanted to. Knowing that, however, did nothing to quell my desire to tie him to one of the monstrous redwoods, cover him with a jar of honey, and let the ants take care of him from there.

Naturally, I would never do such a thing to my husband or hurt him in any way. But it was fun to think about at times like this.

The trail turned out to be a mile in length, hardly long enough to merit being called a hike. Despite some rugged areas, it was more of a leisurely walk than a hike, in my opinion. I was thankful, however, that we'd thought to wear sturdy boots. I could visualize one of us twisting an ankle on one of the numerous tree roots that protruded from the ground. At the end of the Wilderness Trail, Rip commented, "That wasn't so bad."

Considering he'd spent the entire mile moaning and groaning as though I'd signed him up for an Ironman contest, all I could do was shake my head. I definitely needed to encourage him to step up his daily exercise routine. An evening stroll around the campground each night after dinner would be a nice start, eventually working up to a two-mile daily walk that would be beneficial for both of us. I'd bring it up at a later time, I decided.

We stopped at the gift shop next. After using the restroom facilities, we visited "The End of the Trail Museum," which was attached to the north end of the gift shop. I knew Rip would be

interested in one of the largest privately owned collections of arti-
facts from ancient and modern cultures, dating back to the first
Americans. Exquisite burden baskets woven by the Apache tribe,
which were designed to be carried on one's back, animal mounts
and tanned buffalo hides, Navajo pottery, Lakota Sioux death
masks, and even kachina dolls created by the Pueblo Indians were
just a few of the many objects on display. I was particularly fasci-
nated by baskets woven so tightly by the Pomo Indians that they
were naturally waterproof.

The collection was vast and fascinating. Rip had been
enthralled, like an outdoorsman in a Bass Pro Shop, as he took in
all of the exhibits. Exiting the museum an hour later, he said,
"That was worth the cost of admission."

We'd gotten the senior citizen rate of twenty-three dollars per
ticket, which was all-inclusive of the park's amenities, and we both
concluded it'd been money well spent. We'd enjoyed the Trees of
Mystery attraction, but were glad to get back to the campground
and put our feet up while we relaxed over our daily cocktails. Our
primary doctor in our hometown of Rockport, Texas, had allotted
us one alcoholic beverage per day, which I served in quart canning
jars. Not once had Dr. Herron mentioned how large those daily
drinks should be, and not once did I ask. And it goes without
saying I never will.

SIX

The following morning found Rip grumpy and out of sorts. His legs were covered in an itchy rash, and there was a large area on his right arm that was also affected. A subsequent visit to a local urgent care confirmed he'd gotten into some poison oak, which grows as low shrubs in clumps or vines throughout the Redwood National and State parks, the physician explained. I thought back to the previous day's trek through the forest and asked Rip, "Remember yesterday, halfway down the Wilderness Trail, when you declared you couldn't possibly take another step and leaned up against that tree to rest?"

"Yes."

"And do you recall the three-leafed vine snaking up the trunk of that tree that I advised you not to touch? I even recited that old 'leaves of three, let it be' saying to you, but you still insisted on leaning up against it?"

Rip responded with a steely glare but remained silent, rendering my questions rhetorical. It compelled me to get in another jab while I was on a roll. "The fact you were sweaty at the time from all that exertion of walking an entire mile probably didn't help matters any."

Dr. Rand Danko, the ER physician on duty that day, winked at me, laughed at Rip, and said, "Yep, that'd do it!" As a result, he, too, received a steely glare from his patient. It only made him chuckle again. "Poison oak, like its cousins, poison ivy and poison sumac, releases an oil called urushiol, which is absorbed by your skin when you touch the plant. Not all people are sensitive to urushiol, Mr. Ripple, but you are in good company with the fifty to seventy-five percent of adults in this country who *are* susceptible to it. Maybe next time, you should tough it out and walk the entire mile without taking a time out to rest."

Rip didn't bother to respond. But it was obvious he didn't take too kindly to the doctor poking his belly and saying, "A little more exercise would be good for you, Mr. Ripple."

When Rip remained silent, the sassy doctor added, "At the very least, take your wife's advice and don't touch any three-leafed vines."

Dr. Danko, Millie, the attending nurse, and I were all amused by the doctor's advice. But the doctor's petulant patient? Not so much. I adored Dr. Danko at first "slight." Pardon the pun. I wasn't surprised when he prescribed calamine lotion and prescription-strength antihistamine pills to reduce the itching. He recommended applying cool compresses to the itchy rash and long soaks in lukewarm water.

We both nodded. No sense explaining our fifth wheel was equipped with a shower/bath combo that was too small for either Rip or me to sit down in for a long soak. In Rip's case, it'd likely result in a 9-1-1 call and the first responders utilizing the "jaws of life" to remove him from the bathtub. Before Dr. Danko exited the partitioned-off enclosure we were in, he handed Rip a small sample container of hydrocortisone cream and said, "This might help in the meantime. It's for topical use only."

"Oh, darn," Rip said in an annoyed tone. "I was planning on eating it."

Walking back to the truck, Rip muttered, "Well, he was a laugh a minute, wasn't he?"

"I thought Dr. Danko was hilarious!"

"You would!"

"I'm sorry, honey. We shouldn't have poked fun at you the way we did." I really did feel bad about teasing Rip. And I had to admit the doctor had been a little disrespectful. The rash looked angry and I knew the itching made it uncomfortable. "I think Dr. Danko also meant to prescribe you an ice cream cone at the Dairy Queen and just forgot."

Rip's mood brightened instantly. He looked at me, smiled, and said, "I think you're right! I knew there had to be *something* about that doctor I liked, but I just hadn't been able to put a finger on it until now."

Rip pulled into the DQ parking lot no more than thirty seconds later. We both grew up in Texas, where there is at least one Dairy Queen in every town; there are eighteen locations in San Antonio alone. On a normal night in a Texas town that has a population of ten people, you'd find one of them taking orders at the local Dairy Queen, one preparing them, and the other eight citizens sitting at tables slurping on Blizzards, Peanut Butter Parfaits, and Brownie and Oreo Cupfections. The chain is nick-named "the Texas Stop Sign" for a reason, and like any Texan worth his salt, or sugar in this case, we were very familiar with their menu. We hadn't eaten ice cream since before Rip's stent proce-dure. I didn't think having a forbidden treat once in a blue moon was apt to kill him. And if it did? So be it! At least the man would die with a smile and a creamy mustache on his face. "I know you'll want a vanilla milkshake and I'll try one of their new Peanut Butter Puppy Chow Blizzards."

"Peanut butter puppy chow?" Rip asked with a smirk. "What's

it got in it? Vanilla ice cream, peanut butter, and small chunks of Alpo, or worse yet, dog poop?"

"Don't be silly. I'm sure it's better than it sounds."

"I would hope so."

"Order me a small one, please. It ought to have enough calories in it to carry me through next Thursday. Hopefully, the drive-thru line isn't too long."

"Let's order inside and eat our ice cream at one of their tables. There's no hurry to get back to the campground. Her Majesty filled her belly with tuna delight right before we left for the Urgent Care and then curled up in my recliner for a long nap. Besides, I don't want any of the ice cream melting and dripping onto the upholstery of our new truck."

As we drove back to the campground half an hour later, I had polar-opposite emotions about Rip's new poison oak rash. I was discouraged because I knew Rip would milk this minor health concern for all it was worth. He is a man, after all. He'd also undoubtedly use it as a deterrent against taking daily walks this spring, since the physician had informed us that poison oak was very prevalent in the area.

But I was also a tad bit giddy. I knew Rip would be content to have me drive myself to the pharmacy to pick up the antihistamine medication and a bottle of Calamine lotion while he stayed home and suffered in the company of his favorite napping companion, Dolly. I would use this to my advantage, I decided.

As it turned out, the closest pharmacy to the Mystic Forest RV Park was the one inside the Crescent City Wal-Mart, which fit perfectly into my plan. However, since I didn't want to get Rip all stirred up, I simply said, "Looks like the closest pharmacy is in Crescent City, which makes sense because the population of Klamath is no more than a thousand residents."

"All I remember seeing in this town was the Klamath post office, a Holiday Inn Express, and a Laundromat that looked as if it'd gone out of business," Rip replied. "Oh, and that other RV park that looked very quiet and peaceful."

"Yes, Kamp Klamath looked like a very nice place to stay, but they were booked up when I called to make reservations."

"No worries, dear," Rip said as he settled into his recliner. "I'm perfectly content in this campground."

"I am, too. Do you need anything before I leave?"

"A bag of pork rinds would be nice."

"So would a stack of one-hundred-dollar bills, but you're not going to find either one of those things in this fifth wheel. I'll bring you a bowl of carrot sticks instead."

"Swell."

I decided to fix him a bowl of blackberries and strawberries instead because I knew he liked fresh fruit better than carrots. I also wet several washrags with cold water.

"I'll be back in a bit. Try not to scratch and keep these wet cloths on the rash as Dr. Danko suggested."

"Yes, dear. Drive safely."

I knew returning to the scene of my great crime was going to be challenging. After the stunts I'd pulled in the containment/storage/break room, which was an awful lot of hats for such a tiny space to wear, I didn't want to be recognized by the security staff.

I noticed a ball cap Rip had purchased yesterday at the Trees of Mystery gift shop was lying on the back seat of the truck. After I pulled into the Wal-Mart parking lot and found a place to park, I put the cap on and tugged it down to my ears. I then pulled an oversized pair of sunglasses out of my handbag to wear. And, although the Covid-19 pandemic was officially over and face masks had become voluntary at most business establishments across the country, I pulled a black KN-95 out of the glove compartment. It would serve as extra concealment.

I looked in the rearview mirror and thought, *I don't know how Wortal, Tubbs, or the skinny teenager with the bad acne could recognize me. I can barely recognize myself.*

Two minutes later, I strode into Wal-Mart with my head down and my phone in my hand. I pretended to be reading a text. Suddenly, a man stepped right in front of me and, in a familiar voice said, "You again?"

I looked up into Devin Tubbs' eyes and said, "Oh, hello there, Mr. Tubbs. It's so nice to see you again."

My sarcasm was not lost on Devin. "I wish I could say the same."

"Unfortunately, Wal-Mart has the closest pharmacy to the campground in Klamath where my husband and I are staying, and I have to pick up a prescription for him. He got into some poison oak on a hike in the forest yesterday."

"Oh, no," Devin said in a very amicable tone. "I feel for the guy. Not long ago, I did the same thing and ended up with a rash covering about ninety percent of my body."

"That was a lot of rash, wasn't it?" I asked, looking Devin up and down.

Devin stared at me for a few moments as if trying to determine if he should feel offended and react defensively. He chose the high road in the end, as he had a tendency to do, and said, "Yes. It was torture, but witch hazel extract helped a lot. It eased the itching and reduced the inflammation. It also helped heal the blisters. You should pick some up for your husband. It's on the top shelf about halfway down aisle fourteen."

"Hey, thanks for the tip." I was beginning to realize Devin

wasn't such a bad guy. He truly had just been doing his job. If the security guards let every Tom, Dick, or Rapella walk out of the store wearing jackets they hadn't paid for, looking like Minnie Pearl with the price tags still dangling from the sleeves, they wouldn't keep their jobs long. It was my fault I was in such a rush to talk to Amie that I didn't think to remove the jacket before leaving the store. No doubt every woman apprehended by the guards responded in denial as I had. I'm sure the security personnel had heard every excuse in the book, like "I forgot I still had it on" and "I had every intention of returning to the store to pay for it." My personal favorite was "I was overtaken by an evil spirit who forced me outside while I was still wearing this grotesque purple parka."

I felt overwhelmed with a desire to apologize for my audacious behavior yesterday. So I did. Devin accepted my apology graciously and remarked, "No worries, ma'am. Weston and I didn't really believe you would knowingly steal that jacket. You look way too young to wear a purple parka. It looked like something my grandma would wear."

Figuring his granny and I were probably about the same age, I suddenly wanted to kiss Devin Tubbs. And if I wasn't afraid it would traumatize him, I might've done so. "You are a nice guy, Devin. I'm also sorry for the things I did in the containment room. That wasn't cool at all."

"Maybe not," Devin said with a hearty laugh. "But Weston and I thought it was hilarious. I don't think a Wal-Mart containment room has ever been TP'ed before."

"Oh, and in case you haven't noticed it yet, Englebert Humperdinck doesn't actually work here."

"Who's Englebert Humperdinck?" he asked in a serious manner. "Is he that old man who comes in every Tuesday and rings up four bottles of prune juice but leaves with six?"

"Never mind." I shook my head. *What made me think a man in his thirties would know anything about the elderly pop singer from England? I should've put* Bad Bunny *on the time card instead.* "I better go and get that prescription filled for Rip, and then I need to purchase the groceries I left behind yesterday. I'll also pick up some witch hazel extract, as you advised. And, Devin, the next time the prune juice guy comes in, tells him that Metamucil works as well as prunes when you're stopped up like contestants the morning after a cheese-eating contest. I know you like to give medical advice to customers."

"Yes, ma'am, I'll do that." He laughed and tipped his ball cap. His gesture reminded me of how stupid I looked in Rip's "Redwood National Forest" cap, the large sunglasses, and the black KN95 mask. The disguise hadn't fooled the observant security guard for one second.

With the cap, sunglasses, and mask in my hand, I said, "But first, I think I'll go put these in the truck so I don't get stopped for stealing them when I leave."

Devin laughed again and I had to giggle at my foolishness, too.

I shopped for raisins, milk, bread, and a few other items while the pharmacy was filling Rip's prescription. I had no idea what I was going to do with the raisins but felt like I shouldn't go home without them. I then picked up some witch hazel extract in aisle fourteen, hoping it helped Rip as much as it appeared to have helped Devin. I found a blue coat for Rip that was much more stylish than the plain beige one he'd previously selected. Lastly, I found a teal-colored Adirondack-styled jacket I absolutely loved in the women's outerwear aisle. I cursed the rack of purple parkas as I walked by it, as if it was the jacket's fault I'd found myself in such a pickle the previous day. It might not have affected the parkas' disposition one whit, but it made me feel a bit better.

After collecting the antihistamine at the pharmacy, I headed for the self-checkout section, where I found Amie. She was wearing the bamboo cap and appeared to be worn out. No doubt losing her youngest son in such a tragic manner had taken a toll on her.

"Excuse me, ma'am," I said. "Are you Amanda Castonova's Aunt Amie?"

"Yes, I am." Amie was clearly surprised at my inquiry. "Do you know my niece?"

"My husband and I met her the other day when she waited on us at the Annie Creek Café in Mazama Village. Amanda is a delightful young lady."

"I may be a bit biased, but I wholeheartedly agree. Did you enjoy Crater Lake Natural Park?"

"Very much so, and lunch was lovely, too. Amanda told me you recently lost a son, and I just wanted to tell you how sorry my husband and I both are about your loss. We are not supposed to outlive our children, are we? You have my deepest condolences."

"Thank you," Amie said. "It's been tough. My boss offered me some time off to grieve, but I've found keeping my normal schedule to be helpful. It keeps my mind off losing Henry."

"I'm sure it does," I replied. "I think I'd do the same thing if I were in your shoes."

"I'd actually thought about retiring next month, but now I think I'll keep working a while longer."

"Yes, I agree. Staying busy can be a blessing in times like this."

"Exactly!" Amie nodded. "Amanda has been a godsend, too. She checks in on me every evening by phone and has shown up at my house with carryout food several times since the accident. Crater Lake is a considerable distance from here, you know."

"Yes, it is. What a thoughtful thing for Amanda to do, which doesn't surprise me in the least. So you believe Henry's death was an accident?" I'd caught the last word of her remark.

"Of course I do. The police department ruled it as such."

"And just how much investigating did they do before they deter-

mined his cause of death was due to an accidental fall from a thirteenth-story balcony? That just seems so implausible to me."

"You didn't know Henry like I did," Amie explained. *I didn't
know Henry at all*, I could've said, but I remained silent and encouraged her to keep talking. "He'd been known to drink too much at
times."

"I understand." I didn't understand at all. I'd been known to
drink too much on occasion, too, but I can guarantee that no one
will ever see the outline of my body on the pavement below a thirteenth-story balcony. I could be totally blitzed, but I was never
going to crawl up on a railing and accidentally fall off of it to my
death. That was as preposterous as someone saying, "Rapella died
from a bite she sustained while trying to pet a King Cobra after
having a few drinks. Drunk or not, I was never going to pet any
kind of snake, and I was never going to climb up on a thirteen-
story balcony railing, either.

"Excuse me a moment," Amie said. I waited while she helped
an elderly man ring up a couple of bags of produce.

"I didn't know whether this was considered zucchini or
squash," he explained to Amie as he held up a bag for her to exam-
ine. "And I don't even know what these white things are, but my
wife texted me a picture of one and told me to buy three of them."

Amie chuckled and patted the old fellow on the back. "Those
are called pattypan squash."

"Eew," he grumbled in response. "Is my wife actually gonna
expect me to eat this thing?"

"Yes, and she's going to expect you to compliment her on it,
too," Amie told him with an endearing smile. "So buckle up,
buttercup—"

"Oh, no!" the elderly man exclaimed, startling Amie.

"What's wrong?" she asked him.

"She told me to get a buttercup squash too, and I forgot. I'm
not certain I even know what one looks like."

I walked over and told Amie I'd be glad to run and get the gentleman a buttercup squash while she continued to help him and also the lady at another self-checkout stand who was waving her hand as if she was a second grader who knew the answer to her teacher's question.

When I returned with the squash, Amie was pulling a hoodie sweatshirt on over her shirt. I hoped she'd just gotten chilled, but discovered her shift was about to end and she was preparing to leave. It was a nippy fifty-four degrees outside. I knew I only had time for one more question.

"I'm curious, Amie. Does your other son drive a Mercedes convertible?"

"Not that I know of." Amie looked confused. "Unless he just purchased one, that is. It wouldn't surprise me, though, because I know Wilson recently received a substantial check from an insurance company."

"Oh? Had he taken out a life insurance policy on his brother prior to Henry's death?"

It was a bold—okay, brash—thing for me to ask. I expected her to be offended by the intrusive question. Instead, Amie appeared to mull it over for a few moments and replied, "I don't honestly know. He never told me what the insurance payoff was related to and I didn't ask. But I intend to ask Wilson Tuesday night when I see him at the celebration of life being held for Henry at the Moose Crossing Winery. It seems like such an impertinent thing for him to do, yet I wouldn't put it past him. He is all about the mighty dollar."

"Isn't that winery located in Klamath?" I asked. I'd seen a sign leading to the winery on Highway 101. "I think it is right across the highway from the park my husband and I are camping in."

"If you're staying at Mystic Forest RV Park, then yes, that's it. Klamath is where Henry moved after he passed the bar exam, and it's where all of his friends reside. Henry was partial to the winery, so it seemed appropriate to hold his celebration of life there."

"Of course, Amie. It sounds very appropriate," I replied in agreement. *Appropriate for a wedding reception, maybe, but not so much for a celebration of life,* I could've said. But I realized that in a town the size of Klamath, there probably weren't a lot of other options. I hadn't noticed a lot of venues in Klamath with the space and amenities necessary to hold such an event. "I'm not sure you could've found anywhere in that small town that'd be better than the Moose Crossing Winery."

Amie nodded and said she was glad to have met me. I assured her the feeling was mutual. I wished her strength to get through the memorial service for her son Tuesday evening and expressed my condolences once again before she headed to the tiny multi-use room to clock out. I wanted to ask her to pull Englebert Humperdinck's time card and clock him out too while she was at it because I didn't think he needed to be drawing a lot of overtime at Wal-Mart. He surely had a comfortable retirement from making a mint with his singing. I didn't want to delay her any further, though, or explain why the famous singer had an employee time card to begin with. I still had to ring up my own purchases and didn't want Rip to get concerned about how long it was taking me to pick up his prescription.

Another employee arrived to replace Amie in the self-checkout section. I was surprised it was the young man I'd met yesterday who'd stopped me after I'd exited the store still wearing the parka. I could tell he recognized me, too, by the extra attention he gave me as I rang up my purchases. It filled me with rage which I struggled to contain.

The one and only thing I'd ever stolen was a dollar from the collection plate at church when I was nine years old. I'd wanted to buy a tacky bracelet made out of candy at the five and dime downtown. It might've been easier just to steal the bracelet because my oldest brother saw me palm the dollar from the plate and ratted me out. I spent the next week hoeing the garden, gathering eggs, cleaning out the chicken coop, and scrubbing the kitchen floor until it shone, along with doing many other chores. With blistered hands, I sat on the front stoop the following Sunday as parishioners filed into the church. I was holding a sign that read, "I stole a dollar from the house of God last Sunday and as an act of redemption I will be putting it and another five hard-earned dollars into the plate today."

Was I embarrassed? Of course, I was. Did I feel ashamed? Of course I did. Was I ever going to steal anything ever again? Heavens no! I'd learned my lesson and it wasn't one I'd ever forget, thanks to my strict, God-fearing parents. They'd reacted as though I'd whacked Jesus himself on the head with a flaming torch and then cleaned out his pockets while he was down. If Ma and Pa were still alive, I'd undoubtedly be sitting in front of this store with a sign that read, "I tried to steal a putrid purple parka from Wal-Mart . . ."

And now I found my every move being scrutinized by a teenager with bad skin. I was determined to prove to the disrespectful kid I was an honest, law-abiding citizen, so I took special care to scan everything deliberately and carefully. And I made sure he was looking as I scanned each item so there'd be no question I'd paid for it.

A rivulet of perspiration had begun to roll down my chest. The moisture was eventually absorbed by the waistband of my slacks. I was appalled I'd been brought down to this level. I found myself as nervous as a lizard in that chicken coop I'd had to scrub spotless because of a nerdy kid in a Wal-Mart vest who was too young to buy himself a beer. What chapped my hide the most was knowing I had only myself to blame for it. Letting myself get distracted by being totally focused on trying to track down the truth behind a stranger's death had almost got me arrested. A similar situation had happened the previous year in Santé Fe, New Mexico, while I was shopping with my granddaughter Tiffany. Having a one-track mind had been the cause then, too. I prayed it didn't take a third incident to teach me an important lesson.

Suddenly, the young man turned his head away just as I scanned a jar of mandarin oranges. *The scanning machine dinged*, I thought, *but had he heard it?* Knowing he was suspicious of me already, I didn't want to be made a spectacle again by the clerk insisting on digging through my bag to ensure I'd rung the fruit jar up correctly. So, to be on the safe side, I scanned it again, even though the $1.89 fruit jar, which was selling for a dollar before the pandemic, now cost me nearly four bucks. *Thank goodness it wasn't the blades I'm buying for my razor*, I thought. They'd gotten so expensive I'd begun to wonder how truly necessary it was for me to continue shaving. After all, my armpit hair had migrated north to my chin years ago, and Rip wasn't apt to notice how hairy my legs were until the strands got long enough they could be braided into dreadlocks.

As I carried my bags to the truck, I realized that never before had checking out of Wal-Mart been so stressful that it'd caused me to sweat like an iron worker. It had undoubtedly raised my blood pressure to a dangerous level, as well. *From now on, I'm going to go through a regular checkout line no matter how long it takes*, I thought. *If nothing else, it'll help force the store to keep a few humans on their payroll.*

SEVEN

"Wal-Mart?" Rip asked when he scrutinized the bag I was holding. "You actually had the cajones to go back there after what happened yesterday? You have bigger balls than I do, Rapella."

"Thank you."

"It wasn't a compliment."

"I know, but I've chosen to take it as one anyway." I tossed his bag of medications onto his lap momentarily wishing it was an unpinned hand grenade. "Besides, it's the only place within miles to get a prescription filled. I even talked to Devin Tubbs while I was there."

"Who's that?"

Should I have Rip checked for dementia, I wondered, *or does he really just not give a crap what goes on around him?*

"He was the larger of the two security guards who detained me until you somehow got me sprung," I responded. "You must've flashed your sheriff's badge."

"Oh yeah," Rip replied. "Nice guy. And, no, I didn't flash my badge. I explained to the guards that you had a bad habit of sticking your nose into murder cases where it didn't belong and elaborated a little on the death of their coworker's son. I told them you didn't believe the plunge he took to his death was accidental. They were familiar with the tragedy that killed Angie's—"

"Amie, for God sakes!"

"That's right. Her name's Amie," Rip said, as if I was the one who couldn't recall her name. "The security guys agreed with you it seemed unlikely such an accident would occur. They both seemed pleased you were interested in getting involved in the case. I told them I wasn't pleased at all about your intrigue with the man's cause of death, and, at the larger guard's suggestion, they immediately clammed up and released you."

"I see." I liked the friendly Mr. Tubbs even more now. It was nice to have support no matter where it came from. But I was surprised Devin hadn't mentioned anything about me being interested in Amie's son's death when I'd chatted with him earlier that day.

"Turns out the guard you talked to was a close friend of Henry Harpodingle's. He was the last person to see Henry alive," Rip said as nonchalantly as if he'd told me he'd changed the battery in the fifth wheel's two smoke detectors.

"No kidding?" I spoke calmly, even though it was all I could do not to scream that it would've been awfully frigging nice to know that before I conversed with Devin today.

"No kidding."

"Where were they? How did he happen to be the last person to see Henry alive? Did Devin see what happened to Henry? Can he verify it was an accidental fall?" I fired questions at Rip until he held his hand up to stop me.

"I don't know the answers to any of your questions."

"How can you not?" I asked. "Surely you asked him something after he told you he was the last person to see Henry alive. Didn't you?"

84

"No, I didn't," Rip replied. "For one thing, he seemed emotional about it and I didn't want to stir up any sad memories. And for another, I don't care. We are not getting involved in what caused the man's death. Besides, if you remember right, my focus at the time was on trying to keep you from getting arrested for shoplifting."

"Yes, of course," I said, wishing Rip was as inquisitive as I was. "By the way, I had a nice conversation with Devin today and apologized to him for my behavior yesterday."

"That's good." I was convinced steam was coming out of my ears, but Rip didn't appear to notice. I was almost surprised the fifth wheel's windows weren't fogging up. He said, "I would've bet you'd try to disguise yourself and slip in incognito."

"Disguise myself? Don't be ridiculous. That's such a silly notion, Rip," I said while thinking, *I know it's a silly notion because I tried it and it didn't work worth a damn.* "Devin said when he had a bad case of poison oak recently, he swabbed some witch hazel extract on the rash and it helped ease the itching and heal the blisters. There's some in the bag for you to try. He also told me he and Weston thought what I did in their containment room was hilarious."

"Huh? What are you talking about? I'm afraid to ask, but what did you do in the containment room?"

Too late it occurred to me I'd never mentioned anything about that to my straitlaced husband. He'd think my pranks were ridiculously childish, and I'll admit I was usually more sophisticated than that. But I do have my moments on occasion. "Did I tell you I picked up an apple fritter for you as a treat for how well you've done on your diet?"

"Really?" All thoughts of my actions in the containment room disappeared like a ten-year-old who'd just hit a baseball through his neighbor's front window. Having a husband with a sweet tooth the size of Texas could be handy at times. His face beaming, he said, "Whip it on me!"

I had actually bought the fritter for myself and was disappointed I'd had to sacrifice it to pull my ass out of the fire. I had planned to hide it behind the oatmeal box in the cabinet and snack on it later when Rip fell asleep during the NASCAR race with Dolly snoozing on his lap. The two never missed a televised race even though they both were normally cutting Z's before lap ten and woke up with three laps to go and the announcer saying, "Looks like it's going to be a green-white-checkered finish again."

As he relished *my* apple fritter, I reiterated my conversation with Amie about Wilson. I ignored the rolling of his eyes when I'd said running into her was purely coincidental. One has to choose their battles, you know. And a battle I was almost guaranteed to lose was not one I wanted to choose.

"That's kind of odd she didn't know her son had purchased a $138,000 convertible," Rip conceded. "But the man's a lawyer. . ."

Rip appeared to think his five-word remark explained everything. It was if he'd summed it all up by saying something like, "The man's a psychopath. . .," "The man's a walking time bomb. . .," or "The man's a blooming idiot. . ." Out of fear of a liability lawsuit, I'd like to clarify that none of these phrases have anything to do with being a lawyer.

"Enjoy the NASCAR race," I said as I left the living room. "I'm going to sit at the kitchen table and research where we might want to go sightseeing next."

"There's only so much to see and do in the area," Rip replied. "And we have plenty of time to see and do it. Let's take a few days off while my rash clears up."

"Of course. I have a book I want to finish, anyway, so this would be an opportune time to read it." I put the box of raisins I'd purchased in the cabinet, once again wondering if and when I'd ever use them. Months from now, I'd probably discover the dried-up grapes had become dried-up raisins and pitch them. "Don't forget the barbershop quartet has a practice session at the church Tuesday night."

"I know," Rip said around a mouthful of fritter. "Charlie called to check on me while you were at the store. He expected to see us at church today, so I explained that we spent the morning at the Urgent Care. He reminded me of the practice and I told him we'd be there."

"Good."

I recalled then that Amie had told me there was a celebration of life being held for Henry Harpodingle Tuesday night at the Moose Crossing Winery here in town. *Wouldn't you think Charlie Short would be planning to attend the memorial?* I thought. *After all, he did proclaim to be the best friend of the man whose life was to be celebrated.*

It was going to be interesting to see who showed up at practice Tuesday night. I knew how much the quartet wanted to win the singing contest for the third year in a row. *But come on! This was a close friend's life we're talking about. Just how intensely could anyone covet a barbershop quartet championship trophy? It's just a singing contest, for goodness' sake! No doubt the only reward for winning the competition was bragging rights and a sense of pride.*

I woke up Tuesday morning with a bad headache. It bordered on being one of the rare migraines I was occasionally afflicted with. I took a couple of ibuprofen and put a heating pad on my forehead, which did nothing to lessen the throbbing.

The headache lingered on all day and twice again I swallowed two ibuprofen tablets in hopes of it easing up. Rip made himself a sandwich at six o'clock and left for the quartet practice at Pacific Light Church at six-forty-five. We'd already determined I was in no condition to accompany him, and it was really not necessary anyway. Even though I wasn't due to take any additional pain-reducing pills for a couple of hours, I took two anyway, hoping it'd take the edge off. Then I lay back down as I'd been doing the majority of the day.

Suddenly, I sat straight up in bed as though a tornado had startled me by ripping the roof off of the fifth wheel. I grabbed my phone and began Googling. I soon discovered Henry Harpodingle's celebration of life was currently in process barely a stone's throw from the RV park. Rip had taken the truck, but I didn't need wheels to get to the Moose Crossing Winery. It was actually on my list of places to visit while we were here. I had considered asking Rip the following day if he wanted to walk across the highway for our evening alcoholic drinks, substituting our usual cocktails for a glass or two of wine. Maybe we'd even get a chance to each choose a flight of flavors and participate in a wine tasting. I realized that activity would appeal to Rip about as much as attending a quilting bee, but I also knew he would consent to it for my sake.

According to the blurb about the event that I'd found online, the celebration of life began at six and was scheduled to conclude at nine o'clock. Even though my head felt like a woodpecker was pounding holes into it, I got to my feet and immediately fell back into bed. *Vertigo*, I thought. *I should have stood up slower.*

I rose to my feet slower the second time. I felt a bit woozy, but my headache appeared to have eased off just a bit. *Those last two ibuprofen must be kicking in,* I reasoned. I removed my nightshirt and put on a black skirt and a frilly coral and white blouse. I slipped on a pair of black heels, pulled a tube of lipstick across my mouth, and ran a comb through my hair. I glanced into the mirror and confirmed I looked nice from the neck down. From the neck up I looked like death warmed over. I actually looked as if my family should be hosting a celebration of life for me.

But there wasn't much I could do about it. This was too good of an opportunity to pass up. I studied my reflection for a few more moments and questioned my sanity. I wasn't quite sure why this case mattered so much to me. I'd never even known Henry Harpodingle. Still, the more I found out about it, the more intrigued I became, and the more desperately I wanted to get justice for the victim. If justice was due, that is. I couldn't overlook the possibility the drunken klutz didn't suddenly decide to climb up on the railing and pretend he was a California condor. "An attempt to fly gone wrong" could be his actual cause of death, I realized. It was also possible vertigo could've made him lose his balance, much like it'd just done to me.

I knew I'd have to be clever and cunning about it. Rip would be furious if he knew what I planned to do. I didn't want his health affected by any stress I might cause him. Nor did I want to be scolded by him for getting involved. I'd decided it'd be best if he knew nothing about my involvement in the case. *If anyone could pull it off, it's me*, I told myself.

I knew Rip's practice would last about two hours, but I'd figure an hour and a half to be on the safe side. I only planned to see who was in attendance at the celebration of Henry's life. If the opportunity arose, I'd speak with the four likely attendees I was already acquainted with: Amie, Amanda, Wilson, and Devin. Mingling with the crowd, I might stumble onto a suspect I was currently unaware of, or I could learn an incriminating tidbit about one of them I already had on my short list.

Once I was stable enough on my feet to remain upright, I slipped out of the campground in my "Sunday go-to-church" attire and headed toward the winery. As I crossed Highway 101, I thought, *What could possibly go wrong?*

EIGHT

It was a longer walk to the winery than I'd anticipated. Knowing the time restraints I faced, I decided to take the shortcut through the vast lawn rather than the concrete sidewalk around its perimeter. In hindsight, I realized the shortcut took three times longer than the longcut probably would have. I soon regretted my choice of footwear. It had rained earlier in the afternoon, causing the spikes on my heels to sink two inches into the saturated ground with each step. I was relieved when I finally got back to the pavement.

Behind the wine production building and the smaller building where wine tastings and special events were held was a large vineyard. Even at night, it was easy to see it was well-maintained. The most notable thing about the property was the humongous American flag that was flown at the establishment's entrance. It was large enough to engulf a minivan and was hanging limp at the moment atop a flagpole that had to be at least fifty feet tall. *That's got to be the tallest thing in Klamath*, I thought, *except for the towering redwood trees the area is known for.*

That realization brought me to an abrupt halt. I did a complete

360-degree turn, scanning the horizon as I spun. I'd heard the thirteenth-story balcony was part of a hotel suite. His mother said he lived in Klamath. There were no thirteen-story buildings of any kind in this town, hotels or otherwise. There was no town in the vicinity with a large-enough population to warrant a building more than three or four stories tall, and that'd likely be a silo or the town's water tower. I should've realized from the beginning the hotel was not in Klamath. Besides, why would the man rent a hotel room in his hometown unless his own home was being fumigated for pests?

Where exactly did Henry die? I wondered. *Was he on a business trip at the time? A vacation? Attending some other unfortunate soul's celebration of life in another town?*

These were questions I hoped to get answered as I sauntered into the winery. With any luck at all, no one would notice me and inquire why I was attending the celebration of life for a perfect stranger, or at least a stranger. I don't know about characterizing Henry as perfect. Even his mother was aware he had multiple flaws.

My plan was to maintain a low profile, blend into the background like wallpaper, and go unobserved by everyone except maybe the handful of attendees I wanted to speak to. The Robert Burns quote, "The best-laid plans of mice and men often go awry," suddenly came to mind like an ominous intuition. As it would turn out, my best-laid plan took "going awry" to a whole new level.

I was greeted at the door by a distinguished-looking man I'd guess to be in his early forties, despite his silvery facial hair. He had a full beard and mustache of the same color and was built like a WWE wrestler.

"Welcome to Moose Crossing Winery. I don't think I've seen you around here before."

"Good evening. I'm Rapella Ripple. My husband and I just arrived in the area a couple of weeks ago. We're full-time RVers visiting California for the first time. I find the name of this winery kind of baffling because I'd read there were no moose in this region."

"That's true. However, there are a few Roosevelt elk here in Del Norte County, as well as Humboldt and western Siskiyou Counties," the man replied. "They estimate there's around a thousand Roosevelt elk in northern California. But there are also nearly six-thousand Tule elk, the smallest subspecies, in the central part of California, whereas Roosevelt elk are the largest."

"That's interesting, but now I'm even more confused," I told him after he explained more than I ever wanted to know about the elk in the area. "So why didn't the owner name his business Elk Crossing Winery?"

"Probably because *I'm* the owner and although my given name is Anthony Crossing, my parents nicknamed me Moose when I outgrew a size four snowsuit that had belonged to my older brother before he did."

"Moose" laughed and I chuckled along.

"So you go by the name Moose Crossing?" I was still having trouble accepting the fact a man with such classic good looks could go by such an odd moniker. The large, attractive man reminded me of Charlton Heston in his role as Moses in *The Ten Commandments*. It was a movie Rip and I watched every single year during the holidays. We could both recite the entire script along with the actors, and occasionally did.

"Yes, ma'am, I really do go by Moose Crossing." He hunched his shoulders and added, "That's what most people call me, anyway. There's a few folks who call me by even less flattering names, but we don't need to go into that right now. I hate to tell you we're not open to the public tonight because there's a private event going on here."

"Yes, I'm aware," I said. "Henry's mother is a good friend of mine."

Moose nodded at my gross exaggeration. The man who reminded me more of a fox than a moose—a silver fox, to be exact—reached for a glass of wine on a table behind him and handed it to me. "Please try a sample of our signature wine, which is called Moose Crossing Chardonnay."

"No vanity in that," I replied jokingly.

"I agree," Moose said. "But the name has such a memorable ring to it. Taste the Chardonnay and tell me what you think."

He waited as I held the clear glass goblet up at eye level and studied the color and clarity of the beverage. I then took a small sip. I barely managed not to spit it out because of how strong it was. I then sniffed the contents of the goblet, gave the wine a swirl, and finally took a larger sip. I was more prepared this time and swallowed it without gagging. I'd learned the proper way to sample wine while Rip and I were on an Alaskan cruise celebrating our golden wedding anniversary. For the first time since that cruise, I felt thankful for having attended the onboard wine-tasting class, which Rip had predicted would be a colossal waste of time.

"Earthy," I began, "with a hint of pineapple perhaps. I can tell it's been stored in oak barrels by its toasty quality and barely discernible tannic vibe. Your Chardonnay is excellent and would pair well with a chicken dish such as poulet de Bresse."

"Bravo, Ms. Ripple," Moose said with a look of delight. "It's so nice to meet another oenophile like myself."

I hadn't a clue what he was talking about as I'd never heard the term oenophile before. But the winemaker looked impressed by my description of his product, so I smiled and gave him a slight nod.

"The mere fact you know that an oenophile is another term for a connoisseur of fine wines says a lot about you. Have you always been an oenophile?" He asked. *No*, I could've replied. *I've never particularly cared for wine, especially white wine, which I find to be too dry for my liking. I'm more of a connoisseur of cheap tequila, which, when paired with orange juice and a splash of grenadine, suits me just fine.*

I smiled and nodded again. The less I said, the better, or it would be painfully obvious I couldn't tell a glass of Chardonnay from coconut water that'd been stored in an opened bottle for too long. Or even turpentine, for that matter. The Moose Crossing Chardonnay was every bit as overpowering as the paint-thinning solvent. Fortunately, Chardonnay was the type of wine the instructor at the wine-tasting class on the cruise ship had dwelled on the most. I'd paid careful attention and taken notes just in case the occasion ever arose when I wanted to impress someone with my wine knowledge. Lo and behold, that occasion had finally arisen.

"Thank you for the wine, Mr. Crossing." Without giving it any thought, I'd finished off the generous glass of wine Moose had given me. My throat felt like it'd been coated with battery acid. However, when Moose handed me a second glass, I grasped it by the stem as I'd learned serious wine connoisseurs always do. "Much appreciated. It was nice to meet you, Mr. Crossing."

"Call me Moose like all my other friends do," he instructed.

"All right. Thanks." *So Moose and I are now friends?* I thought. *I must've convinced him I was a sophisticated woman who knows a good wine when she tastes one.* I would never pass a "Moose Crossing" sign the rest of my life in Wyoming, Alaska, or anywhere else in the country, where this handsome man wouldn't spring to mind.

"Your friend, Amie Harpodingle, rented out the winery and will be picking up the check for all of the wine and refreshments consumed here tonight, so help yourself to the refreshments and more wine," Moose said. *Very generous of you*, I thought cynically. *How can the poor Wal-Mart clerk afford a tab like that?* Although I was pretty woozy, I tried to focus on the winemaker as he continued.

"She also paid off Henry's debt to the winery, which was considerable. Lawyer or not, he really was pretty much of a drunken loser. I adore his mom, Amie, however."

"So I take it you weren't very fond of Henry?"

"I can see you enjoy the Chardonnay as much as I do." Moose smiled proudly, but was clearly anxious to change the subject. I'd quickly drained the second generous glassful of wine he'd given me, which seemed to please the winemaker. Moose grabbed another bottle off the table, poured two fingers worth of its contents into a clean wine glass, and handed it to me, "Try our Pinot Grigio. It's an ideal sipping wine. I think you'll appreciate the acidic bite it has to it. It pairs so splendidly with Thai or Chinese cuisine."

"I agree completely," I replied after I'd gone through the entire wine-tasting routine again. I'd never heard of Pinot Grigio, much less tasted it. I was glad to discover it wasn't nearly as potent as the Chardonnay that had left a bitter taste in my mouth and an esophagus that felt as though I'd drank drain cleaner instead of wine. Moose seemed to be waiting for my detailed impression of the Pinot Grigio, but I was more concerned about the financial strain this evening might cause the grieving mother who was getting by on a retail clerk's salary. "Perhaps we could take up a collection and all pitch in so Amie's bank account doesn't take such a big hit."

"Oh, come on. You know as well as I do Amie would be offended by the very idea if I even mentioned it to her," he replied with a wink. "Which, my dear, I would never do."

Whatever, I thought. *Perhaps the proceeds of a GoFundMe account are covering the celebration of life along with Henry's other final expenses. If not, I will suggest setting up such an account to her niece, Amanda Castonova, if I see her here tonight.*

With a parting smile, I tried to walk away in such an elegant manner the winery owner would believe I was a member of an elite, high-class, wine-loving society. Still carrying the empty wine glass, I mimicked Naomi Campbell's runway stride as I walked away. I strutted, I sashayed, I swaggered, and then, without warning, I staggered. In the most inelegant fashion possible, I did a face plant onto the tile floor of the winery's main room. I wouldn't describe it as "nailing the landing," either, since all four of my limbs were aimed in different directions as I lay splayed out across the mosaic tile. A wave of dizziness had overtaken me. Between the multiple ibuprofens I'd taken throughout the day and the wine, I was as hammered as if I'd downed four double shots of José Cuervo just before arriving for Henry Harpodingle's memorial service. I could usually handle alcohol much better than this but I didn't usually mix it with over-the-counter pain medications.

So much for maintaining a low profile, I thought. The crowd of about forty guests had grown quiet. I don't know if it was the fall itself or the four-letter expletive that slipped out of my mouth when my face slammed into the tile that had silenced them so instantaneously. And, to be clear, that word wasn't "duck." It probably should've been however, because I knocked over a miniscule elderly man with my right arm as I tumbled. After helping the man to his feet and ensuring he was all right, the entire group stared at me as if unsure of what to do next. I felt like an injured wild animal they couldn't take their eyes off of but were afraid to approach. Just then, several drops of blood dripped out of my right nostril, which is what usually happens when you try to break a fall with your nose. The silence in the room was broken by a man, who sounded even more blotto than me, when he hollered, "Cut her off!" Everyone snickered and refused to make eye contact with me. I'm sure it was to avoid feeling guilty for making my embarrassment even more intense.

Looking around, I was surrounded by a zillion tiny shards of glass from the long-stem wine glass I'd been holding when I fell. Beyond humiliated, I refused to even glance at the winery owner. Alas, it was Moose Crossing himself who rushed to my side, asking me if I was okay and handing me a wad of tissue to staunch the bleeding. I'm not sure if it was because he genuinely cared or if he was just concerned about an impending personal injury lawsuit I might file with Henry's brother as my attorney. I could guarantee him no lawsuit would be filed. To me, it would be akin to suffering a serious burn injury after spilling coffee on your lap and then suing McDonald's for serving it to you hot.

I was astonished by how quickly a young man carrying a broom and dustpan arrived to clean up the broken glass. After assuring Moose I could stand under my own power, he helped me to my feet. Once it became clear to the other attendees the inebriated old broad hadn't broken a hip, they lost interest and began chatting amongst themselves again. Thankfully, a new batch of mourners had entered the winery, and Moose left me to greet them. I hurried to the opposite side of the room, trying not to make eye contact with anyone I passed on the way.

I walked over to look at the framed pictures of Mr. Harpodingle at different stages of his short life and other items of memorabilia spread out on a table. Behind the table, a continuous stream of photographs of Henry with family and friends were projected on a white sheet that'd been tacked to the wall. I noticed both Charlie Short and Devin Tubbs in several of the photos. Those were the only two indications I was at a celebration of life. There were no eulogies given, no minister reciting prayers for the dearly departed, no moments of silence to honor the deceased, not even a stack of pamphlets bearing his photos and details about his life and death. People were mingling and imbibing as if at a cocktail party. On occasion, they'd swing by a strategically-placed bowl of cheese chunks, mixed nuts, or butter mints and grab a snack. *I should've eaten something today to absorb the wine*, I thought as I ambled toward a bowl of fancy soda crackers. I hadn't had a morsel of food all day.

As I inhaled a handful of crackers, I gazed at the slide show on the wall. Two photos of Henry and Wilson as young boys showed the brothers with their arms around each other. They were laughing and obviously enjoying themselves. A picture of Amie with her two sons, all arm-in-arm and dressed nicely as if attending a church service, flashed up on the wall. Amie had long, beautiful blonde hair, and the teenage boys looked like twins. Next was a photo of Henry holding up a framed attorney license he'd received when he passed the bar exam and then a photo of him in a football uniform as a high-school athlete. It made me sad. It was evidence of a man living a good life that was cut too short.

I could hear laughter breaking out in various clusters of guests. Something told me they were chuckling about an anecdote involving Henry that someone had shared. It was unlike any celebration of life I'd ever been to. At Rip's and my age, funerals and celebrations of this sort comprised a huge hunk of our social schedule. Without them, our social outings would be pretty sparse and primarily health-related.

Why not bring in a band so folks could dance? Maybe even hold a karaoke contest, I thought. *And why not? It's not like this event is anything but an excuse to gather with family and friends and enjoy free wine.* They could all just as well have been celebrating the fact it was Tuesday, the hands-down favorite to win a dullest day of the week contest.

I felt a tap on my shoulder. I turned to see a look of concern on Devin Tubbs's face. "Are you okay, Mrs. Ripple? That was quite a spill you took."

"Yes, I'm fine, Devin. Nothing injured but my pride. I must've tripped over something." I took one last dab at my nose before stuffing the tissue in my pocket. Fortunately, my nosebleed hadn't turned into a major gushing episode, like a hemophiliac who'd gashed an artery. "My husband told me you were the last individual to see Henry alive. Is that true?"

"Yeah," he replied. His eyes misted over as he explained. "Henry was my best friend. I'd accompanied him to his brother's bachelor party, which was held at a bar in Sacramento."

"Why was it held in Sacramento?"

"No reason that I know of. Henry arranged it. He wanted Wilson's bachelor party to be memorable. I'll have to admit, it was definitely a party none of us who attended will ever forget."

"Where is Wilson, by the way?" I asked. "I would've expected to see him at his brother's celebration of life."

"Yeah, you'd think so," Devin replied. "They had each other's backs, but they were never exactly close. That's why I was so surprised that Henry was asked to be his best man and that he wanted Wilson's bachelor's party to be a more memorable evening than if they'd had the party anywhere in this vicinity. Like I said, the night was unforgettable, but for a whole different reason than its location."

"Such a shame," I said. "So what happened to Henry? It seems so absurd that he'd accidentally fall off a thirteen-story balcony."

"Are you all right, Mrs. Rapella?" Devin asked again.

"Yes, of course. Didn't we just go over that?"

"I'm not referring to your fall," he replied. "It's just that you seem to be slurring a lot of your words."

"Really?" I asked. "I thought my words sounded perfectly enunciated. In my head, they did anyway. Clearly, one should not mix ibuprofen with a couple of large glasses of Chardonnay."

"No, definitely not. One glass of Moose's Chardonnay is strong enough to kill an actual moose. Honestly, I can't believe you're still standing."

"So continue with what you were saying," I prompted Devin. I didn't want our conversation to veer away from what had happened to Henry. "You were responding to my query about the unlikelihood of a person accidentally falling off a thirteen-story balcony. What exactly *did* happen that night?"

"I'm not entirely sure." Devin pulled a handkerchief out of his pocket and blew his nose. He wiped his eyes before elaborating on what had occurred that evening that had left his best buddy dead.

"The party was crazy fun. Henry had booked a stripper and rented a private nightclub for the party. We drank a lot, stuffed dollar bills in strippers' garters, and Henry even danced on a table at one point. I cut myself off after three beers, but Henry got so trashed I was afraid to let him drive back to the hotel where we'd all booked rooms for the night. I took his keys and stuffed him in the back seat of my pickup."

"It sounds like you behaved very responsibly, Devin."

"Yeah, for what good it did." Devin paused as if the next part of the story was tough for him to verbalize. "Once we got to the hotel, I helped him up to our room—"

"You shared the hotel room with him?" I interrupted.

"Yes. It was so expensive we decided to share a room with two q-q-queen b-b- beds." Devin sounded defensive, especially when he stuttered his way through the words "queen beds." It was as if he felt I might be judging him for sharing a hotel room with another man. I didn't care if Devin identified as gay, bisexual, transgender, or as any other letter in the LGBTQIA acronym. I believe God created us all equal, and we each have the right to love who we choose without prejudice or persecution. If I'd felt differently, I might have just as well disowned my brother Billy from Mora, Minnesota, decades ago. And that will never happen! I love both Billy and his husband Bryce to pieces, figuratively, of course. My objection was not to Devin's sexual orientation but to how he could share a hotel room with the deceased and not know exactly what, or who, had killed him.

"Of course," I said with a smile. "Sharing a room is what I'd have done too in your shoes. As cheap as I am, I'd have shared the room with everyone at the bachelor party if I could, even if I had to sleep in the tub." Devin grinned and his tension appeared to ease up when he carried on with his story. "So, after I'd gotten Henry safely into the room, I had to take a leak. . ."

Devin stopped speaking as though he was afraid he'd offended me.

"Of course, you had to pee," I said. "You just said you drank three beers. I'd be up all night peeing."

"So, anyway, I discovered the toilet in our room was clogged up. I left Henry nearly passed out on one of the beds to go down to the front desk to get a plunger, a bag of chips out of the vending machine, and to put in a wake-up call while I was at it. I assumed he'd be so fast asleep he'd never even realize I was gone."

"That's what anyone would've assumed, Devin. Go on," I prompted, when Devin hesitated. I could tell it was the next part of the story that was really eating Devin up inside, like a dozen tapeworms had taken up residency in his belly.

"When I got back to the room, Henry was missing. At first I thought he might have gotten a second wind and gone down to the bar in the hotel. At the time, the idea angered me. But now I wish it'd been exactly what he'd done."

"I understand completely."

"Then I noticed the balcony door was open. I walked out to look over the edge with an instinctive feeling of dread. That's when I saw his body sprawled out on the pavement below. Several people were gathered around him, but from that height I couldn't make out what they were doing."

"Oh, my, Devin. That's just awful." I gave the heartbroken man an impromptu hug. "I'm so sorry for your loss and what you went through. I can't imagine losing your best friend so tragically, and at such a young age. Do you know what preempted his fall?"

"No. I have no idea."

"If you had to guess, then, would you suspect his plunge off the balcony was an accident, suicide, or at the hands of someone else?"

"Am I being interrogated?" Devin asked with a wry grin.

I laughed along with Devin and jokingly asked, "Do you have

an alibi that'll account for your whereabouts at the time of Henry's death?"

My question must've come out sounding more accusatory than teasing, as I'd actually intended, because Devin stopped laughing. "Of course I do. I chatted with the hotel clerk manning the front desk for probably half an hour, during which time Henry's death occurred."

"I was only joking with you, Devin," I explained as I ran my right hand up and down his sleeve. "It was insensitive, especially considering the reason we're both here, and I apologize. I most certainly was not inferring in any way you might've had something to do with Henry's death. It's quite the contrary. Taking his keys away so he didn't decide to go bar-hopping and get involved in a wreck or picked up for a DUI is all the proof one needs to know you were very protective of your friend."

He nodded. It would've been even more insensitive for me to repeat my previous question or to ask him anything further about his buddy's death. So, instead, I said, "Again, I am so sorry for your loss. Just out of curiosity, how did Henry's death affect Wilson's wedding?"

"Well, since Henry was to serve as his brother's best man, and it didn't seem right to go ahead with the wedding without him, it's been indefinitely postponed. It would've been a joyless ceremony, so I'm glad they put it off for a while."

"Yeah, I'm glad too. That wouldn't have been a very auspicious beginning to the couple's marriage."

Devin agreed, and we parted ways. I'd just spotted Amanda Castonova coming in the front door of the winery. I was thankful she'd missed out on the scene I'd created earlier.

"Hello, Amanda," I greeted her a few minutes later. "Do you remember me?"

"Of course," she responded. "You and your husband came in the café the other day. I'm sorry, but I've forgotten your name."

"It's Rapella."

"Oh, yes, that's right," she replied, as if assuring me that even in my current state of drunkenness, I'd correctly remembered my own name. She appeared to have no trouble remembering my husband's name. "Where's Rip?"

"He had to attend practice for the upcoming barbershop quartet competition."

"I might've already told you, but both of my cousins were involved in that competition. Henry competed with the Klamath team before his death, and Wilson sings baritone for the Siskiyou County team. The competitiveness between the brothers bordered on insane. A huge wager was placed between the two every year, too. Since Henry had won the bet the last two years in a row, Wilson was out for blood this year. Naturally, the contest became a moot point after Henry's death."

"Yes, of course." I gave her a hug and offered my condolences.

Insane competiveness? Out for blood this year? Those two phrases bounced around in my mind for a few seconds, along with random alcohol-induced hallucinations. *Is it even worth considering that the wager between the brothers could've had something to do with the tragic "accident"?* After some consideration, I decided it wasn't likely.

"Are you all right, Rapella?" Amanda asked.

"Yes, I'm fine. Like I just told Devin, I'm learning that ibuprofen and wine do not mix well. So pardon me if I seem to be slurring my words."

"Well, yes, there's that," she conceded, "but I was referring to the fall I heard you took before I arrived."

Swell, I thought. *I'll be fortunate if someone didn't catch my stumble on video. If so, it's undoubtedly already gone viral. If that was the case, Regina would've already seen it on her phone and informed her father about it, and Rip will be apoplectic by the time I return home.*

"Yes, I'm fine. It was just a little stumble." Amanda looked skeptical. To change the topic, I asked, "How did you first hear about your cousin's passing?"

"I was out of town that night, but I got a call from Aunt Amie who had just been notified of her son's death by the local sheriff."

Just then, we looked across the room as Amanda's Aunt Amie passed out and crumpled to the floor. Somehow, Amie's fall resembled a graceful ballerina dissolving in slow motion, where mine was more reminiscent of an inebriated lumberjack pitching face-first into a lodge-pole pine tree. Thankfully, no one laughed or made rude remarks following Amie's collapse, such as, "Cut her off!"

"Oh, my!" I exclaimed. "Your poor aunt must have been overcome with emotion at the loss of her son."

Amanda shook her head. "Nah, I doubt it. I imagine it's a reaction to the chemo treatments she's been undergoing. They've made her weak and light-headed."

"Chemo treatments?" I thought back to the bamboo cap Amie had been wearing when I spoke with her at Wal-Mart. When I'd seen the photos of her with beautiful long blonde hair in the slide show, I'd wondered why she'd cover it with a cap. "Oh, no. Has she been diagnosed with cancer?"

"Yes," Amanda replied. "It's an aggressive form of liver cancer. Stage four, I'm afraid."

"That's incredibly sad." I hugged Amanda again. "I'm so sorry. I thought she looked fatigued when I ran into her at Wal-Mart, but I had no idea she was sick. Is she still working due to financial issues, like paying off steep medical bills? I was thinking about setting up a GoFundMe account for her."

I was surprised when Amanda laughed at my suggestion.

"Aunt Amie would be furious if someone did that." Amanda followed her response with one of her adorable snorts. "She's loaded! My late uncle invented some kind of adhesive that went effing nuts on the QVC channel when it first came out. It made him a millionaire practically overnight. But he was killed in a car wreck two months later. Aunt Amie inherited the patent and his entire estate. Trust me; she's not still working for the money. She just needs to keep busy so she doesn't sit around and mope and think about her. . ."

Amanda's explanation of her aunt's financial status explained Moose Crossing's earlier remarks when I suggested everyone should chip in on the cost of the celebration of life event. When Amanda paused and began to cry, I said, "I know, honey. I'm so sorry. What a heartbreaking time for your entire family. With Henry's death, and what's likely to be your Aunt Amie's imminent passing, it's a lot of grief for a family to absorb."

"Yes, it is," Amanda said through her tears. "Fun fact: Aunt Amie has donated every penny she's earned from her current job to a local pet rescue charity. She owns nine cats herself."

"Ah-ha! The crazy cat lady." I instantly felt remorseful for my quip. "I'm sorry. That was insensitive."

"No, it wasn't." Amanda had stopped weeping and was able to snicker. "That's exactly what everyone in the family and probably most of her friends call her. She'll probably leave her entire estate to them, or at least to someone who'll take care of them after she's gone."

Her last remark opened up the water faucet again. A tear rolled down her cheek. Hoping to make her laugh again, I said, "Maybe you should volunteer for the job so you can quit your job and build that dream home on Mad River."

It worked. Amanda laughed and replied, "Trust me, I have volunteered. But after I killed my own cat by closing the garage door on him, I doubt she'll give my offer serious consideration."

I didn't know if it was appropriate to laugh about her dead cat, or not, but since she was chuckling, I did too. "I'm sorry about your kitty's death, but you'd think she would've heard the door coming down and skedaddled."

"Tinkerbell couldn't hear the door." This time, Amanda's voice sounded solemn. I sensed guilt was setting in. "She was pure white with two blue eyes. Fun fact: up to eighty-five percent of white cats with blue eyes are born deaf. The congenital deafness is linked to something called a 'W gene.'"

"That's interesting." Amanda's fun facts reminded me of the Sheldon Cooper character in the *Big Bang Theory* sitcom. "I didn't know that about white cats. Did you know that ninety-nine percent of calico cats are female?"

"Yes." Amanda nodded. "The one percent that's male doesn't live long because of a chromosomal abnormality. They're also sterile. I learned that from Aunt Amie, of course."

I nodded. As I was listening to Amanda expound on "fun feline facts," I glanced over her shoulder and saw Stanley Ledge, Buster Boeing, and Charlie Short stroll through the front door. *Oh good!* was my first thought. I was relieved Henry's singing companions had made it to his celebration of life. *Oh, crap!* was my next thought. If the rest of the barbershop quartet was here, that meant Rip was undoubtedly back home in the fifth wheel, at least thirty minutes earlier than even my most conservative estimation. He had to be frantic about my disappearance. I was actually surprised he hadn't tried to call me. I realized then it was loud in the winery with so many conversations taking place at the same time, so I checked my phone for missed calls and found none.

I quickly told Amanda I needed to head home and asked her to please not mention seeing me at her cousin's memorial service if and when Rip and I showed back up at the café to try the brisket and fries basket. She promised she'd never reveal having seen me at the celebration of life, even though she looked perplexed by the necessity of it. Thankfully, she didn't ask me to explain.

I raced across the room and out the front door, with barely a wave at Moose Crossing, who was still manning the front door. I slipped off my heels, and carrying one in each hand, began to sprint across the damp lawn. I'm not sure my top speed at seventy-two years old would actually qualify as sprinting. It might be more aptly described as scampering, or more accurately yet, laboring. Regardless, I was hoofing it as best I could, given the circumstances. While running across the vast lawn, I had to stop twice to puke. I also tripped and fell three times. At least the landings were much softer than the tile floor had been. I couldn't recall feeling this intoxicated since my senior prom. My stomach was churning like a freight train chugging up a steep incline.

Although it was hard to maintain a train of thought for more than a few seconds, I tried to think of a plausible explanation for where I'd been. My destination had to be important enough I'd felt determined to go to Henry's celebration of life at the winery with no vehicle at my disposal, even though it was close enough to walk to. Rip knew I'd been under the weather all day. That left two places: the campground's putt-putt course and the winery. My astute husband would rule out the putt-putt course immediately. Because, let's be real, who plays putt-putt in the dark? With no other options, I'd have to tell the truth, I realized.

"I walked to the winery," I'd say.

"Why?" he'd most certainly ask.

"Because my headache had abated and I was bored. Since I was anxious to explore a place with a crazy name like Moose Crossing Winery when there are no moose in northern California, I thought, why not walk over and check it out?" My explanation would satisfy Rip about as much as a kale salad when he's craving a t-bone.

The inspiration made me feel even more panicky than before I'd tried to concoct some believable justification for my being out and about afoot after dark. My goose was not only cooked; it was deboned, diced into tiny chunks, and devoured. There was no other possible outcome for this harebrained notion I'd had. I didn't know if the burning in the pit of my stomach was from the anxiety of disappointing Rip or a result of the booze and pain-reducing drugs I'd ingested. *It's mostly likely a combination of both*, I thought.

I've been told on numerous occasions, by numerous individuals, after numerous self-inflicted kerfuffles, that I was my own worst enemy. I'm beginning to think there might be something to that.

When I reached the RV park, I tore off my muddy and shredded pantyhose and tossed them in a dumpster as I sped by it. When I reached the fifth wheel, I looked in the window. I was surprised to see Rip munching on a pork rind in his recliner. Clearly, he hadn't even bothered to check in on me when he'd returned from practice. He also clearly had a hidden bag of forbidden pork rinds in the trailer, which irritated me even though I frequently hid some of my favorite food items from him.

I watched as he handed Dolly a green dental treat before snatching another pork rind from the bag for himself. *Good Lord*, I thought. *No wonder they're both overweight.*

After Rip handed Dolly's next "greenie" to her, he got up and traipsed into the bathroom, leaving the restroom door ajar. *This is my chance*, I thought.

I eased the door of the trailer open, slipped inside, and quickly tiptoed down the hallway to the bedroom. With his back to me as he urinated into the toilet, he had no clue I wasn't sound asleep in bed as I quietly passed by the open bathroom door.

I climbed into bed and pulled the bed covers up to my chin. As I suspected he might do, he glanced into the bedroom after he'd finished in the bathroom. Most likely, he wanted to ensure he hadn't awoken me so he could continue to pig out on the fatty pork rinds. He certainly didn't take the time to put a mirror under my nose to see if I was still breathing or anything of that nature. I found that disheartening. My heart was full again when I barely heard him whisper, "Love you, honey," before backing out the bedroom door. I whispered, "Love you more," once the door had closed behind him.

After Rip had returned to the living room to resume his snack-rotating game with Dolly, I changed clothes quickly in the dark and crawled back into bed. All the while, I was thinking I needed to scratch the Moose Crossing Winery off my list of places to visit while staying at the Mystic Forest RV Park. It wasn't because I'd already been to the winery, but because I didn't want to have to explain to Rip when the winery's owner met us at the door and asked, "Have you recovered from the nasty fall you took here the other night, Mrs. Ripple?"

"You must've mistaken me for someone else," I'd have had no choice but to reply, "Someone who's ironically also named Mrs. Ripple."

Nope! I thought. *Not ever stepping foot on Moose Crossing's property again!*

NINE

I woke up the next morning with a horrible hangover and an ugly bruise on my right cheek, the kind that slowly transforms from purple to orange to yellow before finally fading away. My right nostril was caked with dried blood, as well. I was fortunate a raccoon was not looking back at me from the mirror. Years ago, after I'd undergone deviated septum surgery, I'd ended up with two black eyes, due simply to their proximity to my nose where the operation had taken place. If there was any way to disguise the discoloration on my face, I would've, but there wasn't near enough foundation in my makeup bag to cover it up.

When I walked out to the kitchen, Rip looked up at me in alarm. "What in tarnation happened to you?"

It's hard to explain how a person can sustain a bruise like mine while lying in bed, and I hate to tell my husband bald-faced lies unless it's the last resort. So I told him the absolute truth, but in a very evasive way.

"I got up in the middle of the night to pee." I actually *did* get up to tinkle at around midnight. I had to pee again at three-thirty.

And then pee once more at five. After all, I had drunk what seemed like a gallon of wine before going to bed.

"When did peeing become a contact sport?" Rip asked.

"I made a misstep and took a tumble." And as you know, I *did* stumble and fall at the winery a few hours earlier. So, unless I'd omitted the period after "pee" and combined those two sentences with a conjunction, such as the word "and," which I had not, there was no lying involved in my response.

With my ugly bruise and Rip's poison oak rash, we decided it was best to just chill in the fifth wheel all day.

"We're a pair to draw to, aren't we?" Rip asked. "We have plenty of time left to see all we want to see in the area. It makes sense to take a day off now and then to rest, relax, and enjoy the comforts of our new RV. I'm fixing to watch a Gunsmoke marathon and you're probably looking forward to doing a load of laundry today, anyway."

There was so much I wanted to say in response. *Have you not seen every one of the 635 episodes of* Gunsmoke *a dozen times already?* And, *the washer and dryer could be made of solid gold and serve me tequila sunrises and beer nuts while I worked, and I would still never "look forward" to doing laundry. I'd definitely be more willing, however.* Those were just a couple of the responses that immediately came to mind.

Instead, I just nodded and began to prepare us each a small bowl of oatmeal and a couple of slices of cantaloupe. Rip groaned when he saw that, once again, bacon, eggs, and biscuits and gravy were not on our breakfast menu. I ignored him. I'm sure he felt as though our random days of R&R in the fifth wheel should be accompanied by greasy, cholesterol-laden meals that'd ascertain his arteries would clog up like the toilet in Devin and Henry's Sacramento hotel room.

We spent the next few weeks alternating between busy days of touring the area to check "places to visit" off my list and quiet days spent lounging around the campground and getting to know some of our fellow campers. There was one particular couple named Jack and Janet Wright, whom we became quite fond of. Jack was of average height and weight and wore his hair in a buzz cut. Janet was about five feet two, had long blonde hair and hazel eyes, and was extremely attractive. In one of those "small world" coincidences, they were from the same subdivision in Shawnee, Kansas, that our friend, Lexie Starr, and daughter Wendy, lived in prior to moving into the Alexandria Inn in Rockdale, Missouri, with Lexie's new husband, Stone Van Patten.

One Tuesday morning, while Rip was in town washing the truck, I called Lexie. While chatting with her, I mentioned the Wrights.

"Of course, I know Jack and Janet!" Lexie exclaimed. "They are so much fun! Sheila Davison will always be my BFF because I've known her forever and we've always been like twins separated at birth, but Janet is a close second. Tell them hello for me and that I miss them dearly."

"I will do that this evening when we join them for dinner at the historic Requa Inn on the Klamath River. The inn's been in operation for over one hundred years."

"Being an inn owner myself, it sounds very intriguing," Lexie replied. "You'll have a blast going with the Wrights. But, then, you'd have fun with those two just going to a service station to get an oil change. I'm so jealous right now. I truly have a major case of FOMO."

FOMO was one of the acronyms I'd learned from a gal named Harlei Rycoff while visiting our granddaughter in Albuquerque last October. Harlei found using real words to be too time-consuming, I think, because she used acronyms instead whenever possible. "I hate that you're missing out too, Lexie. Maybe Janet and I can facetime you from the inn."

"Oh, please do!" Lexie insisted. "After dinner, you should all find a bar, or maybe a winery, to go get a drink. That'd be right up the Wrights' alley. Jack actually retired from a major beer company. Jack and my best friend Sheila are both die-hard Miller Lite drinkers. And, by the way, just saying that makes my FOMO flare up even fiercer."

We laughed, and I replied, "We might go to a bar, maybe. There's only one winery in town and I've been forced to ban myself from it."

"Oh, no," she responded in an amused tone. "Rapella? What. Did. You. Do?"

After making Lexie promise to keep my story confidential, I reiterated my experience at the Moose Crossing Winery. After I first mentioned the name of the winery, she asked, "Have you and Rip seen any moose since you've been there?"

"No. There are no moose in northern California."

"Then why—?"

"It's a long story and not particularly important. Rip might be back any minute, so I can't waste time explaining it."

"Oh, no," Lexie repeated. "Hence the reason I've been sworn into secrecy. If this is one of the stories I can't bring up around Rip, I know it's got to be a dandy. Is it as bad as what happened to you when you went dumpster diving to find two cookies in Rochester, Minnesota?"

"It's comparable," I replied. "Ironically, I was just thinking about that humiliating experience earlier today."

"You've got to share that story with Janet. It's hilarious."

"And terribly embarrassing," I added."But I'll think about it. The point I was trying to make was that I'm trying to look into this man's death without alerting Rip. I think I might've promised him I wouldn't get *us* involved in another murder case. However, I don't think I promised him that *I, personally,* wouldn't get involved in another one."

"Yeah," she said knowingly. "I believe I made that same promise to Stone. Three or four times, at last count. I won't say a thing. I swear."

"Thank you, Lexie. I *would* like to keep my vow not to get 'us' involved, if at all possible. I don't even want him to know I've gotten myself involved in Henry's death." I looked at my watch and continued. "Now, hush up, so I can tell you what happened and what's going on that preempted my visit to the winery."

I was able to tell her the *Reader's Digest* condensed version of everything I remembered from first hearing about the death of Henry Harpodingle up to sneaking back into the fifth wheel while Rip took a leak. I had to pause on occasion to wait for her to stop snickering. I finally asked, "How am I going to be able to tell you this entire tale before Rip gets back if you keep laughing?"

"You expect me to be able to refrain from laughing after you tell me that in your tanked-up condition you did a face plant in the middle of a somber celebration of life ceremony?"

"Well, I wouldn't exactly call it a 'somber' ceremony—"

"Seriously, pal?"

"Okay, okay." I consented. "It is kind of amusing now, but it sure wasn't very funny when it happened."

"You know what?"

"What?"

"I know Janet would be more than happy to pitch in and help if you need assistance with anything while you're investigating the case. And I also know she won't spill the beans to Rip, or even Jack."

"That's great to know." I felt a sense of relief and had a hunch I'd be calling on Janet Wright to help me out before all was said and done. "Thanks for the suggestion."

Just then, I saw the new Ram truck rumbling up the road. I

ended my call with Lexie and went inside to do a load of laundry. After all, I'd been *looking forward* to it all day.

Dinner that evening with the Wrights was a lot of fun. As an appetizer, we all shared a plate of cold smoked steelhead trout with cheese and crackers, and each of us ordered their evening special as our entrée. Rip had been craving steelhead trout since Amanda had mentioned it at the Annie Creek Café. And the special, consisting of braised beef shoulder, carrots, and mashers, sounded as delicious as it had actually turned out to be. We chatted and laughed and truly enjoyed each other's company. I'd insisted Rip wear his hearing aids so he was able to fully participate in the conversation.

At one point, Janet suggested we stop at the winery after supper to participate in a wine tasting. She'd been anxious to check the place out. Rip and Jack nodded in agreement and I shrugged as though I was indifferent. When the two men stepped outside to view the beach at Requa Inn where the Klamath River met the Pacific Ocean, I said, "Janet, I need to tell you something while the men are outside."

I proceeded to tell her an even more condensed version of the implausible death of Henry Harpodingle and my visit to the Moose Crossing winery. It was so condensed I left out the face-plant part of it completely. I explained why I didn't want Rip to know about my involvement in the case and why, due solely to that reason, I couldn't be seen at the winery ever again.

"I understand completely," Janet replied. "My lips are as sealed as if I'd super-glued them together. If you ever need any help—"

The men appeared over my shoulder just then and Janet ceased talking abruptly. I winked at her and nodded and she nodded back. Relief flooded through me, knowing I had a helping hand if one became necessary. A couple of clichés came to mind. Two heads were always better than one and misery loves company. The latter was in the event everything came crashing down, landing us in deep doo-doo, which was never beyond the realm of possibility when I was involved in a murder case. I had a notion both clichés would come into play in the near future.

A few minutes later, Rip remarked, "Are you folks ready to head to the winery? If I'm not mistaken, it's one of the places on Rapella's list she wants to visit while we're here."

I turned into a pillar of stone, but Janet, bless her heart, responded, "I have a better idea. We've been to the winery and it's not much to brag about. I wouldn't bother even going there if I was you."

Rip nodded, clearly forgetting this was the woman who'd earlier suggested we go to the winery because she'd been anxious to check it out. Jack appeared dumbfounded by Janet's remarks, as Rip asked, "Okay. What do you have in mind?"

"Let's pick up a six-pack of Miller Lite at the liquor store and then explore the Klamath River. I read online that people can walk to a hidden beach and sometimes you can spot black bears swimming across the river."

"Oh, yes!" I exclaimed a little overzealously. "That sounds like fun! Let's do that instead of going to some old winery. Rip and I aren't big wine drinkers, anyway."

"Great," Janet said. "And one day this week, I'd like to take Rapella to this really unique shop I heard about the other day. It's in Eureka, about an hour or so south of here. You men are more than welcome to go along, but—"

"That'd be a hard pass for me," Jack replied.

"I'm with Jack on this one," Rip added.

As it turned out, we didn't see any swimming bears, but we did see a mother river otter interacting with her baby. Mama otter appeared to be teaching her offspring how to break a crab apart by floating on her back, placing the crab on her chest, and smashing it with a rock pulled from under her arm. It was fascinating to watch and we did so for at least fifteen minutes.

Later, we were all startled when a dark brown deer-like animal with an impressive set of antlers ran out from behind a large conifer tree.

Rip exclaimed, "That's the largest elk I've ever seen!"

"It must be one of those Roosevelt elks that are found in the rainforest regions of northern California, specifically Del Norte, Humboldt, and western Siskiyou Counties," I said with an unmistakable hint of smugness in my voice. "Interesting fact: there are approximately a thousand of them in northern California and nearly six thousand Tule elk that are more centrally located in the state. Roosevelt is the largest elk subspecies and Tule elk are the smallest."

Rip looked at me as if I'd just explained how supersymmetry was related to the string theory. "Where'd you learn all that?"

At the winery, while I was speaking to a fellow oenophile named Moose about elk and how nicely an earthy Chardonnay pairs with a chicken dish such as poulet de Bress, I could've said had I wanted to blow Rip's mind into a zillion gooey pieces. But I didn't want to share any of that, so I simply stated a fact. "Rip, you know I enjoy Googling interesting local facts about areas we're visiting."

"Yeah, right." Rip raised his eyebrows. "And, by the way, fun or interesting facts coming from a young lady on a waitress's salary whose head is in the clouds and thinks she'll one day be able to afford a dream home on the Mad River is cute. But coming from a mature woman with more common sense? Not so much."

I felt properly censured. Once again, I had only myself to blame. Trying to show off my knowledge about an animal I should have absolutely no idea even existed was a stupid error in judgment on my part. *I won't make that mistake again*, I vowed to myself. *If I want to keep Rip unaware of my involvement in investigating the truth behind*

Henry Harpodingle's death, I'm going to have to be more cunning and a whole lot craftier.

A few minutes later, while the men were checking out the hidden beach, I was able to draw Janet aside and ask, "What shop were you talking about taking me to?"

"Shop?" Janet asked with a laugh. "There actually is a cute shop in Eureka that Jack knows I thought was interesting, but I have no intention of taking you there. I just thought it'd be a good opportunity to do some investigating into the death of that Henry fellow with the odd last name. Surely by then, there'll be someone whose potential motive and possible alibi you might want to check into. I'm anxious to help you. I always marveled at how Lexie was able to track down a killer when even the local detectives were having no luck."

"Lexie's the one who got me into this exciting world of amateur sleuthing. I'm not sure if I should love her or hate her for that. Even though I've had some pretty hairy life-or-death moments, I still find it thrilling to be able to get justice for a victim and closure for their family. Just knowing the truth can make all the difference in the world for the victim's loved ones."

"I can't wait to get involved in Henry's case with you." Janet was beaming from ear to ear, like a kid about to go on their first pony ride.

"And I can't wait to go 'shopping' with you," I said with a chuckle and air quotes.

Janet smiled again and held her beer can up in the air to clink against mine. As a toast, she said, "To justice!"

I barely knew this woman and already adored her. I had a gut feeling that, like my relationship with Lexie, we'd be friends for the rest of our days on Earth.

***

It was three days later when Janet and I went "shopping" at the Annie Creek Café in Mazama Village at Crater Lake National Park. I'd had a sudden hankering for a barbecue brisket sandwich and asked Janet to join me. Jack had planned to play a round of golf with another gentleman he'd met at the campground, so Janet said she was delighted to come along.

"Janet will be picking me up in a few minutes," I told Rip. "There's some leftover spaghetti in the refrigerator for you if you get hungry."

"There *was* some leftover spaghetti in the refrigerator, but I ate it before you got out of bed this morning." I flinched at the thought Rip was up chowing down on spaghetti at six o'clock in the morning, and then gobbled down his breakfast an hour later. But I didn't want to squabble with him about his atrocious eating habits, so I remained silent while Rip continued. "I'll have a can of Vienna sausage with a handful of saltines for lunch. So, where are you two ladies off to?"

"Remember when we were out with the Wrights the other night and she said there's a cute shop in Eureka she wants to take me to?" I made certain I didn't actually state we were going to the shop Janet had mentioned.

"Oh, sure. Have fun."

"Thanks, honey. I'm sure we'll have a good time."

"Love you, babe," Rip said.

I walked over, gave Rip a kiss, and said, "Love you more."

I then stepped out of the fifth wheel and sat down in a lawn chair on our concrete patio. At straight up eleven o'clock, Janet arrived in her Hyundai Veloster. She and Jack towed the sporty yellow car behind their Winnebago motorhome. Soon, we were off on an adventure. I hadn't actually planned for the day to turn into an adventure, but as they say, shit happens! And in this case, the phrase was not figurative, but rather, spot on!

TEN

Janet was about my age and had a bubbly personality that reminded me of our mutual friend, Lexie Starr. It was no wonder they were such good friends. As she pulled out of the campground, she asked, "So where are we really headed this morning?"

"I wanted to treat you to lunch at a cozy little café in Crater Lake National Park."

"Cool," Janet replied. "It kind of makes me wish I hadn't just eaten a ham sandwich."

"No problem, Janet. I've already eaten, too," I admitted. "But nothing says we can't have a cup or two of coffee."

"Count me in," she said. "I never say no to coffee."

"Then you must stay fully caffeinated when you're with Lexie. She drinks more strong brew than anyone I've ever met."

"You're telling me! Even I can't compete with her when it comes to downing coffee by the potfulls."

I laughed and asked, "Is 'potfull' even a real word?"

"It is when you're with Lexie," Janet replied. "I take it by the fact you also ate before we left that lunch is not the true reason we're going to the café. Am I right?"

"You are absolutely right! There's a waitress there I hope to get some valuable information from while we linger over coffee."

"I'm quickly learning there's always a hidden agenda when it comes to you."

"Shrewd observation, Janet."

We carried on in the same jocular vein until we reached Annie Creek Café in Mazama Village. Amanda was ringing a customer's bill up at the cashier stand when we entered. When she spotted me, she waved enthusiastically.

I introduced Amanda to Janet as she set us at a window table with a beautiful view of the lake. We ordered coffee: mine black, Janet's with copious amounts of sugar and cream. I was amused to discover there wasn't much room left for caffeine once she'd doctored up her drink.

I was glad to see the restaurant wasn't excessively busy, so speaking to our waitress whenever possible wouldn't keep her from waiting on her other customers.

"That was quite an unusual celebration of life the other night, wasn't it?" I asked Amanda. "I'd never been to one before that was so casual and, to be honest, so dispassionate. If one didn't already know, they'd have thought they were at a cocktail party."

"Yes. But that's exactly the way Henry would've wanted it," Amanda explained. "He never took himself, or anything else, very seriously. Henry liked to entertain clients at the winery and would tell the server there to put it on his tab. Trouble was, he never seemed to pay off that tab. It had grown ridiculously large. Between having that huge bill paid off, and the cost of the celebration of life at the winery, Henry's death was a real windfall for Moose."

It was the tone of her voice that made me wonder if Amanda

had some reason to believe the winemaker might've played a part in Henry's death. Mr. Crossing had appeared to me to be a laid-back, introspective type of guy, incapable of taking another person's life. *But,* I reminded myself, *according to the old adage, you can't judge a winemaker by his low-key demeanor.*

"I can see why the winery owner would be anxious to get his money. Wasn't Henry an attorney?" I asked Amanda, even though I was well aware of the answer.

"Yes. He mostly represented women in divorce court. I think he then bedded most of his newly divorced clients." Amanda rolled her eyes. "My cousin was quite the player. He'd shower these women with lavish gifts, fancy dinners, and expensive wine. Wine he never paid for, of course. But after a couple of months, he'd get bored with them and move on to the next divorcee. Henry spent money faster than he brought it in."

"Or didn't spend money, as in the winery's case," Janet replied.

We all chuckled at her remark. Then I asked Janet, "Do you remember I told you about a man we met at the Pacific Light Church in Klamath?"

"Yes, of course," Janet responded. "Wasn't his name Charlie Short? And didn't he ask Rip to replace Amanda's cousin Henry as the tenor in their barbershop quarter?"

"Exactly," I said. "Charlie's wife Fern told me Charlie and Henry were best friends. A security guard at the Crescent City Wal-Mart named Devin Tubbs also told me that Henry was *his* best friend, so apparently, Henry had a lot of best friends."

"He was everyone's best friend," Amanda said. "Or so he made them believe. He was my best friend throughout my entire child-hood. To this day, he was my favorite relative, which is why his death has hit me so hard. I can't believe anyone would kill a fun-loving, laidback guy like Henry."

"I can only imagine how hard it's been for you and for your

Aunt Amie." I didn't want the conversation to get sidetracked, so I reverted back to the former topic. "Anyway, Fern said she felt Henry was a bad influence on Charlie. Henry was a swinging single and acted as though Charlie was unencumbered with a spouse as well. She said Henry liked to frequent strip bars and places of that sort. Like you, Amanda, Fern thought Henry was a womanizer."

"Henry does sound like a ladies' man," Janet agreed. "My guess is he broke a lot of women's hearts with his love-'em-and-leave-'em lifestyle. Is there any chance it was one of them who pushed him over the edge, literally?"

"I wondered about that too," Amanda said. "But there were so many of them it'd be hard to guess which one would've been devastated enough to kill him."

I hadn't considered that angle, and the idea was discouraging. It sounded like there were a lot of potential suspects with identical motives, and I had no way of knowing who to question or where to find them. I felt like I'd just slammed up against a rock wall. Then Amanda spoke again.

"He had a tendency to wear out his welcome pretty rapidly when it came to women."

"That's probably pretty common with a ladies' man," I said.

Amanda nodded and said, "If I had to suspect one of them, it'd be his last fling."

"Who's that, Amanda?" I asked, anxious to get a good lead on who Henry's killer might've been.

"He had an affair with Buster Boeing's wife not long before his death. It caused quite a stir in the little town of Klamath."

"Buster Boeing?" Janet asked Amanda. She then turned to me and asked, "Isn't that the man you said sings lead in the same barbershop quartet Rip will be singing tenor? I believe you said he's a hefty man without a hair on his head."

"Yes, that's right." Stunned, I could barely focus enough to respond to my new friend. When I didn't continue, Janet asked, "Are you all right, Rapella?"

"Yes, I'm fine. Amanda's last remark took me by surprise. I was going to say Buster is about three decades younger than Rip, but the two men are built exactly the same. If you were to wrap them both in tin foil from the forehead down, tossed them in a bag and shook it up, and then dumped them out on the floor, you wouldn't know which man was which."

"Wow! That'd be an awful big bag. Not to mention, quite a few rolls of tin foil," Amanda said, cracking us all up.

"So Buster found out about the affair?" I asked once the laughter stopped.

"Yes. Buster and Clara Boeing ended up getting divorced," Amanda replied. "Guess who represented Clara in divorce court?"

"Are you kidding?" Janet and I asked in stereo. I added, "That was terribly ballsy of Henry. The fact the two men sang in the same quartet and were friends should've definitely put Clara in the no-fly zone for Henry."

"You'd sure think so, wouldn't you? Can you guess what happened next?" Amanda asked Janet and me.

"What happened?" We both responded in unison again.

"Henry dumped Clara almost as soon as the ink was dry on the Boeings' divorce decree and hooked up with his most recent client, whose divorce he'd handled in court."

"And who was that?" I asked.

"I don't remember her name, but they had already split anyway."

"Oh. My. God!" I exclaimed. "The list of people who had a motive to kill Henry just keeps growing. It's got to be as lengthy now as my grocery list for Thanksgiving dinner."

"I don't seriously believe Clara would've retaliated against Henry. It didn't take her long to get her fill of him, and she seemed happy to have that relationship in her rearview mirror." Amanda studied our expressions and appeared to feel the need to throw a bone Henry's way. "Despite everything, however, I adored my cousin. I loved both of them, actually. Wilson, who's forty-two, is just as good as his younger brother was at blowing money as fast as he makes it. I'd guess knowing their terminally ill mother is a multi-millionaire has something to do with it. But of the two of them, I've always been closest to Henry. It's probably because I'm closer to his age than Wilson's. I'm thirty-five and Henry was thirty-eight. Wilson's seven years older than me and pretty uptight. Henry was always a lot of fun. Wilson was not. He was always focused on where his next dollar was coming from."

"Didn't Wilson just buy a costly convertible?" I asked Amanda, even though, once again, I already knew the answer. "He told Rip he used money he received from an insurance payoff. Did you know anything about that?"

"I knew he bought a new Mercedes at a dealership called Hubbard's German Auto in Eureka." Amanda shook her head. "I have no clue where the cash came from, though, but money has never been an issue for him. He spends a lot, but he makes even more. Like Henry, Wilson's a lawyer. Insurance claims and lawsuits fund his lavish lifestyle. You should see the mansion he owns in Somes Bar."

I turned to Janet and added, "Wilson sings for the Siskiyou County barbershop quartet."

"Really?" Janet asked.

"Yep!" Amanda answered for me. "Fun fact: barbershop quartets can be traced back to African-Americans in the mid-to-late 1800s. One of the unique qualities of that style of music is the barbershop chord, also known as the ringing chord. The four voices reinforce each other so strongly sometimes a ringing tone is actually heard by listeners. I've heard it too. It's freaky cool. Listen for it at the contest."

"I will." With my focus on Amanda, I said, "You told me at the celebration of life the brothers were ultra-competitive when it came to the annual competition between counties."

"Ultra-competitive is an understatement." she replied. "Henry and Wilson were like two gladiators pitted against each other in the Roman Coliseum. Every year it was like a fight to the death kind of match between them."

Janet took the words right out of my mouth when she asked, "Is it possible it turned out to be an actual fight-to-the-death competition between your cousins?"

Amanda shook her head. "Nah. I can't imagine Wilson could want to win a silly singing contest badly enough to harm his own brother to achieve that goal. Or hurt anyone, for that matter. Wilson's not the violent type at all. He and Henry fight like little kids arguing over a toy sometimes, but they were always the first to defend the other if anyone else said or did anything bad to their brother. Wilson would never have killed Henry, for any reason whatsoever, and I can assure you of that."

"That's good," I replied. I was glad to know I wouldn't have to add either Wilson or Clara to the list of suspects I kept in my little notebook. Lexie convinced me to buy the notebook when we'd solved our first murder case together. That notebook that I used to keep in my nightstand, I now hid in a cabinet behind my bottle of laundry detergent. I knew Rip would never, ever touch or move that bottle and discover the notebook. "By the way, Amanda, as far as our hubbies are concerned, they think Janet and I are shopping in Eureka right now. So if you see Rip, could you please—"

"Like I told you before," Amanda cut in, "I'll never mention having seen you since that first day you and Rip came in and had our chili for lunch. Fun fact: the town of Eureka got its name from a Greek word meaning 'I have found it!' Eureka is also California's official motto. I think it had something to do with gold miners."

"Interesting," Janet responded. I nodded my head in agreement.

Amanda had to excuse herself to wait on a family who'd just entered the café. After her departure, Janet said, "I can see what Rip meant about fun facts being cute coming from a young waitress with her head in the clouds. But, one more fun fact and that cuteness is going to disappear faster than those two cups of coffee we just guzzled."

I agreed and was surprised when Janet asked, "Should we get one more refill before we leave?"

One more refill turned into two. We were both so wired by the time we left that the two of us could've provided the entire town with electricity.

Traveling south on Highway 101, Janet and I discussed all we'd learned. From what Amanda told us about her cousin, there were a number of other scorned lovers that might've wanted Henry dead too, but I had no way of knowing all of their names. I had to agree with Amanda, though. Most of them had probably had enough of Henry before their relationship with him had run its course. Janet and I decided not to pursue any motives from his ex-flings.

"Amanda's a sweet young lady, isn't she, Rapella? But if I ever say 'fun fact,' slap me, won't you?"

"Only if you promise to do the same to me." We both laughed. "Like Rip told me, it's not so adorable coming from a seventy-two-year-old."

"Hey, that's my age too. We be like twin sistas from different mistas."

I groaned. "Would it be okay if I slap you right now? Just for practice, of course."

After Janet stopped snickering, she said, "Sorry, I couldn't help myself. But I do like Amanda a lot. Don't you?"

"Yes," I replied. "Rip and I both found her charming the first day we met her in the café."

As I'd responded, Janet was careening around a sharp, narrow curve. I had a firm grip on the "oh shit!" handle above the passenger-side window.

All of a sudden, Janet whipped the steering wheel to the right to avoid something in the middle of our lane. I barely caught a glimpse of a large moving mass before the car slammed to an abrupt stop. We were nose down in a ditch, about ten miles north of Klamath. I was surprised we both hadn't been punched in the face by deployed airbags. Shaken, I asked, "Are you all right, Janet?"

"I'm good. How about you?"

"I'm fine too. What the hell was that?"

"It was a black bear with two cubs."

"Oh, m-m-my goodness," I stammered. "What were they doing in the middle of the road?"

"It looked as if the cubs were wrestling with each other while their mama was leaving a calling card on the pavement. An extremely big calling card, to be sure."

"I thought bears pooped in the woods," I replied.

"Usually, perhaps," Janet said. "But, like us humans, when you gotta go, you gotta go."

"I guess you're right. I usually pee in a restroom. But I have a vivid recollection of having to squat behind a gas station one time when their restroom was locked and—"

"Stop right there!" Janet said as she put out her hand like a traffic cop stopping vehicles at a school crossing. Her fingers were trembling as though she was afflicted with palsy. Or, more likely, the combination of caffeine overload from four cups of bold Columbian coffee and a near-death experience. She went on to say, "I don't want a vision of you squatting behind a gas station in my mind that I can't unsee. Besides, we need to get out of this car and summon help."

"I'm not getting out of this car," I insisted.

"Why not?"

"According to you, there's a mama bear with two cubs nearby. Like all mothers, they can be very protective of their offspring. I don't want my DNA to be present in that bear's next calling card. That's why not!" I said emphatically. "Rip and I came face-to-face with a bear in the Big Horn Mountains of Wyoming. We're lucky one or both of us didn't get mauled to death that day. I've seen what a bear can do to a body and I want no part of it. But I will call Rip and ask him to arrange for a tow truck for us. There's no way we're getting this car out of the ditch without one."

"Yeah, you're right. Go ahead and call Rip."

Calling Rip was more difficult than I'd expected. Getting a signal in the area proved impossible on either of our phones. "We'll have to get a message to them some other way," Janet said.

"What did you have in mind?" I asked. "Smoke signals?"

"Good point," Janet conceded. "Got any ideas?"

"Just one, but it ought to work."

A few minutes later we flagged down a young couple who were slowing down anyway to stop and see if we needed assistance and make sure we weren't injured. I gave them Rip's number and asked if they'd mind calling him once they were near a cell phone tower. They assured me they would.

When a tow truck pulled up on the shoulder beside us about forty-five minutes later, Janet said, "That was a spark of genius you had to have that young couple call Rip for us."

"Not my first rodeo," I replied.

We finally felt comfortable enough to get out of Janet's Veloster. Walking around the car, I was surprised to find no apparent cosmetic damage to the exterior, which was a relief to both Janet and me. We'd yet to see the front end of the vehicle though.

I then studied the tow truck. It had a bright paint job and had "Boeing Towing" plastered on each side. I didn't normally believe in coincidences, but this seemed too flukish to be anything but a twist of fate. I knew instantly it was Buster Boeing, and that he'd brought Rip along with him, when the two men, who in profile looked identical, stepped out of the truck to stare at the yellow car in the ditch. I heard Janet whisper, "Now I can definitely see how wrapped in tin foil it'd be hard to tell those two apart."

After Janet explained to the two men what happened, Buster walked over to his truck to fiddle with what he referred to as a "winch-out cable." Rip asked Janet and me, "How'd you two end up north of Klamath? I thought you were going shopping in Eureka."

"We were," Janet replied. "But we decided to grab a cup of coffee first."

Rip looked at me, skepticism etched in his face. "Seriously?"

"Yes. There's a nice little café north of here. We enjoyed a few cups of coffee before heading south to go shopping." I didn't tell him the name of the café and he didn't ask. As Rip glanced at his watch, presumably to calculate how much coffee we must've consumed considering the amount of time we'd been gone, I gestured toward the Veloster. "And then this happened."

To steer the conversation away from the café and why we'd traveled north rather than south, I'm certain, Janet added, "I probably over-reacted because I was a bit jittery from all of the caffeine I'd just ingested. But I sure didn't want to hit a bear and possibly hurt or kill her and her babies."

"Not to mention, damage your car. As it is, the car appears to be intact. And hopefully there are no dings or dents in the front end." I smiled at Janet. "We can always go shopping another day.

I'm just glad neither of us was injured and neither was your cute car."

"Me too," she replied.

I then turned to Rip. "So Buster owns a towing company? How ironic is that?"

"I remembered him mentioning it at my very first practice with the quartet. So I called him and he picked me up on his way out of town to pick up Janet's car. He thought it'd need to be towed to a body shop. As long as there's no damage to the front end, engine or drive train after Buster gets it out of the ditch, it may not have to be towed back to Klamath after all. But they'll still be a charge for the service call and pulling it out of the ditch."

"Of course. That'd be great if it's still drivable." After my response to Rip, I walked over to chat with Buster while I had the opportunity.

"Hello there, Buster. Remember me?" I asked.

"Of course," he said. "You're the woman whose singing voice sounds like a house cat in heat."

"Um, yeah." I'm not sure which is the most horrendous sound-ing, a cat in heat or one hung up in a barbwire fence, but I did know neither comparison was flattering. "I didn't know you owned a towing company."

"Well, I own half of a towing company," he explained with a scowl. "My ex-wife Clara owns the other half. Our twenty-year marriage crashed and burned about six months ago."

"Oh. I'm so sorry to hear you and your wife divorced. That must be difficult."

"It has been hard," he agreed. "What was even harder for me, though, was not to retaliate against her and that jerk that I caught her hooking up with, which led to Clara and me splitting the sheets. And the towing company."

"Oh, no!" I reacted as if it was the first I'd heard about the affair between Henry and Clara. "Did you know the jerk?"

"Yeah, I knew him. Very well, in fact. It was Henry Harpodin-gle, who your husband replaced on our barbershop quartet after Henry was killed. Had he not died, I would've quit the barbershop quartet. As far as I'm concerned, Henry got what he had coming to him without me having to lift a finger. We ended up with Rip singing tenor, too, who we all believe is a much better singer. So it was a win-win situation for me."

"Yeah, I guess so." It was hard for me not to sound appalled at Buster's callousness. The fact he'd used the word "killed" rather than "died" had caught my attention as well. The official cause of death was still listed as accidental. I couldn't resist asking, "It wasn't exactly a win-win situation for Henry, though, was it?"

Buster shrugged and turned to Janet. He was clearly done conversing with me. "Can I see your AAA card please, ma'am, before we yank that little four-banger out of the ditch?"

"It might only have four cylinders, but it's turbo-charged," Janet said defensively. "It can really scoot when I want it to."

"Whatever," Buster replied indifferently. "Stand aside, ladies."

As it turned out, the Hyundai Veloster was not only drivable; it was nearly unaffected by its nosedive into the ditch. Buster explained that a small hole had been punched into its exhaust system by a piece of metal that'd been lying in the ditch and the muffler would need to be replaced. I was extremely thankful. I would've felt responsible for any damage to the car because Janet had volunteered to drive as she assisted me in my covert investiga-tion. I offered to pay for the new muffler and Janet declined. "It'll give Jack something to do one day and get him out of my hair for a couple of hours."

"Hmm," I replied. "Maybe I should punch a hole in our truck's muffler so I can get a short reprieve, as well."

That night, as I lay in bed waiting for sleep to come, I thought about how the day had not gone as planned. But, yet, Janet and I had still uncovered quite a bit of useful information. Buster's statement about not having to lift a finger to get revenge against Henry made me want to eliminate him from my suspect list. However, his obvious resentment of the man who'd destroyed his longtime marriage and his use of the word "killed" instead of "died" made me decide to leave it be. And due to the accident we'd been involved in, which had interrupted our shopping plans, we'd have an excuse to go to the cute little store in Eureka again.

ELEVEN

We got up a little earlier than usual the next morning. We'd been lazing around the campground for several days, playing corn hole and a card game called Spades with the Wrights. We also made use of the putt-putt course, which was an unusual amenity to find in an RV park.

But it was time Rip and I did something more active. So we decided to drive the ten-mile Newton B. Drury Scenic Parkway, which we'd heard was even more amazing than the Avenue of the Giants, which we'd driven the previous week. The picturesque drive snaked through the ancient redwoods. We also planned to stop and walk the eighth-of-a-mile trail in Prairie Creek State Park to the Big Tree wayside. There, we'd utilize a viewing platform to see some stunning old-growth redwood trees, including one called "Big Tree" that was more than fifteen hundred years old. At seven o'clock, we headed out to enjoy a day of much-anticipated sightseeing.

Just as we hit the road, my phone dinged and I looked down to see I'd received a text from Janet.

> I thought I'd run over to the Boeing Towing office to pay my bill in person. Is there anything in particular you'd like me to ask Buster while I'm there?

> Yes

I'd already paid the towing bill, but didn't mention it to Janet.

> See if you can find out where we could locate his ex-wife, Clara. I'd like to question her if possible. I think we might find out more information about Buster from Clara than from Buster himself.

> I agree, I'll see what I can find out. I'll also try to find out where Buster was at the time of Henry's death. If he was in Sacramento at the time, he should move to the top of our suspect list, right above Moose Crossing.

> Yes, we should. Great thinking, Janet. Thank you so much.

> My pleasure. Have fun sightseeing today.

"Who was that?" Rip asked when I stowed my phone away in my purse.

"Just Janet telling us to have fun sightseeing today."

***

We enjoyed driving the Newton B. Drury Scenic Parkway, which took us about an hour because we'd decided to take advantage of several pullouts along the way. I took photographs of the spectacular scenery from those viewpoints. We also stopped at the Prairie Creek Visitor Center. There, we learned the man the parkway was named for had spent forty years of his life preserving these kinds of forests and had been awarded a silver Pugsley Medal in 1940 and a gold medal in 1950.

"What's a Pugsley Medal?" I asked the gentleman behind the information desk.

"They are named after the Honorable Cornelius Amory Pugsley," he explained. "The purpose of the awards is to honor outstanding contributions in parks and conservation."

"Very interesting," Rip replied. "Wasn't Cornelius Pugsley a one-term Democratic congressman from New York in the early 1900s?"

"Why, yes, indeed," the visitor's center employee responded with obvious surprise. Even though I've always been amazed at Rip's knowledge about a myriad of subjects, I was no longer taken aback by it. "I'm impressed, sir. I haven't found many visitors who were familiar with the one-term politician."

"I'm kind of an historian at heart and am particularly interested in politics," Rip responded.

By the time we finished the picturesque drive and walked the short path to the Big Tree wayside in Prairie Creek State Park, I'd taken a dozen beautiful landscape photos and Rip and I were both hungry.

"Jack told me about a restaurant he and Jane tried called Snack Shack that's only about ten minutes from here," Rip said. I would've corrected him on Janet's name, but rarely was he only one letter off. I let it pass and listened as Rip continued to speak. "Jack said the hamburger and fries basket he got was delicious. Do you want to stop there for lunch?"

"Okay," I agreed reluctantly. "Maybe they offer something a little healthier we can order besides hamburgers and fries."

"They probably do." Rip's tone was downtrodden, as if he was the male version of the Poor Pitiful Pearl doll I'd owned when I was a child. He didn't have to say so in words, but I knew he was praying they didn't offer salmon, kale, or a Cobb salad. He'd recently complained his last lab work results indicated he was now seventy percent human, twenty percent rabbit, and ten percent grizzly bear.

We ended up ordering fish tacos, which I found to be delicious, and Rip declared to be a fine way to ruin a traditional Mexican favorite.

Forty minutes later, we were on Highway 101, heading back to the campground. I was anxious to speak with Janet to find out if she learned anything beneficial from Buster Boeing.

That evening we joined the Wrights around a common fire pit to enjoy the camaraderie of our fellow campers, roast marshmallows over the flame, and make s'mores. I had bought all of the ingredients several weeks prior, but had forgotten to buy roasting sticks. Fortunately, the Wrights had seven or eight of them in their camper. S'mores had been a staple of my childhood. If my four brothers and I were all well-behaved the entire week, on Saturday nights we were allowed to roast marshmallows for the coveted treats over flames in our backyard hand-dug fire pit. No thanks to my ornery siblings, we only got to make s'mores about once a month.

After I explained our day of sightseeing to the Wrights, Janet told us about how she and Jack had visited a local pet shelter that morning and adopted a two-year-old Great Pyrenees. They'd sent a photo of their new family member to their granddaughter, Cora, who named the dog Barkus. Jack and Janet hoped the large, clumsy dog was a good traveler. Janet walked over to their motorhome and returned with Barkus. She held on to his collar while he squirmed like a child during a church service. He reminded me of a wild hog in a tea cup factory, but what did I know? Perhaps the Wrights could stir Valium in Barkus's food every morning before hitting the road in their motorhome.

I was content to travel with a tabby. I didn't have to take Dolly outside to do her duty three times a day. And somehow, the chunky house cat could waddle across a table loaded with fragile trinkets and not disturb a single item.

Just then, another camper's Jack Russell terrier, which was being walked by its owner, barked and scared the bejesus out of all of us. Barkus leaped out of Janet's grasp and took off like a squirrel chasing another squirrel with an acorn in its mouth. Jack and Rip were tasked with catching him, which was free entertainment for us ladies. It was like watching a herd of old elephants trying to run down a young Grant's gazelle. We couldn't help but laugh at our winded husbands, who were too spent to realize the dog was playing with them and believed evading them was part of the game. Had they stopped pursuing him, he would've walked right up to either one of them to be coddled. Janet told me the big oaf clearly thought he was a Chihuahua.

With the men scurrying around the campground trying to catch Barkus, Janet and I took the opportunity to discuss the case we were investigating. I asked, "Did you learn anything interesting from Buster today?"

"Yes, I learned a few things from him. First, he told me that his ex-wife Clara is a massage therapist at a place called Tree House Massage and Spa in Crescent City. She works Tuesdays, Wednesdays, and Fridays from ten to five. He also said that free massages were the only thing he missed about his ex."

"What a loser," I replied. "Clara's better off without him."

"Agreed," Janet said. "We should book massages with Clara. I'm guessing she'd be an open book when it comes to dishing on her ex-husband."

I wasn't keen on getting a massage. If I caught Rip in the right mood, I could get him to grope me for free. Paying someone to manhandle me just wasn't on my bucket list of things I wanted to do while in northern California. But Janet was able to twist my arm and get me to relent. She would book the massages for us, she said. "It will be a lot more enjoyable than you think, Rapella. I'll bet you'll leave wondering why you've never treated yourself to a massage before."

"Fat chance. But I can't think of a better way to get Clara's undivided attention."

Just then, we were distracted by Rip, who hollered, "I've got him!" We all looked in his direction, only to see Barkus slip through his hands as though he'd been dipped in a vat of vegetable oil. I was glad it was a false alarm so Janet would have time to tell me what else she'd learned from Buster.

"Buster told me he was in Sacramento when Henry died. He said he wasn't invited to the bachelor party and wouldn't have gone even if he had been. He wanted nothing to do with Henry, he said." Janet paused for effect before continuing. She reminded me of myself when she said, "So why was Buster in Sacramento, you're probably asking yourself. Well, when I asked him that very question, he claimed he was attending a business-related seminar at Woodbine Park, which is in Sacramento."

"The man owns a towing business," I said. "What kind of seminar would a tow truck driver attend?"

"A fabricated one, probably," Janet replied. "Wasn't he questioned by the homicide detectives?"

"I doubt it." I shook my head as I pointed to our gasping husbands who currently had the frisky dog pinned down. The Great Pyrenees emerged from their grip with what I'd swear was a taunting smirk on his face. Janet and I howled in amusement at the men's frustration before I continued. "Henry's death was classified as accidental. I don't think anyone was questioned. The police department measured his blood alcohol level and determined he was stinking drunk, and therefore determined his plunge from the balcony was attributed to his intoxication."

"Sounds like pure laziness on the police department's part to me," Janet said.

"Me too," I agreed. "And that's the main reason I feel so compelled to pursue this investigation into what, and who, was behind the man's death."

"My sentiments exactly," Janet replied. "Oh, and the office lady told me the towing bill had already been paid when I pulled out my MasterCard. When I asked her who paid it she replied, 'Your friend who looks like Jamie Lee Curtis.' And now that I think about it, that's exactly who you remind me of."

"Thanks." I grinned. "I get told that a lot and consider it a high compliment. I stopped by Boeing Towing yesterday and paid the bill. Buster wasn't there, though. You surely didn't think I was going to hang you with that expense *and* the cost of a new muffler, did you? But I didn't mention paying the bill earlier because I thought if you stopped in you might get lucky enough to converse with Buster."

Janet had no idea that being such a spendthrift went totally against my normal nature. But even though I was a penny-pincher, I never wanted to be seen as the type of person who would take advantage of another individual. And especially not of someone who was going way out of their way to help me.

"Thank you, Rapella. That was totally unnecessary but very kind."

"It was necessary to me."

The two men returned to the fire pit, panting and holding their sides. I was afraid Rip would experience another heart attack, so I jumped to my feet and helped him into his chair.

"Thanks," he said between wheezes. "Pardon my pun in advance, but I am dog-tired."

"No doubt." I glanced at Janet and noticed the former nurse was eyeing Rip with concern. However, she didn't seem at all troubled by the fact Barkus was still racing around the campground, as though she were a human two-year-old trying to burn off excess energy. "Barkus led you two on a merry chase. I hate to say it, but you men were kind of underdogs in that contest. Rip, you haven't run that much in a dog's age. I'll bet your dogs are barking."

"Rapella, please," Rip pleaded with a chuckle. I was relieved to see he'd stopped struggling to catch his breath.

"All right," I said. "You were wheezing and I was just trying to take your mind off the fact you were having trouble breathing. I think anxiety only exasperates the problem."

"Thanks. You must be right because it worked. I'm fine now."

"Good. At least you'll probably sleep like a dog tonight."

Rip gently turned my chair over on its side, spilling me out onto the grass like a toppled basket of dirty laundry. He then got up to help me to my feet. "Sorry, dear, but every dog must have his day. And that was mine!"

All four of us were laughing heartily by now. Jack said, "You have the balls of a brass elephant, my friend. I'd be fixing myself a bowl of cereal for supper for the next month if I did that to my wife."

"And don't you forget it," Janet quipped.

While we all chortled, Barkus sauntered back to the fire pit area and walked straight up to Janet, who hugged the dog tightly to her chest. Barkus glanced from Jack to Rip with a look of superiority that cracked all of us up again. A couple taking their own dog on an evening stroll walked by and stared at us wistfully as if wishing they were enjoying our merriment with us. I waved them over.

"Would you folks like to join us for s'mores? We've got more than enough to share."

Bill and Kathy Stryker, vacationers from Bemidji, Minnesota, and what Kathy called a Havanese named Ellie, fit right in with the rest of us. Rip and I enjoyed the evening immensely. It was nearly midnight before we all called it a night and returned to our respective RVs.

The next day was Tuesday, and I received a text from Janet early that morning.

> Want to go shopping in Eureka today, Sherlock? I have massage appointments for us at one-thirty. I'll drive.

> Absolutely, Dr. Watson. I'll be waiting with bells on. Let's leave early and stop for lunch. My treat.

> Yes, on lunch. I'll pick you up at eleven. No, on the bells. My car is loud enough until I can get the muffler replaced.

I went outside to inform Rip that Janet and I would be making another attempt today at going shopping in the cute little shop in Eureka.

Rip nodded after I told him of my plans and then cursed at the screwdriver he was using to tighten a screw. He was having trouble keeping the tool in the screw's slot. I took the screwdriver from his slightly trembling hand, tightened the screw with it, and handed the tool back to Rip. He grunted in response.

"You're welcome," I said and returned to the fifth wheel to get ready for another adventure with my new friend.

TWELVE

Having met Buster, Clara Boeing was a lot better looking than I'd expected. Tall and willowy, she had brown hair, blue eyes, and a megawatt smile. Her porcelain skin looked as if it'd never spent an hour outdoors in the sun. Considering Buster's looks and personality, I'd have been less surprised to see Rosie O'Donnell's doppelganger when I entered the massage parlor. After introductions, Clara said, "You two can disrobe in the individual dressing rooms and lock your clothes and valuables inside."

"Disrobe?" I asked in disbelief.

"Yes. It means undress," Clara replied.

"I know what 'disrobe' means." My tone was much sharper than I'd intended. However, being talked to like I was a kindergartner had a tendency to tick me off. "I'm just wondering if you were serious about us taking all our clothes off." *Does she truly expect me to prance around her spa in my birthday suit? No way, sister. This seventy-two-year-old body ain't going to be on display for anybody's amusement.*

"Duh," Clara replied rudely. "You expect me to give you a massage while you're wearing that fur-lined Adirondack jacket?"

Janet noticed my uneasiness and handed me a robe off a pile

beside her. She whispered, "You can leave your underwear and bra on and wear this robe until she takes you back into a private room with a massage table. My body's as old as yours and hardly center-fold-ready, but it's worth a bit of embarrassment. Trust me."

I did trust Janet. So I stripped down to my bra and panties, thankful I'd worn a brand new pair of underwear and my lacy Cross-Your-Heart brassiere. Once *disrobed*, I donned the plain white robe. Usually, when a situation like this arose—such as recently when the two cops found me shirtless in a dumpster behind a cardiac cath lab in Rochester, Minnesota—I was wearing the oldest, rattiest brassiere I owned. The cops probably thought I was hoping to find a bra that was less than two decades old while I was dumpster diving. Not that it would've been any less embarrassing than when they discovered I was actually looking for two chocolate chip cookies. Not to eat, mind you, but I couldn't tell the policemen they were potentially the cause of a man's death. Lexie had insisted I tell this story to Janet, but I'd yet to do so. I felt I owed it to her at this stage of the game and decided I'd share it with her following our visit to the massage parlor.

When Janet and I walked back out of our dressing rooms in the robes we'd been given, Clara pointed to me and said, "You're with me."

"All right." *Perfect,* I thought.

Then Clara pointed at Janet and said, "Bridget will do you in room three."

Do you? What has Janet got us into?

Janet agreed and looked at me with a nod and three words of encouragement. "You got this."

I knew what she meant. She wasn't going to get an opportunity to speak with Clara about her husband, so it would be up to me to dig as much information out of the massage therapist as I could. I returned Janet's nod and followed Clara to massage room one.

Clara had me lie face down on a padded table with my face

positioned in an opening in the chair. I was staring at a white-tiled floor that could use a good mopping. Clara squeezed my shoulders once and stopped.

"You're too tense," she said. I knew my muscles were as tight as a size six bikini on a size ten body. But how could I be anything but on edge when I'd never experienced a full-body massage before? She advised me to "relax and enjoy."

"Okay, but," I began, "I'm just, ooohhh. Aaahhhh. Uummm. Wow, that feels so good. Don't stop."

As Clara began to knead my shoulders, I unhooked my bra and flung it across the room. *Modesty be damned. This feels amazing*, I thought. I could feel the tension leave my body like oil draining out of a car into a pan. I was so relaxed I almost forgot I wanted to ask Clara about her ex-husband.

Finally, I said, "Clara, I noticed your last name is Boeing. It's probably just a coincidence, but my husband is singing in a barber-shop quartet in Klamath with a guy named Buster Boeing. Is he by chance any kin of yours?"

"Nope," she replied. I knew the answer but was fishing for more information. Clara added, "Used to be hitched to the prick, but not anymore."

"Oh." It wasn't the cleverest response, but it was all I could come up with at the moment. "I'm sorry to hear your marriage didn't work out."

"Thanks," Clara replied. "I'm not sorry we split up at all. I'm just sorry it was because of a guy who was an even sorrier son-of-a-bit—"

"Ouch!" I exclaimed. What felt like a bolt of lightning went through me when Clara pressed down on my lower back. It was as if she'd pressed a live wire up against my spine. Luckily, the pain subsided quickly.

"Sorry about that," she said. "You may want to get checked for arachnoiditis. It's a rare pain disorder caused by inflammation of the arachnoid."

"I thought an arachnoid was a spider."

Clara laughed. "A spider is an arachnid. Arachnoid is the name of the middle of three membranes, or meninges, which surround the nerves of the spinal cord. Lhermitte's sign can also cause a short, intense electric-shock-like sensation in the lower spine. But then it can be a symptom of multiple sclerosis, as well. Consider bringing these three disorders up with your primary doctor the next time you go in for a checkup, won't you?"

"Sure." I hadn't come to the massage parlor for a medical diagnosis and wasn't thrilled about having three new health issues to worry about. At my age, every unexpected twitch and odd sensation was cause for concern. Also, because of my age, I might remember MS, but was sure I'd forget the other two disorders, arachnoiditis and Lhermittes sign, before Clara finished massaging my back and started on my thighs. "It sounds like you've had medical training, Clara."

"I have. I worked in a physical therapy facility for years. I just recently opened up this spa. Being your own boss isn't always a stroll down Easy Street, but it beats working for someone else."

"I'm sure it does." I could think of no reasonable way to segue back to the previous subject, so I just plowed ahead. "You were talking about some guy who was even more of a jerk than your ex-husband before you were interrupted."

"Oh, yes," she said. Without mentioning his name, I knew she was referring to Henry Harpodingle. "The slime ball broke up my marriage and then dropped me like I was a bucket of pig slop afterward. He's dead now, though, so I guess I got the last laugh."

"How'd he die?" I asked, hoping she'd admit she shoved the "slime ball" over the railing of a thirteenth-story balcony.

But instead, Clara said, "He's dead. That's all that matters. Now, you need to hush up and let me do my job. I need to put a lot more pressure on your muscles to loosen up the tightness I feel in them. It'll help relieve the obvious stress your body's under. Deep muscle massage is also helpful in improving the work of the immune system, which will be beneficial if you have MS, arachnoiditis or Lhermittes sign. The latter can also be a symptom of Behçet disease or Arnold-Chiari malformation."

"Good to know." I would've liked to get more information out of Clara, other than grim statistics about serious medical conditions I might or might not have. I have to admit, though, as I lay on that table, loose as a frigging goose while she manipulated my muscles, it was pure heaven. She squeezed hard enough at times to make me grit my teeth in anguish. *Who knew pain could feel so glorious?* I thought.

As Janet had predicted, I was wondering why I'd never tried a massage before. I knew without a doubt this would be just the first of many to come in my future. For a second, I almost wished I had one of the conditions she'd mentioned so I could justify weekly deep muscle massage treatments. If I'd learned anything besides how much I enjoyed having a trained professional poke and prod my muscles to the fine line between bliss and pure agony, it was that Clara Boeing's name should be on the list in my notebook. Clara should be listed right below her ex-husband. I wasn't certain now if she shouldn't be Janet's and my prime suspect. I knew her fingers were definitely strong enough to dump Henry over the railing of a balcony.

After our forty-five-minute full body massages, Janet and I met up again in the spa's lobby. I laid a credit card down on the checkout desk and motioned for Janet to put hers back in her wallet. "It's the least I can do since you won't let me pay for a new muffler."

"But you paid for lunch, too," Janet said.

"That's right. Have you priced a new muffler recently?"

As we pulled out of the Tree House Massage and Spa parking lot, I reiterated my conversation with Clara to Janet, sans all the medical disorders that I might be harboring. When I was done, Janet told me she might've found out something more significant from Bridget about Clara than I had learned from Clara about Buster, which was basically nothing.

"What?" I hoped she didn't drag out the intriguing information like I often did to Lexie.

"Bridget told me she was leaving this Friday on a week-long Caribbean cruise with her husband of two years. It seems they'd never had the opportunity to take a honeymoon, so this would be like a belated one. She said they'll be sailing out of Miami and making stops in Antigua, Barbados, the British Virgin Is—"

"Janet!" I exclaimed, deciding at that moment I was never going to put Lexie through the agony of waiting for me to get to the point again. "I don't care if Bridget and her hubby plan to stop in North Korea to have afternoon tea with the Communist dictator, Kim Jong Un. Cut to the chase!"

"Oh, yeah. Sorry," she said with a chuckle. "So, anyway, I asked Bridget if Clara would be able to handle all the massage business with her gone for a week. Bridget replied, 'It'll be a busy week for her, but I covered for her in early March when she was gone for a week.'"

"Okay." I tried not to sound let down, but I wasn't sure how knowing Clara took a week off work would aid our investigation into Henry's death.

"There's more," Janet said, sensing my disappointment. "I asked Bridget where Clara had gone, and she said Clara took a last-minute trip to Sacramento when she heard her ex-husband planned to be in that town the same week. The woman had as big of an ax to grind with Henry Harpodingle as she did with Buster, if not bigger. Didn't you say Henry's death occurred in Sacramento on March 6th? March 6th was the only Sunday in March that could be considered 'early March.'"

I still didn't see how Clara's vacation had anything to do with Henry's death, but I wanted to show my appreciation for Janet's hard work.

"Good job, Dr. Watson! I apologize for my impatience earlier." I felt bad I'd snapped at Janet, who was only trying to help me get to the bottom of the late tenor's death. "I'm really sorry, and I truly appreciate your assistance in this case."

"No worries, Rapella. I shouldn't have strung you along like that to build up your anticipation. It's a bad habit of mine."

"You're preaching to the choir, my dear. I've been known to do the exact same thing to Lexie, although I've just recently sworn off doing it again." I glanced at Janet and winked. "As you said before, you and I are like sistas from different mistas."

We both laughed before I returned to the previous subject. "I definitely think Buster should be moved to the top of our suspect list. Don't you?"

"Absolutely," Janet said. "He merits extra attention."

"I agree. Let's take a look at our list of suspects in my notebook."

"That'd be very helpful."

"Actually," I said, "we only have Moose and Buster on the list so far."

"What about Henry's brother, Wilson?" Janet asked. "I'm not convinced he shouldn't be on the suspect list."

"After talking to Devin and Amanda about the brothers' relationship, I'd pretty much decided Wilson wouldn't kill Henry."

"What about Clara?" Janet asked. She sounded disappointed. "Doesn't she merit extra attention, though?"

"I'm not sure. But I'll talk to Fern Short about Clara at Rip's next quartet practice. She might have an idea of whether or not Buster's ex is capable of murder. I'll bring up Wilson, too. I'm going to talk with Fern about who she'd most suspect of murdering her husband's best friend. She's a good source of inside information."

After Janet quit laughing hysterically at my dumpster-diving story, which I related soon after we left the massage parlor, we discussed the next steps in our investigation into Henry's death. While we were in Crescent City anyway, Janet and I decided to stop at Wal-Mart to pick up a few things we both needed. If Amie was on duty, we thought we might even engage her in a short discussion about her son, Wilson.

The young man with the bad complexion greeted us at the door but didn't seem to recognize me. He looked as if he was bored out of his gourd. I could've walked in dressed as the Grinch with Janet dressed in Catholic school attire and screaming, "This dude stole my Christmas!" The skinny Wal-Mart greeter would probably have just nodded at us and said, "Welcome to Wal-Mart."

Janet and I both picked up one of the handheld baskets, and after collecting the few items we both needed, we met at the self-checkout stands. Janet beat me there and I was surprised to find her chatting with Amie. This time, I noticed the cashier was completely bald, although the bamboo cap made it almost unnoticeable. It made me very sad to think the nice lady was dealing with cancer and undergoing chemo treatments. To watch her smiling and laughing with Janet, you wouldn't think she had a care in the world. It was a testament to Amie's fortitude and positive nature.

I didn't want to interrupt, but I did want to eavesdrop, so I stood behind Janet and scrutinized the selection of candy bars on the rack next to the cashier stand. The way I stared at them, one might've concluded I feared selecting a Butterfinger when I should've opted for a Snickers Bar could potentially be a life-altering mistake. I picked up a Mounds bar and pretended to read the ingredients, calories, and other information on the label before putting it back and picking up an Almond Joy. An elderly lady behind me tapped on my shoulder and said, "The only difference is the almonds on top of the Almond Joy."

"Thank you," I said politely. If I wasn't trying to hear what Janet and Amie were talking about I'd have corrected her. The coconut filling in an Almond Joy is covered with milk chocolate, whereas a Mounds bar is topped by dark chocolate. I knew this because Rip once asked our primary doctor which candy bar would be the healthiest for him to eat. She'd replied, "That's like asking me whether I recommend you take up bull fighting or motorcycle racing at your age." Dr. Herron had studied Rip's protruding paunch for a moment and added, "As well as your condition." Rip had visibly blanched at the physician's response. He'd faced down a lot of scary characters during his lifelong career in law enforcement, as well as in his four-year stint in the military. No one had ever made him more uneasy than Dr. Herron. I've seen him cowering in the corner, dressed only in a paper gown that left little to the imagination, after Dr. Herron had walked into the room and demanded he drop his drawers and bend over. I was surprised she didn't reward him with a lollipop after managing to give him the penicillin injection in his right cheek to treat his strep throat.

Over the constant beeping of the self-checkout machines and the din of customers conversing with each other, it was very difficult to make out what either Janet or Amie was saying. They were animated and looked as if they were having a lively exchange. But I knew the topic had switched to a more somber one when their body language abruptly changed from joyful to morose. It was time for me to step in.

"Oh, hello, again, Amie," I greeted the clerk. "Do you remember me?"

"Of course. You're Rapella Ripple."

"Good memory," I replied. "And I see you've met my friend, Janet Wright."

"Yes. We were just talking about a pain in the rear end."

Guessing who Janet was referring to could result in a large hole I had to dig myself out of, so instead, I asked, "And who might that be?"

Janet and Amie both cracked up. Finally, Janet explained as she pointed toward a thin middle-aged male customer. "Not who, but what? I'm referring to piles."

"Piles?" I was still confused.

"See that guy over there?" Janet pointed to the skinny man again, and continued. "Amie told me he comes in every Wednesday and buys ten tubes of hemorrhoid cream."

"Oh, that kind of piles. Ten tubes seem like a colossal amount," I replied. "Can you make meth or some other kind of drug out of *Preparation H?*"

"I don't think so," Amie said with a chuckle. "I believe you're thinking about Sudafed or anything with ephedrine in it. My guess is that either he or his wife has hemorrhoids the size of buttermilk biscuits. And by the way he walks, I'm betting on him."

We all watched as he gathered up his bag and yanked his receipt out of the machine. As he waddled off like a hen with an egg about to slide out of her, the three of us struggled to contain our laughter. Once he'd exited the building, we cackled like a gaggle of amused geese.

"Come to think about it," Amie began once we'd all regained control. "Janet and I were actually talking about two pains in the butt. I was telling her that I was joining my son Wilson for supper at a restaurant near his office in Brookings, Oregon, later on today. When he's not working at his home in Somes Bar, he's at his office in Brookings. Most of his clients are Oregonians. Apparently, Oregon citizens are very clumsy, which makes it a great place for a personal injury lawyer to hang up their shingle."

We laughed again, and then I asked Amie how she was feeling. I explained that her niece Amanda had told me she was fighting liver cancer. Amie tried to smile, but the smile didn't reach her eyes. "I'm hanging in there. I've had a couple of rough days this week. I had to call in sick twice, which I hate to do."

"Amanda told me you didn't need to work and that you donate your entire pay to a pet shelter charity," I said. "Maybe it's time to quit and spend the time taking care of yourself instead of taking care of Wal-Mart customers and stray animals."

"Finding a forever home for animals is a passion of mine. That's how I ended up with nine cats. A tenth one joins the herd this weekend. She's blind and lost a front leg when she was hit by a car. I call her Lucky. The shelter hasn't been able to find someone willing to adopt her, so I guess I will. I can empathize with her. Lucky reminds me of myself. In my condition, no one would want to adopt me either. Besides, when you already have nine cats, what's one more? I only adopt cats from the shelter because, being litter-box trained, they are more self-sufficient than dogs. I couldn't work eight-hour shifts with a house full of peeing, pooping pooches. As far as quitting my job, I can't do anything at home I couldn't do here, except sit around and brood over the fact I lost my son and this cancer is going to kill me. Sooner, more than later, I'm sure."

"Not necessarily," I replied. Janet and I both hugged her. I had tears running down my cheeks for this kind lady's plight. I asked if there was anything the two of us could do for her, and Janet nodded in consent.

"Actually, there might be," Amie replied. "I need to make some changes to my will and would like someone to go with me because my attorney is in Trinidad, which is about forty-five minutes from here. I also want to stipulate how my rescued kitties will be taken care of when I'm gone. Amanda volunteered to drive me there but can't get down here for another two weeks. I will pay for your fuel and buy lunch for you both. In a pinch, I could always book a ride with Uber, but I'd kind of like some company."

"There's no need for that. We'd be more than happy to take you. Is there a reason you don't want to wait two weeks?" I asked. "You might feel more comfortable if your niece took you."

"Look at me, Rapella!" Amie said ruefully. "I'm at the point I'm afraid to buy green bananas. I want to be certain it's done before. . . well, just before."

Her unfinished remark struck me in the gut like a foul ball in any of California's five Major League Baseball stadiums. My tears began to flow again, and seeing me weep made Janet begin to blubber, too.

"Come on, ladies. Please don't cry," Amie said. "And don't feel sorry for me. I have accepted my fate and I'm ready to go home. Besides, if my boss sees customers in the self-checkout area sobbing, it might reflect badly on my next employee evaluation report."

This did the trick in changing our moods. We knew she didn't give a rat's behind about her next evaluation report but was only trying to make us laugh. And we did so loudly. I could see the area was getting busy and two customers were waving at Amie to come help them with a difficult purchase. I told her to let us know when she needed us to drive her to Trinidad, because we would be happy to do so.

"Thanks," she said, as I wrote my name and phone number down on a post-it note. "With my husband deceased, and only one son remaining, I don't want the state of California to have anything to do with my estate. I have no other relatives aside from Wilson and Amanda. Amanda's mother was my sister Susan who has also predeceased me. Ironically, she died of liver cancer, too."

"You haven't died of liver cancer yet, sweetheart," I reminded Amie. "Keep the faith!"

Amie nodded. Her expression was more one of acceptance than hopefulness. This made me even sadder. To change the topic, and hopefully the melancholy mood, I asked, "Isn't Wilson a lawyer? Can't he draw up your will for you?"

"No."

Apparently, my quizzical expression following her one-word response was enough for her to address my unspoken query. "For the same reason I didn't have Henry draw up my original will. It would've only caused friction and unpleasant discourse in the family, which I wanted nothing to do with. There was enough competitiveness between my sons already."

Before I could question her further, Amie told us goodbye and walked over to assist a lady who was holding up a clump of kohlrabi and summoning Amie to come help her ring it up.

"I bet she doesn't know what it's called," Janet said.

"Or she does know what it's called and doesn't know how to spell it," I countered.

As we walked by Amie and the young shopper toward two open stands so we could ring up our own purchases, we heard the lady ask, "Does kohlrabi start with a 'c' or a 'k'? I'm having trouble looking it up on this machine. I don't think it knows how to spell."

Well, clearly, someone doesn't, I thought.

As we carried our groceries out to Janet's Veloster, I said, "That was an interesting conversation with Amie, wasn't it, Janet?"

"Yes. Very much so. How ironic is it that Amie's sister died of liver cancer? Do you think it's a genetic thing?"

"Maybe," I replied. "But I was actually referring to the fact

Amie didn't want either son to draw up her first will because it would've caused even more friction between her sons."

"Do you think she might've left everything, or at least the bulk of her estate, to one son over the other?"

"It's possible. I also think it's possible she left her entire estate to the pet rescue charity she donates her check to every payday. Amanda was only kidding, but she said she wouldn't be surprised if her Aunt Amie left her fortune to her nine cats or to someone who'll take care of them after she's gone."

"I'll take care of them," Janet said with a chuckle. "And I'm allergic to cats. With enough loot in the bank, I can overlook the hives and constant sneezing."

"You're a hoot, Janet." We both laughed, but then I came to an abrupt stop in the middle of the Wal-Mart parking lot.

"Are you okay?" Janet asked. "You look like you just had an epiphany. Or a stroke."

"I definitely didn't have a stroke," I replied. "But I did have a great idea."

"I haven't known you very long." Janet looked as if she'd just seen Charles Dickens' Ghost of Christmas Past gathering up carts in Wal-Mart's parking lot. "But I just felt a shiver run up my spine as though I'd stuck my finger in a light socket."

"Do you have to be home at any certain time?"

"For some odd reason, I'm compelled to lie and say I do, but no, I'm free all day," Janet answered honestly.

"Cool. I'll text Rip and tell him we're enjoying our day so much, we're going to check out some stores in another town."

"Oh, boy."

THIRTEEN

"So you see, Mr. Harpodingle," I said to Wilson, "my friend Janet was shopping in this cute little boutique in Eureka about two weeks ago. She didn't realize there were three cats in the shop until her windpipe swelled nearly shut and she could barely breathe. She almost died right there in their changing room. If another customer in the store hadn't been carrying an epi-pen with her, Janet probably *would* have died."

We had driven up to Brookings, Oregon, after I'd found the address of Wilson's office online. No surprise, it was listed under Wilson Harpodingle Esq., Personal Injury Attorney-at-Law. It was only about a half-an-hour away from Crescent City. After Wilson nodded and motioned for me to continue, I asked, "Do you have any idea how much an epi-pen costs these days? And obviously, Janet had to reimburse the kind lady who likely saved her life. If you remember right, my husband met you when you almost drove your new Mercedes into the rushing water at—"

"I remember. Go on with what happened to Ms. Wright."

"You told my husband you were a personal injury attorney, and I thought perhaps Janet had a case against the shop for not warning their customers that there were multiple cats on the premises."

"Umm, I'll have to do some research. This is a new one for me."

"Are you saying it's all right for a shop to subject their customers to something that could cause them to go into anaphylactic shock if they happen to have a cat allergy?"

"No, I'm not saying that," Wilson replied. "I'm just not sure if a case like this has enough meat to merit filing a lawsuit. After all, Janet could have left the shop when she noticed there were cats present.

"What?" Janet gasped. "And not buy those swanky black heels while they were forty-percent off? I'm not nearly as flush with cash as you must be."

"And I'm not in the habit of taking on cases that might get thrown out of court by a judge."

"I see." Janet looked irate. She was playing the part perfectly.

My tone was intentionally judgmental when I spoke next. "I'd heard you were one of those ambulance chasers. I suppose Janet would've had to have a clothes rack fall on her, severing her arm before you felt her case had enough 'meat,' as you put it."

I glanced at Janet, who nodded in agreement. Wilson clearly wished both Janet and I were knee-deep in bombed-out rubble in some third-world war zone. Before he could boot us out, I said, "I also heard you were engaged. Congratulations."

"Thanks, but that engagement is up in the air right now."

"Oh, I'm sorry to hear that," I said with as much phony empathy as I could muster.

"Shit happens." Wilson wrote something down on a memo pad and then said, "Now let's get back to—"

"I'm also sorry you lost your brother in such a tragic way." I interrupted Wilson because there was nothing more I could add to the fictional anaphylactic shock story.

"Like I said, shit happens. If I'd had a cat allergy, I'd have never survived my childhood. My mother was a cat hoarder. She collected stray kitties like some ladies collect tea cups. I couldn't stand those hairball-hacking freaks of nature. I actually tossed a cat that whizzed on my pillow into a dumpster and let Mom think it'd run off."

After that horrific admission, I was too disgusted to express my thoughts out loud. *Wow! You are a complete jerk, and a horrible monster to boot. I'm sorry the loss of your brother and the upheaval in your relationship with your fiancée that ensued afterward have caused you so much emotional turmoil. Your sorrow is underwhelming! It makes me wonder how much distress your mother's cancer diagnosis is causing you, knowing you're her sole beneficiary. Unless of course, Lucky is about to get even luckier, and along with her nine step-siblings, destined to become one of the wealthiest cats in all of California.* I came out of my seething reverie when Wilson spoke.

"Now let me explain the reservations I have about taking on this case." It was evident the attorney was focused on whether or not he wanted to take on a lawsuit that pended on a cat allergy. I'm certain he was thinking in dollar signs. This case probably wasn't going to bring in the kind of money for him to purchase a second Mercedes convertible for his garage, and that's obviously all he cared about. Before he could cast us aside like we were two of those stray kitties his mom had rescued, I wanted to save face.

"Never mind, Mr. Harpodingle," I said as I stood up. Janet happily followed suit. She'd clearly wanted out of that office too, still outwardly seething at the idea Wilson had mercilessly killed a kitten. "We have changed our minds about retaining you for this case. We'll find another attorney who's interested in more than his own bottom line."

We walked out of Wilson's office. As I closed the door, loudly, behind us, I heard him laugh and say, "Good luck with that, ladies!"

I hope your mother's entire estate goes to those hairball-hacking freaks of nature! I wanted to scream. *But not before every single one of them whizzes on your pillow!*

Janet and I were both fuming as we exited Wilson's office. She looked like a volcano that was fixing to blow and I felt like my ears might melt from all of the steam emitting from them, leaving me with cauliflower ears like a pro wrestler. "What do you say we stop and get a sundae at that Slugs'n Stones Ice Cream Cones shop we passed driving into town? We could both use something to cool us off."

Janet agreed. "A sundae sounds great. I'd also like to ask where the name of the shop originated from."

"There better not be a slug in my sundae," I replied with a wink.

"Don't worry, Rapella. A slug can't eat all that much. The bulk of it will still be yours to enjoy."

On our way back to Mystic Forest RV Park in Klamath, I admitted it probably hadn't been worth the time and effort to drive to Brookings to talk to Wilson. "I don't know that we got any beneficial information out of him."

"Maybe not," Janet concurred. "But it seems obvious to me Wilson couldn't care less that his brother died so tragically, and I wouldn't put it past him to have killed Henry himself to become his mother's sole beneficiary."

"Assuming Lucky and the other—"

"Well, yes," Janet began, "but do you really think Amie would leave her fortune to cats? Who does that? Except maybe the most eccentric of characters, and Amie didn't appear to me to be all that peculiar. My guess would be that she'd originally planned to leave more to one son—probably Henry—than the other, and that's why she was afraid it'd cause friction between the brothers. Now that Henry's dead, it stands to reason she'll make Wilson her sole heir."

"Yeah," I agreed. "You're probably right. But it's possible she decided to add another heir to her will."

"That's true. But I still think, at this point, Wilson should be our number one suspect. Don't you, Rapella?"

"No, not really," I replied. A gut feeling told me Wilson could be the world's biggest dweeb and have killed one of his mother's cats, but he would never kill his brother. Not for any amount of money. They had both been raised by too kind of a woman to stoop *that* low. "I know all about sibling rivalry, having grown up with four brothers. I often thought they'd kill each other in an argument that had turned into a brawl. But I also knew if another man had laid a hand on one of their brothers, they'd be all over that man like fresh tar on a roof. I strongly believe blood truly is thicker than water in this case. I think Wilson's nonchalant attitude about Henry's death is nothing more than a typical man's desire to hide his true emotions. I doubt being a grown man crying in front of two women would sit well with Wilson. It's obvious he's got a lot of pride."

"Yeah, you're right," Janet agreed. "But I still don't think Wilson should be removed from the suspect list."

"I agree. Just not at the top of it."

"You got home just in time," Rip said as I walked in the door about forty-five minutes later. He looked slightly perturbed. *Had my text about going shopping in another town not gone through?* I wondered. *Maybe that's why he hadn't responded to it.*

"I got your text," he replied, as if reading my mind. "But I had no idea you two girls would shop that long. Our quartet practice is at the Shorts' house in about fifteen minutes. Fern asked specifically at our last practice to bring you along to this one. She has something she wanted to talk to you about. I guess I should've texted you back and reminded you. My bad."

"No problem." *You can't "remind" me of something you never told me about in the first place,* I wanted to say. But I didn't want him asking too many questions about how Janet and I had spent the day. I'd just been about to apologize to Rip when he'd turned the tables and apologized to me. I love when that happens. "I'm here now and ready to go whenever you are. I'm curious what Fern wants to talk to me about."

"She probably has some new cookie recipe she wants to share with you."

I nodded but knew it had to be something more stimulating than a cookie recipe. *Do men really think all we women think about are cooking, cleaning, and shopping? I suppose I should leave shopping off that list since, as far as Rip knows, Janet and I have made a habit of shopping in cute little shops recently. You'd think he'd wonder why I'd yet to purchase a single item.*

But thinking we'd gotten caught up in shopping had kept Rip's blood pressure at a healthy level and kept me from having to explain why I felt the need to get involved in Henry's death. I'm not sure I knew the answer to that question myself. But I think it was the absurdity of homicide detectives declaring his death an accident that had me determined to prove otherwise. Grown men, drunk or not, do not normally fall off thirteen-story balconies without the help of an individual who wants them dead, flattened on the ground like a cow pie run over by a tractor numerous times.

"Yeah, she probably has a new recipe for me to try out. After all, what else could it be?"

"Exactly," Rip said. "I'm ready to go. If we leave right now, we should arrive about five minutes early. I don't want to be late."

"Rapella!" Fern exclaimed before enveloping me with the kind of bear hug you'd greet your husband with when he stepped off the airplane following a year-long stint of military service abroad. "It's so good to see you again."

She was holding me so tightly I could barely breathe, but I managed to choke out, "It's good to see you too."

Her reaction to seeing me again had me baffled. No doubt she was a friendly, affable person, and we'd clicked at our first meeting, but her overstated greeting had made me uncomfortable. Then she leaned toward me in such a way I thought she was going to kiss my cheek, and after the hug she'd given me, it wouldn't have surprised me. But, instead, she whispered in my ear. "Stay in the kitchen with me. I have something important to tell you."

I gave her an almost undetectable nod. I'd planned to stay with her anyway. After being accused of sounding like a cat hung up in a barbwire fence, I didn't think the four singers would welcome my presence while they were practicing. The men hung around in the kitchen for about ten minutes, snagging pastries off the tray Fern had set out for them. Rip clutched onto a glazed doughnut like a drowning man might grasp a floating life preserver ring. Not unexpectedly, he avoided catching my eye the entire time he was inhaling it. It was almost amusing, but not quite. Men act like naughty little boys sometimes. But then, I'm sure all women already know that, and every man would deny it.

As the men munched on the refreshments, they chatted among themselves. Tonight was the next-to-last practice before the competition, so they'd all chose to wear their vertically-striped red and white shirts. Fortunately, Buster had a spare shirt for Rip to borrow. I made it a point to only wear vertical stripes because, as opposed to horizontal stripes, they were thinning. But on Stanly Ledge, the vertical stripes almost made him disappear. The ultra-thin bass singer was the only one not indulging in the sweet treats. If he turned sideways it'd be hard to distinguish Stan from a barbershop pole, which seemed very fitting.

Stan asked Rip, "So, what do you plan to do with your $25,000 if we win?"

Rip swallowed his mouthful of doughnut so quickly it's a wonder someone didn't have to perform the Heimlich maneuver on him. At the time, I didn't realize this was a prophetic perception and I'd find myself in a similar situation the next time we came to the Shorts' house.

Appearing stunned, Rip finally asked, "There's a cash prize for the winning team?"

"Yes, of course." Stan stared at Rip as though he'd just stripped off all of his clothes and begun twerking on Fern's kitchen table. "You didn't know that? The first-place team wins the $100,000 purse and a trophy, of course. Second place gets the honor of saying they were runners-up and a cheap medal. Third place gets an even cheaper ribbon. Why else would we all be so determined to win?"

Rip was rendered speechless. Charlie laughed at his reaction and said, "I guess I forgot to mention that to you, Rip. That's the reason we'd do almost anything to win again this year. And with you singing in place of Henry, who was only a mediocre tenor at best, I think we stand a very good chance. Our only real competitor will be the team from Siskiyou County."

"Doesn't Henry's brother sing for that team?" I asked, feeling as shell-shocked as Rip.

"Yes," Charlie replied. "He's the backbone of that team."

"I see." What I really saw was that I might've overlooked a few people with a motive to eliminate Henry, the mediocre-at-best singer on their quartet. The weak link, you might say. Stan had seemed delighted that Henry was no longer on the team, and Charlie had said they'd do anything to win. It looks like they not only had a motive, but they'd had 25,000 motives. Is it possible that Wilson's life was in jeopardy? If Buster, Stan, or Charlie were guilty of killing Henry, could they be planning the other Harpodingle brother's demise as we gathered in the Shorts' kitchen? I was even more anxious now to discover what Fern had to tell me. To prod the men to leave the room, I said, "Shouldn't you fellows be practicing? I don't think stuffing your faces with doughnuts is going to do much to help you win the lucrative contest."

The men skedaddled out of the room so hastily it was like flushing a covey of quail out of a brush pile.

———

"When I talked to you before about Henry's death, it was obvious you thought foul play must've been involved," Fern told me in a soft voice after the men had left the kitchen. "And Charlie told me that Rip had mentioned you had an inclination to butt into murder cases."

I was instantly offended by Rip's description of me and wanted to defend myself. But I wanted to hear what Fern had to say even more, so I nodded and prompted her to continue. "And very successfully, I might add. Go on, Fern."

"My friend, Cindy Travis, works for the police department," she began. "I joined her for lunch the other day and she told me that the cause of Henry's death has been changed from accidental fall to homicide. They are keeping it on the down-low for the time being. Cindy said there are details about his death they don't want the public to know because it might interfere with their investigation."

"Really?" I was surprised to hear that the detectives had been investigating the case at all. I'd thought they'd written it off as a "stupid drunk doing stupid drunken things" kind of tragedy. That information should've made me feel relieved enough to step aside and let the authorities take it from there. Instead, a sense of competitiveness washed over me. I knew from past experience it likely meant the situation could turn into a "stupid amateur sleuth doing stupid amateur sleuth things" kind of tragedy. "What happened to make them change the COD?"

"Apparently, they'd ordered a tox screen report on Henry," she explained. "The results just came back showing he had Flunitrazepam in his system."

"Flunitrazepam? What's that?" I asked. "And what significance does it play in Henry's death?"

"It's what they call a 'roofie,' or a common date rape drug."

"Henry was raped before he was killed?" I asked without giving it much thought.

Fern laughed. "No, he wasn't raped, Rapella. But the tasteless, odorless drug is a central nervous system depressant about ten times more potent than valium. When mixed with alcohol, or copious amounts of alcohol in Henry's case, it can be lethal. I recall the young men who witnessed Henry's fall from the balcony told the police they didn't hear Henry make a sound while on his descent from the thirteenth floor. No screaming or flailing, more like a mannequin falling out of the sky."

"So you think he might've been dead before he fell from the balcony?"

"My guess is whoever slipped Henry a roofie tossed him off the balcony after he died from the aftermath of the drug interacting with the alcohol in his system. I doubt it was an intentional murder, but I think the plunge from the balcony was a means of covering up this individual's part in Henry's death."

"Wow!" I exclaimed. "You might be on to something. I know Devin Tubbs was supposedly the last person to see Henry alive. He's the one who helped him up to their shared room. He told me he then went down to the front desk and found his friend dead when he returned to their room. Could he have 'slipped Henry a roofie' as you put it, and then pitched him off the balcony to save himself from prosecution?'"

"It's possible, but highly unlikely," Fern replied. "Charlie and I have met Devin. He seems like a very responsible guy who's too kind to intentionally harm anyone. I can't imagine what kind of motive he'd have, either. I know Devin was almost as close to Henry as Charlie was. I truly don't think Devin would hurt a flea, much less Henry."

He hurt my pride when he placed me in Wal-Mart jail for forgetting to take off the repulsive purple parka before I raced outside to join my husband as he conversed with the victim's mother, I could've said. But I knew Fern was right. Devin was a very conscientious, caring individual who I could never imagine slipping a date rape drug in anyone's drink.

"Do you know who all attended Wilson's bachelor's party in Sacramento?" I asked.

Fern momentarily looked surprised I knew so much about the night of Henry's death. She paused for a moment as if unsure she should share any additional information with me. *Is she worried about my safety if I get more involved in this case?* I wondered. *Her concern is considerate but unnecessary.*

Finally, Fern responded. "I'm not sure of everyone who attended the party, but I know Stan, Devin, Moose Crossing, and Wilson were there. I believe there were a few other men at the party, but I don't know their names. Moose Crossing owns the winery across from the RV park you're staying in."

"Yes, we've met. But please don't mention that to anyone, especially Rip or Charlie."

Fern nodded in accord. "I won't."

"Didn't Charlie attend the Bachelor party?" I asked.

"No. Charlie wasn't particularly close to Henry's brother, even though he and Henry were best friends. Besides, my husband had a work event to attend that evening here in Klamath."

"And Buster?"

"Charlie told me he heard Buster had to go to a seminar in Sacramento that same evening, but he wasn't invited to the party. After Henry had an affair with Buster's wife, Clara, Buster wouldn't have attended the Bachelor party even if he *had* been invited."

"I can't blame Buster for wanting nothing to do with Henry after the man destroyed his marriage. In fact, I'd have been shocked to hear Buster attended a party Henry arranged. I would have been less surprised to find out Buster was behind Henry's death."

"It wouldn't surprise me to discover that either. Nor would I be shocked to hear Moose Crossing killed Henry. I still can't believe he had the gall to show up at the bachelor's party." Fern shook her head. "Why do you want to know who was at the party? Are you actually butting into Henry's case, like Rip told Charlie you have a habit of doing?"

"I was just curious," I said, clenching my false teeth together with a jaw strength similar to that of an alligator's. I didn't want to appear irritated by Fern's question or appear to show too much interest in the party's guest list. But, like Fern, I found it interesting that Moose Crossing was present at the party, considering the fact Moose had spoken of Henry with such disdain—a 'loser,' he'd called him. Fern had made it clear Charlie played no part in Henry's death. She'd also indicated she thought either Buster or Moose could be responsible. I almost wished I'd brought along my notebook so I could jot down all of the useful information she was sharing with me. "Is that all you wanted to tell me, Fern?"

"No. There's more." Fern looked around as if concerned Charlie had stealthily slinked back into the kitchen to snag a doughnut when she wasn't looking.

"Is everything okay?"

"Yes," Fern replied. "But Charlie gets upset when I gossip. He considered Henry his closest friend and it upsets him when I talk negatively about him. Just as I promised not to tell anyone what you've said to me tonight, please don't tell anyone, especially Rip, what I told you about any of this. I'm afraid he'd mention it to Charlie."

I could've told Fern someone could lash me to a tree surrounded by fire ants and pour honey over me while playing hard rock music at the loudest decibels possible, then water-board me at the same time, and I'd still not utter a word of what she told me to Rip. His disappointment in me would be more painful than any kind of physical torture ever could be.

But instead, I told Fern, "I can promise you I won't mention a word of it to my husband. He gets equally upset when I get caught up in a murder case I have no business getting involved in." I refrained from adding "or anyone else" to my vow, because I had every intention of telling Janet what I'd learned from Fern. This way, I wouldn't be guilty of lying to Fern.

"Okay, good. Thanks, Rapella."

"No problem. So what else did you have to tell me?" I asked.

"Charlie told me that Stan has amassed a gambling debt of $19,500 and has been getting pressured by his bookie to get the debt paid off, or else."

"Or else what?"

"Use your imagination, Rapella," Fern said. "I'm sure it wouldn't be pretty."

"Is his wife aware of his gambling debt?"

"Stan's never been married. He's a bit of an oddball. Not to mention, he has the looks and personality of a broomstick. I don't mean to imply Stan's not a nice fellow. He's just not marriage material, in my opinion."

"I don't think I've ever seen a skinnier man. Broomstick is a fitting analogy for the guy."

"I often make doughnuts, cupcakes, and other treats for the

guys when they meet here to practice. I've never seen Stan take a bite of anything. I think he believes sugar is akin to the devil."

"Is he diabetic, by any chance?" I asked. "That would explain his avoidance of sugar."

"I don't know," Fern replied. "But I'd think he'd be more likely to have hypoglycemia, or low blood sugar."

'Does Stan have other unusual idiosyncrasies?"

Fern shrugged. "It depends on what you'd consider an idiosyncrasy. He has plenty of quirks and weird anomalies. For example, he never wears matching socks."

"Maybe he's colorblind." I thought of Rip's recent remarks about his socks and added, "Or perhaps Stan just doesn't give a fig if his socks match."

"I suppose," Fern agreed. "He also never steps on a crack."

"Maybe he's afraid he'll break his mother's back."

"His mother died two decades ago of a heart attack."

"Those are strange quirks, for sure. But I was thinking about more sinister behavior. For instance, do you think Stan would be capable of killing off Henry so the quartet could replace him with a better singer?" I asked. "He sounds desperate to get his gambling debt paid off. I would be too if what my imagination came up with is anywhere close to being what his bookie has in mind for him."

"I don't know him all that well, but I guess I wouldn't put it past him." Fern was nodding agonizingly slow as she spoke even slower.

"Do you think Wilson would kill his own brother?" I asked.

"No. Wilson and Henry were competitive, for sure, but deep down, they loved each other."

"Fern, do you think Stan might try to eliminate Wilson so the Del Norte County team will be a shoo-in for the prize money?" I asked in a whisper.

Fern's expression was unreadable. It was as if an imaginary light bulb had been switched on above her head. She mulled over my question for at least fifteen seconds before she said, "Stan seems harmless, and a little on the delicate side, but I wouldn't rule it out."

We spent the rest of the evening discussing things to see and do in the area that I might have overlooked. That exchange added two tourist sites and three restaurants to my list of things to do while in northern California. And our earlier conversation put Stanley Ledge at the top of our suspect list. The suspect list was becoming similar to an escalator, with no suspect remaining on the top step for very long. The list currently contained four names: Stan, Buster, Clara, and Moose. And they were listed in that precise order.

It was going to be hard to keep the interesting information from Rip, but for my own sake, I would. I could hardly wait to share it with my new partner-in-crime-solving, Janet Wright.

FOURTEEN

"What would you do with your share of the prize money if your team wins the competition again this year?" I asked Rip on the drive back to the campground.

"I'd use it to help build up our nest egg again," he replied. We had paid cash for the new truck and fifth wheel, but it had put a major dent in our emergency fund. There was nothing we needed at the time, so I was satisfied with his response. "Can I buy a new can opener? The one we have isn't worth the two dollars I paid for it at a garage sale."

"Honey, you can buy a new can opener even if we come in dead last. If that bankrupts us, we're paupers already and just don't know it. I have to ask, though. What exactly were your expectations for a can opener you picked up for a couple of bucks? I'm sure it found itself on a card table in the seller's garage for a reason."

"Actually, it worked like a champ for five years. It's only been in the last month or so that it's gotten a little cantankerous." Rip rolled his eyes, so I reverted back to the previous topic. "I can't believe not a single one of the men in the quartet ever mentioned before there was a significant windfall at stake in all of the practices you've gone to."

"Stan might have mentioned wanting to win the money at one of our practices, but I thought he was talking about a game of gin rummy, so I pretty much just toned him out."

Gin rummy? How can you get gin rummy out of a conversation about a cash prize in a singing competition? I wondered. *I guess it's easy to do when your hearing aids are safely stashed in your nightstand, where they won't get worn out from overuse. I don't know why I don't just sell the costly dang things. After all, Rip wouldn't even notice they were missing and I could advertise them as being in "like new" condition.*

The evening had given me two things. One, a bellyache from overindulging in doughnuts, and two, a lot of things to think about concerning the death of the quartet's former tenor. In the event Stan was behind Henry's death, I sure hoped he didn't become displeased with Rip's singing skill before May 14th.

———

At the table the next morning, after Rip grumbled about the Honey Nut Cheerios and banana I'd served him for breakfast, he asked, "What's on tap for today?"

"I hadn't planned anything," I replied. "Was there something special you wanted to do?"

"No. But I know there's still a lot of things you want to do while we're here, and I thought today would be a great day to check one or two of them off your list. I know you wanted to visit the Plianki Falls in Crater Lake National Park."

"Yes, I did," I began, "but I crossed it off the list when I discovered that getting to the falls and back was a two-mile hike. I didn't think you'd be up for it."

"You were wrong. I *am* up for it. If it's something you want to see, I want you to see it. I'm so proud of you for not surrendering to your dark side and getting involved in Henry's death. The least I can do is make sure you get to visit all the places on your list." Rip reached across the table and squeezed my hand. I hoped my trembling fingers didn't give away the guilt I was feeling. "Are you cold, babe? Your hands are shaking."

"Just a little," I responded. "They'll warm up quickly when I wash the breakfast dishes. Are you sure you don't mind a two-mile hike?"

"I might not be able to sprint to the waterfalls and back, but I can definitely handle two miles of strolling."

It was a reminder of how lucky I was to have found this man over fifty years ago. Rip would walk through fire on a bed of nails for me. That's why I was so determined not to distress him with the knowledge Janet and I *were* looking into who and what was behind Henry Harpodingle's death. "You are the best, my love. Should we stop by the Annie Creek Café, like we promised Amanda, and try out their brisket basket for lunch?"

"Didn't she say the sandwich came with the best French fries in all of Oregon?" His question was voiced the same rhetorical way someone might ask, "Is the Pope Catholic?"

"I believe she said they were the best in Klamath County."

"That's good enough for me," Rip said with a smile. "It's a date."

"I love you, Rip." I returned his smile and patted his hand as it rested on top of the table.

"I love you more." Rip stood up with a half-full bowl of cereal in his hand. He tilted the bowl and drained the remainder of the milk into his mouth, then emptied the leftover Cheerios into the trash can. Apparently, with the promise of a brisket sandwich and Klamath's best fries for lunch, he didn't feel the need to finish his breakfast.

Pliakni Falls was gorgeous. The trail was well-maintained and fairly easy to walk. The path meandered through hemlock and fir trees and we saw large cliffs in the distance and wildflowers along the way as we sauntered beside Sandy Creek. Rip appeared to be enjoying the hike as much as I was. He took several photos along the way, as did I.

"Be careful not to touch any of the poison oak," I warned him. "I've noticed a number of patches of it and I just plucked a tick out of my wrist."

"Trust me," Rip said. "I'm not getting anywhere near anything with three leaves. One episode of that intense itching was more than enough. By the way, did the tick's head come out with its body?"

"Yes," I replied. "I yanked on it before it'd had time to get dug in good and tight."

Rip had no trouble walking the two miles. I'd noticed he'd been taking short walks around the campground the last few weeks. The ER physician had irritated Rip when he'd poked his belly and told him exercise would be good for him. But Dr. Danko had obviously made an impression on my husband, and for that, I was very thankful. I wanted Rip to be around for as long as I was. My plan was for the two of us to die together instantly in a freak "falling boulder" accident when we were in our mid-nineties. Earlier in age if either one of us was confined to a wheelchair and sat around in it all day like a head of cabbage. That wasn't too much to ask for, was it?

We returned to the truck at around eleven-thirty and headed to the Annie Creek Café for lunch. We were glad to find Amanda was working that day. She seated us at the same table she'd put Janet and me. It had the window with the beautiful view of Crater Lake.

"It's so great to see you two again," she said with an effervescent lilt to her voice.

"Likewise," I said. "We have come to try the brisket basket you told us about the last time we were here."

"Awesome. Will it be water with two lemon wedges for you, Rapella, and unsweetened ice tea with no lemon for you, Rip?"

"Yes!" I exclaimed. "You have a great memory, Amanda. You may look forward to quitting this job one day, but you are an excellent waitress."

"Thanks. Waiters and waitresses prefer to go by 'server' these days, but I'm not sure why. 'Server' sounds more like 'indentured servant' to me than 'waitress.' But I agree having a good memory is a real bonus. I used to not even write orders down on paper, but it seemed to make my customers uneasy, convinced I'd bring them meals that in no way resembled what they'd actually ordered. Sometimes, I just doodle on the order pad as they tell me what they want so they don't get nervous. The cooks are used to it."

We all laughed at her admission. There was only one other couple in the restaurant, so we had time to chat with Amanda. We told her about our morning in Crater Lake National Park.

"Pliakni Falls is one of my favorite sites in the park. Toketee Falls is awesome, too. It's my favorite of the two waterfalls. And the hike to it is less than half as long as the one to Pliankni."

After Amanda's comment, Rip looked at me as though someone had gifted us with a fifty-five-gallon barrel of Dingdongs and I hadn't told him about it until after I'd polished off the final one.

"Sorry, honey," I said. "I didn't know about the Toketee Falls or that it required less walking. Maybe we can hit that after lunch."

Now, he looked at me as if I'd missed the point entirely. I could tell he wasn't up for another hike, so I let it drop and asked Amanda, "Is Mad River worth visiting? I know your dream is to build a home overlooking it."

"Yes, it's amazing." The waitress had a dreamy expression as she continued, "Fun fact: the Mad River was named in memory of an incident when an explorer, Dr. Josiah Gregg, lost his temper when his exploration party didn't wait for him at the mouth of the river. He died after falling off his horse near Clear Creek due to starvation."

"Speaking of passing away," I said, hoping my segue to another topic sounded smoother to Amanda than it had to me. "My friend, Janet, and I ran into your Aunt Amie at Wal-Mart the other day. She said you were going to take her to Trinidad in a couple of weeks so she could get her will updated. That's awfully sweet of you to do."

I made certain not to make eye contact with Rip. I could hear his mind whirring like a ceiling fan set on low. He was clearly wondering when Janet and I had gone to the discount store in Crescent City.

"I'd do anything for my aunt. She's like a second mother to me. I lost my mom years ago to the same cancer Aunt Amie has now."

"That's what Amie told us. I'm so sorry for your loss. Cancer sucks, doesn't it?"

"Very much so."

"Your aunt also asked if Janet and I could take her to Trinidad sooner than two weeks because I think she fears she'll die before then and leave the fate of her estate up in the air." I tried to give off a nonchalant vibe. I noticed the more I talked, the louder the whirring in Rip's mind sounded, as if someone had cranked the ceiling fan up to high. Of course, that could've just been my imagination in overdrive due to my sense of guilt.

"Oh, dang." Amanda looked sad. "I didn't know she was so worried about it. I'll try to see if I can get a day off later this week. There's no need for you two to have to make that drive. I'm sure she wants to make sure Wilson doesn't have to deal with her estate going through probate and all that nonsense. I can't say I blame her."

"Neither can I. Janet and I wouldn't mind taking her," I said.

"But I know the time spent with your aunt would mean a lot to both of you, so we will step aside unless you find out you can't get the day off to take her yourself."

"Thanks. When I spoke to Wilson yesterday, I asked him why he didn't attend Henry's celebration of life the other night—"

I shot her a warning look, to remind her not to mention seeing me there. She gave me an almost imperceptible nod in return and continued, "It was at the Moose Crossing Winery, by the way. Wilson told me he was too busy to go. How can you be too busy to attend your own brother's memorial? I was beyond furious."

"It's nice to hear they held a celebration of life for your cousin, but it makes you wonder if he didn't have something to do with Henry's death, doesn't it?" I tried to come across as just mildly interested in the subject so as not to get Rip's panties in a twist. Wilson was not on our suspect list, but I wondered for a moment if he should be. Amanda shot that idea down quickly.

"No, it's not that." Amanda's cheerful personality had become downhearted in the blink of an eye. "It's just that Wilson's so caught up in his job he never has time for his family. Family should come first above all else. I feel so sorry for my aunt."

"I do, too, sweetie. But I'm sure the detectives are working hard on this case."

"Well, they did alert Henry's family to the fact he was slipped a roofie and the cause of death was changed to homicide, even though the news has not been released to the public."

"Exactly, Amanda," I replied. "Now that they know your cousin was murdered, I believe they'll have a suspect in custody before long."

"I sure hope so," she replied.

"I'm sure Rapella is right, Amanda," Rip added. "The detectives are obviously pursuing the perpetrator."

I nodded, but was still hoping to solve the case myself. It had become almost an obsession with me for some reason. I didn't want to think about what that reason might be or what my fixation on the case said about me. I was starting to scare myself.

Amanda excused herself to go pick up our brisket baskets from the order window. She didn't want our meals to become cold, and neither did we. Fortunately, with a basket of food emitting a delicious aroma in front of him, Rip was too distracted to ask me about Janet's and my visit with Amie at Wal-Mart that I'd never mentioned.

As we ate, I saw Amanda speaking with the lady behind the cash register, who I assumed must be the café's owner. When the waitress stopped by to see if Rip needed a refill on his empty tea glass, she said, "Good news! My boss said I can have Friday off to take Aunt Amie to Trinidad. She's going to have Belinda fill in for me that day."

"That's great," I said, even though I had mixed emotions about her announcement. I'd kind of looked forward to taking Amie to see her lawyer because it would've allowed Janet and me time to get a lot of information out of her during our time in the car. Just then, I recalled Amanda telling us at our first visit to the café that Wilson lived in Somes Bar, which wasn't too far from Trinidad. "I assume Wilson will meet you two at her attorney's office?"

"I doubt it." Her response was brief, but her expression was one of anger. She quickly left our table to welcome a family of four who'd just entered the restaurant. "I don't think Aunt Amie wants him there."

Her answer to my question left me stymied. *Could Amie seriously be planning to leave her estate to her feline friends and is afraid it'd upset her oldest, and only remaining, son?* But I knew asking her would raise the hackles on the back of Rip's neck. I'd already pushed the envelope as it was. So, instead of inquiring further, I simply said to Rip, "What a bizarre family the Harpodingles are, don't you think?"

"Yeah, I guess." Rip was solely focused on his lunch. I felt as though I could've asked him if he was all right with going bungee-jumping after lunch, and he would've replied, "Yeah, I guess." But then he made it apparent he really had been paying attention when he said, "But what I really think is that these truly are the best French fries in all of Oregon."

As we headed to the truck in the restaurant's parking lot, I was shocked when Rip asked, "So, which way do we go to get to Toketee Falls?"

"I don't know, but I can use my WAZE app if you really want to go. I figured one hike today would be all you were up for. You certainly don't have to go there today on my account. We've got a couple of more weeks here. I'm sure we could fit it in on another day."

"No. I'm up for it." Rip appeared offended by my inference that he wasn't physically capable of going on another hike that was less than a mile in and out. "Besides, we're here. Why make another trip to Crater Lake National Park to see the Toketee Falls when we could mark that off your list right now?"

I agreed, and we spent the rest of the day hiking to Toketee Falls, visiting a couple of gift stores, and making another drive around the lake on Rim Drive. It was so scenic it was more than worthy of doing again.

On the way back to the campground, I got a strange text from Amanda's Aunt Amie.

> Amanda just called and told me she was going to take me to my attorney's on Friday. I thought you and Janet would be taking me and I was going to tell you then about something that has me concerned, but I'll tell you now instead. Janet told me at the store the other day that you and she were doing some snooping into the death of my son.

"Who's that?" Rip asked.

"Just a friend checking in." I was being totally truthful because I now consider Amie a friend. I just wished Janet had thought to tell me what she and Amie had been discussing before I was able to join in on their conversation.

"Okay." Rip looked down at his phone. He was using the app I'd mentioned for navigational assistance back to Mystic Forest RV Camp. We had gotten off the normal path following our final stop at a lookout point that offered a great view of the park's volcanic formations.

I sent a return text to Amie while he was preoccupied.

> I'm not sure snooping is the correct word, but there's certainly no reason for you to be concerned. We just feel as though Henry deserves justice and you and your family deserve closure, as well.

I agree. I appreciate you two looking into his death. It's just that I was taken aback by Moose Crossing's attitude when he told me about the substantial debt Henry owed his winery. I paid it off, of course, but was alarmed at how hateful he appeared to be when it came to my son. And now, I've learned from a friend that Moose has closed up the winery and left the state. No one seems to know where he went, but it makes me feel like he has something to hide.

That is odd. I've had reservations about the man myself. Has he listed the winery for sale?

Yes. My friend Sammi saw a real estate sign in front of the main building. She stopped and went inside and said there were several men loading bottles of wine into boxes. She asked one of them if Moose was available and he said he'd already moved across the country. I don't know if that means he moved to the East Coast, or not, but I do know he grew up in Myrtle Beach, South Carolina. I just think it's peculiar that he left Klamath without telling anyone. Sammi spoke to numerous people about it and none of them had heard anything about Moose leaving. Why would he slither out of town like that unless he was running from something or someone?

Rip was pulling onto Highway 101 now, and I didn't want to have to explain what I'd been texting "my friend" about, so I told Amie we'd look into it and thanked her for the information. I then asked Rip, "So which of the two waterfalls did you think was the most impressive? I think I have to agree with Amanda. I thought the Toketee Falls were absolutely amazing."

"Me too," he agreed. "We aren't that far away from the last gift store yet. Are you sure you don't want that beautiful blue benitoite necklace? The sales lady said it was the official gemstone of California and only found in a small area of San Benito County."

"Yes, I heard her. But it's because it's one of the rarest gemstones in the world that it's outrageously expensive. I'd be afraid of losing it."

"You could keep it in that safe I had built into the floor under the bed."

"And what fun would that be?" I asked. "You are so sweet to offer to buy it for me, honey, but I don't need to own something I'd be afraid to wear because of its value. That sapphire necklace you bought me for my birthday last year is just as pretty, and I feel comfortable wearing it when we go out."

My text exchange with Amie was completely forgotten by Rip but gave me something to deliberate on as we traveled back to the campground. I was glad Janet had clued her in on our quest to get to the bottom of Henry's death and that Amie was okay with it. Her information might prove beneficial in our investigation. I would check out the real estate sign in front of the winery and call the agent who'd listed it. Maybe if I pretended to have an interest in purchasing the business, I might be able to find out why the owner had decided to sell it.

While we rolled down the highway, Rip was jabbering on about the upcoming barbershop quartet competition, while I was thinking about Amie's last comment. "Why would he slither out of town like that unless he was running from something, or someone?" *Why, indeed?* I thought. Just then, something Rip said brought me out of my reverie.

"Charlie told me that all three of the guys were glad I was on the team now instead of Henry. He said, 'If Henry was still alive and we did win the championship, my twenty-five grand would've probably gone to Fern in our divorce settlement.' So, I asked him if they were splitting the sheets."

"Wow!" I exclaimed with a chuckle. "At least you were tactful about it. You may want to have your sensitivity chip checked out. I think it might be broken."

"You think?" Rip laughed. "I'm sorry, but that's just how we guys talk to each other, honey."

"Yeah, okay," I replied dryly. "So, what was Charlie's response?"

"He said no, they weren't divorcing, as far as he knew, but Fern had threatened to leave him if he didn't put a stop to his gallivanting around with Henry. Charlie claimed that as much as Henry's death had devastated him, it had probably saved his marriage."

"I'm not surprised. During one of our conversations, Fern expressed displeasure with the way Henry acted as though Charlie were as single and unencumbered with a partner as he was. She thought Henry was a bad influence on Charlie."

"No doubt." Rip pointed to a highway sign advertising the best ice cream on the West Coast. "Wanna stop and see if that's true? The Main Street Creamery is right off the next exit."

"Sure. Why not?" I felt Rip had more than earned a rare treat, having completed two hikes with me that day. And, to be honest, a chocolate ice cream cone sounded pretty darn good to me, too. "I would sure hate to take a billboard's word for it."

With several suspects vying for the top spot on our suspect list, I didn't know which lead Janet and I should follow next. Perhaps a call to the realtor who'd listed the Moose Crossing Winery could solve that conundrum. And, if not, maybe a chat fest with Fern at the quartet's last practice the following evening would do the trick.

FIFTEEN

"David L. Colmer, broker. ReMax Realty," the real estate sign read. The agent's phone number and the address of his office were also listed on the sign. As Rip was turning left into the RV park, I snapped a photo of the real estate sign in front of the winery. I wanted to call Mr. Colmer the first opportunity I got.

"What'd you take a picture of?" Rip asked curiously.

"I thought I saw a snake, but looking at the photo now, I can see that he already left the area." A snake *had* left the area, just not the type of snake Rip was envisioning. It was a snake—a hot, sexy snake, to be precise—who I intended to hunt down and catch if it turned out he was behind the untimely passing of Moose's heavily indebted customer. No matter how much money Henry owed Moose, murder was not the answer. Murder was *never* the answer. That's why God created lawyers. Lawyers like Wilson and Henry Harpodingle.

I looked up from the cozy mystery I was reading when I heard Rip snore. It was so loud and unexpected; it scared me and pissed off Dolly, who was awakened from her own catnap by the sound. She hissed at Rip, glared at me as if it was my fault I let him fall asleep, and turned over. Within seconds, she resumed purring.

I put down my book and picked up my phone. As quietly as possible, I went outside and walked up the path toward the park's putt-putt course. When I was certain I was out of hearing range of any of the other campers, I dialed 141 to conceal my cell number and then David Colmer's phone number.

"ReMax Realty, Dave Colmer speaking. How can I help you today?"

Just then, I heard a man holler, "Fore!" milliseconds before a golf ball flew by my head like it'd been shot out of a rifle, missing my right temple by mere inches. I looked up to see a young man wearing a red Polo shirt and blue jeans that'd been constructed out of more rips and holes than denim. He had to have whacked the ball like he was teeing off on a five-par hole at the Masters Tournament in Augusta, Georgia.

"What part of 'putt-putt' don't you understand?" I hollered back before I stepped behind a tree to proceed with my phone call.

"Excuse me?" I heard a male voice emitting from my phone. "Were you talking to me?"

"Oh, no. I'm sorry, Mr. Colmer. I nearly got beaned by a golf ball."

"Are you all right?"

"Yes, I'm fine. The golf course marshal shouldn't have let those amateurs on the course to begin with." I let him believe I was in the middle of a round of golf at a ritzy country club. "I was a bit shaken up there for a moment, but I'm okay now."

"I'm glad you weren't injured," the realtor said before repeating his former question. "How can I help you today?"

"My name is Joyce Mauer, of Mauer's Refining Corporation,

and I'm interested in a piece of property you have listed." I thought the "oil money" reference might make the realtor more willing to give me some useful information about why Moose Crossing left the state so abruptly.

"Please call me Dave, Miss Mauer, and I'll call you Joyce. There's no need to stand on ceremony." At my concurrence, he asked, "Are you from this area?"

"No, I'm from Texas." That was true enough. Plus, Texas is a large state with a lot of oil refineries. More than any other state in the country, in fact. If I'd said I was from Florida or Georgia, and the realtor had any knowledge about oil production, the cat would've been out of the bag. There are no oil refineries in either state.

"Ahh, Texas. Of course. Everything's bigger in Texas, including oil production." Dave's response made me glad I'd not said I was a Floridian. He then asked, "Which piece of property are you referring to, Joyce?"

"I'm interested in purchasing the winery on Highway 101. Moose Crossing, I believe it's called."

"Yes, that's correct. It's listed at two-and-a-half-million. Everything but the wine stock conveys with the sale. When would you like to see the place?" Dave asked.

"Before I arrange to tour the property, I'd like to know a little bit more about it. For instance, why is the current owner selling? Is the company in financial straits or has the owner fallen ill? I'd like to know what would cause a person to walk away from a business that by all accounts appears to be successful."

"All the owner, Moose Crossing, told me was that he needed to move back home to take care of his ailing mother."

"Did I hear you right?" I asked, pretending to be in the dark about the origin of the winery's name. "The owner's actual name is Moose Crossing?"

"Yes. That is his real name." Dave laughed. "Believe it or not, Joyce, there are no moose in northern California."

"Yes, I'm aware. But you do have Roosevelt Elk in—"

"How does this afternoon at two o'clock sound for a showing, Joyce?" Dave cut in. He was obviously not interested in wasting his time discussing the elk population of California. "I'm certain you'll want to get a contract drawn up before someone else snatches this golden opportunity out from under you."

David Colmer was like a Peregrine falcon zeroing in on the kill. But I was craftier than your average pigeon.

"I'll have to check my schedule and get back with you," I replied. It was apparent the realtor knew little more than I did about Moose Crossing's motivation to flee California. He was going to be of no help to me, so it was time to end the charade. "Thank you for your time."

"Can you give me your phone number?" Dave asked quickly before I could ring off. "It isn't showing up on my screen for some reason."

"Yes, of course. It's (361) 555-1022," I said and ended the call. The 361 area code was used in Corpus Christi, Texas, where a lot of refineries were located, and the exchange code of 555 was often used in movies and books because it wasn't a working number. It prevents people from getting unwanted calls from movie-goers and readers. But I didn't want to stay on the line long enough to see if Mr. Colmer was aware of that fact.

The real estate agent had been more than happy to tell me all he knew about the winery's owner. But unfortunately what little he knew wasn't very useful. "Going home to take care of an ailing mother" was a handy excuse if one doesn't want to explain the real reason he's "slithering" out of town, as Amie had put it. And using the term "home" rather than "Myrtle Beach, South Carolina," was an evasive maneuver too.

I realized it was reasonable for Dave Colmer to believe his

client had turned his back on his successful business to rush back "home" and care for his ill mother. But I knew that wasn't true about as much as I knew an expensive white tablet three times a day was not going to make me lose five to ten pounds a week. I was smart enough to know it was the "with diet and exercise" addendum tacked on in small print to the miracle weight loss drug's advertisement that made the pounds fall off. And I was also smart enough to know Moose Crossing didn't just close the door on his winery and flee the state in the middle of the night. He wouldn't be leaving behind everything he owned, other than the wine stock, to care for a sick mother. And how do I know this, you might ask? I know this because I'd spent over an hour that morning searching the internet until I found an obituary for an Opal Marie Crossing of Myrtle Beach, who died of viral pneumonia on June 15, 2013, leaving behind two daughters and one son named Anthony (Moose) Crossing.

As I was walking back to our campsite, I saw Jack and Janet sitting at a wooden picnic table outside their motorhome. I stopped to say hello. I was about to ask how they were doing, but I could tell by their somber expressions something was wrong. "Is everything all right?"

Janet wiped a tear from her cheek and said, "We had to take Barkus to see the vet today. He developed a persistent dry, hacking cough like he had something caught in his throat. When he refused to eat and began throwing up a white foamy substance, we rushed him to the *Four Paws Pet Hospital* in Crescent City. Dr. Cruzer did some blood work and ordered a chest x-ray. He diagnosed Barkus with an infectious respiratory disease known as kennel cough. He said he probably caught the virus at the rescue center. Dr. Cruzer decided Barkus's symptoms were severe enough he needed to keep him in the pet hospital for a few days on intravenous fluids and antibiotics."

"I'm so sorry to hear this," I said. I had a tear threatening to run down my cheek now, too. I'd grown fond of the big, dopey dog. "Does Dr. Cruzer think Barkus will be all right after a few days under his care?"

Jack nodded at the same time Janet shook her head. Although those two opposing reactions made for an ambiguous answer, it was clear to see which of the two was the glass-half-full type and which was the opposite. Janet clarified it for me. "Well, the vet didn't actually specify one way or the other, but I got the impression the vet felt as though it was a precarious situation."

Jack looked at his wife as if wanting to ask her what vet she'd been listening to, before saying, "I didn't get that impression at all, Janet. I thought Dr. Cruzer was very optimistic about the outcome but only wanted to keep Barkus a few days out of an abundance of caution. I think you were just reading him wrong because of your emotional attachment to Barkus. I'm sure he'll be just fine, sweetheart."

Janet's face brightened considerably at her husband's words of encouragement and both hers and my tears quickly dried up. I grabbed her hand and squeezed it. "I'm sure Jack is right about this. The vet would've surely told you if Barkus's diagnosis was that dismal. I'm certain your furbaby will be home and right as rain in a couple of days."

I could relate to how two people could come away from a medical appointment with two very diverse outlooks. Earlier this year, the cardiologist in Minnesota had explained to Rip he needed an arterial stent inserted near his heart. Rip had acted as though the doctor had told him he needed a dab of Neosporin and a Band-Aid. I, on the other hand, was convinced Rip would be dead by Tuesday and I'd be shopping for a new black dress the following day. It'd be a slimming dress I could also use for a cocktail party or a Bar Mitzvah if either occasion arose in the future. I'd be broken-hearted and completely distraught, naturally, but that doesn't mean I'd spend good money on a dress I could only use for one purpose.

Rip was still asleep when I returned to the fifth wheel. Now Dolly was stretched out on his belly, snoring almost as loudly as he was. Neither had a clue I'd been gone for thirty minutes, which was exactly what I'd hoped for. I tip-toed into the kitchen to scour through my refrigerator and cabinets for something I could throw together for supper. Between the brisket baskets and ice cream cones, I wasn't even hungry, but I knew Rip would be like a bear awakening after a long hibernation. As expected, when he woke himself up snoring again, he asked, "What's for dinner?"

Dolly was startled awake again too. She leaped to her feet as if a mouse had just spit in her ear. Or, to be more accurate, she struggled to her feet as quickly as a twelve-year-old, twenty-pound house cat is able. She hissed at Rip again and climbed up on the back of the couch. I don't think cats are capable of rolling their eyes. But I knew she would've if she could've, and I agreed she should've if she could've. Regardless, she'd made it clear she didn't appreciate having her twelfth nap of the day disturbed.

SIXTEEN

I texted Janet the next morning and asked her to meet me at the campground's laundry facilities. I wanted to wash the comforter on our queen-sized bed and it was much too large for our apartment-sized appliances. She claimed to have a load of delicates she wanted to wash and with Jack playing another round of golf, the timing couldn't be any better.

After a brief hug, I explained to Janet everything I'd learned about our various suspects since I'd last seen her. When I finished, she asked, "So, what are you thinking?"

"Frankly, I don't know what to think. It seems as though Moose and Buster are the only two suspects with a viable motive to want Henry eliminated."

"Don't forget about Stanley Ledge's 25,000 thousand reasons to want Henry dead. If his bookie threatened him with bodily harm if he didn't cough up the money he owed, it'd make for serious incentive to kill the man who might stand in the way of him getting the cash he needed. There's no telling how far a man might go to save his own skin."

"That's true, Janet." I stuffed the comforter into the large load washing machine and said, "It seems like all motives boil down to four things: love, money, fear, and anger."

"That just about covers it, Rapella. But which of those motives are the most compelling? In this case, would it be Buster's anger or Stan's fear?" Janet asked as she shoved quarters into a washer. "And what about the winery owner?"

"That's just it. Although Moose Crossing appears to have the strongest evidence of guilt, he also seems to have the weakest motive. If people killed off every individual they had an issue with, there wouldn't be too many people left walking this Earth. The human race would've been erased from the planet like the dinosaurs were, except by other humans rather than impact with an asteroid or large-scale climate change."

"You're right," Janet agreed. "But why would he leave town practically in the middle of the night and not tell anyone where he was going if he wasn't trying to escape someone or something?"

"That's almost exactly what Amie said. I suppose there could be any number of reasons. Maybe he owed a lot of money to someone like Henry had owed him. Perhaps that debt was so overwhelming he felt he had no other option. If that was the case, I can understand why he wouldn't want anyone to know why he left or where he went. Or, perhaps he got caught banging some other man's wife and was worried about the man retaliating. He could have even got some kind of offer he couldn't refuse back on the East Coast."

Janet nodded. "I see your point. If we stopped and thought about it, we could probably come up with a dozen or more possible reasons for him to disappear like he did, reasons that don't involve something as drastic as murder. If he'd been behind Henry's death, you'd think he would've skipped town that very night."

"Yes. I agree. Let's pretend Moose is a great, big, handsome elf and put him on the shelf for now. We'll concentrate on the other two suspects instead. I believe both Buster and Stan have strong motives for murder."

"We'll have to eliminate them from our list one at a time. Rapella, didn't you say you are going to be seeing Fern again tonight?"

"Yes. It's the quartet's last practice before the competition on Saturday."

"You see what you can glean about Stan and Buster from talking with Fern tonight and I'll make another visit to Boeing Towing this afternoon and see what else I might learn directly from Buster."

"All right," I replied. "That's a great idea. I might even get a chance to talk directly with Stan and Buster myself. What will you use as an excuse to drop by Buster's shop?"

Janet shrugged and let out a long exhalation. "I don't know, but I'll think of something."

"What I do in situations like that is think WWLD."

"Don't you mean WWJD?" Janet looked puzzled.

"No, but you've got the right idea. Instead of 'What would Jesus do?' it stands for 'What would Lexie do?'"

"Ahh, yes. That's exactly what I'll do. I might even give her a call and see if she has any clever ideas."

"Oh, they'll be clever, no doubt. But they might also be risky, or even downright dangerous."

"Is it cold in this room?" Janet asked.

"I don't think so. Why do you ask?"

"Because I just felt a shiver run up my spine again." Janet shuddered dramatically, like she was sneaking up on a pack of polar bears in the Arctic Circle.

"If you used to hang out with Lexie as much as you said you did, you should be used to that by now."

We were both laughing as we sat down in a couple of rickety old chairs to wait for our washers to quit agitating.

At the Shorts' house that night, everyone gathered around a plate of lemon bars, rum balls, and apple tarts in the kitchen. Fern was a first-class hostess and an accomplished baker. As before, Rip avoided eye contact with me as he gobbled down one of each. And also like before, Stan ate nothing, opting for a cup of black coffee instead. I walked over to engage him in some small talk.

"How are you doing, Stan?"

"I've been better, but I'm getting by. How are things going for you and Rip?"

Saying everything was just fine sounded like boasting after Stan's response, so I replied, "We're hanging in there."

"That's good. How is that rum ball you're eating?"

"I haven't actually tasted it yet, but it looks delicious. Why don't you try one?" I asked.

"I'd love to, but I've been a type-one diabetic since I was nine."

"I'm sorry to hear that, Stan. It must be tough." I thought back to when I'd asked Fern if Stan was diabetic. As the hostess, you'd have thought Fern would be inclined to ask him about it after he refused to eat her pastries several times in a row.

"It's tough at first, but you get used to it," he answered with a smile.

"I suppose so. We all learn to adapt to whatever life decides to throw at us." *Enough small talk*, I thought. I was curious if Stan would be honest with me when I asked, "So what do you plan to spend your share of the cash prize on if you men win the singing competition again this year?"

Surprisingly, he was honest. Honest to a point, at least. He replied, "I have some debt I'd like to get paid off."

"Oh? Like credit cards?" I asked, even though it was none of my business whatsoever.

"Something like that." His answer was vague, but he didn't seem put off by my nosy inquiry.

"I know your team is hoping for a three-peat. What did you spend your winnings on last year and the year before that?" Again, it was none of my business what the scrawny fellow spent his winnings on.

"Same thing as I'll spend it on this year if we do manage to win for the third year in a row," Stan said. So far, my conversation with the bass singer had yielded very little beneficial information. All that changed when Stan said in an almost giddy manner, "Thank God we have your husband on the team now instead of Henry. After a few beers, that man couldn't carry a tune in a dump truck, much less a basket. And keeping the dude sober was near impossible. If not for that stroke of good fortune, we wouldn't have had a chance of pulling it off again this year."

Henry's death was a stroke of good fortune? I wanted to ask. But I couldn't because Stan's remark had made me choke on the rum ball I'd just stuck in my mouth. As I struggled to dislodge the pastry from my throat, Rip walked over and pounded me twice on the back. The rum ball popped out on his second thump and fell to the floor like a gut-shot deer as everyone else in the room stared at me in stunned silence. I was thankful Rip had been cognizant enough of my dilemma to react quickly. If I'd had to rely on any of the others in the room to save me, I'd have been flat on the floor, unresponsive, before any of them had the presence of mind to come to my aid. I was even more grateful Rip hadn't had to perform the Heimlich maneuver on me. The choking incident had been embarrassing enough as it was.

Many moments later, as if a delay switch that'd been activated was turned back off, everyone started firing questions at me all at once. They were asking me if I was okay, if I needed a glass of water, and if I wanted to sit down while I recovered from the near catastrophe. Buster even had the audacity to ask me if I wanted another rum ball to replace the one that was still lying on the floor like a fallen soldier. I shook my head a dozen times. *What I'd really like right now*, I wanted to say, *is to disappear like a full-sized airplane in a David Copperfield magic show.*

What bothered me even more than the humiliation of having to have a pastry pounded out of me by my husband was that now I no longer felt comfortable resuming my conversation with Stan. *Damn*, I thought. *Just as I was beginning to get some very telling information out of him, I had to go and poke a run ball in my pie-hole.* For a split second, I even wished I was the diabetic instead of Stan. If that were the case, I'd have never put the pastry in my mouth to begin with.

Fern appeared to recognize my unease. She shooed the men out of the kitchen and picked the rum ball up off the floor with a napkin. To ease my embarrassment, she said, "I'm so glad Rip was on his toes. That happened to me once when I hiccupped and inhaled a lemon drop I had in my mouth at the time. We were in the women's clothing section of a Macy's Department Store. Charlie stood motionless like he was one of the store's mannequins until I folded my hands and pretended to give myself the Heimlich maneuver. By the time he caught on, my face was blue. Thankfully, it flew out on Charlie's first attempt to free it. I haven't touched a lemon drop since, and that was ten years ago."

As serious as the incident had been, I couldn't help but laugh at the humorous way she'd described it. She joined in my merriment, clearly relieved she'd helped alleviate the humiliation I'd been experiencing. I was appreciative of her thoughtfulness and told her so.

"Like I said before, I've been there, Rapella. I know exactly how you were feeling." As she spoke, Fern rubbed my back as though she was trying to erase the hard whacks Rip had been forced to use to dislodge the rum ball blocking my airway. "Now, let's get a cup of coffee and go sit on the porch so we can talk."

After we got settled into some comfortable padded chairs on the Shorts' back porch, I asked her if she and Charlie were getting along okay. When she gave me a surprised look, I explained that Rip had told me about her threatening to divorce her husband if he didn't stop gallivanting around with Henry. Again, it was none of my business whatsoever, but I knew I wasn't going to garner any useful information by asking Fern what she used to get blood stains out of her son's baseball uniform. Jacob, she had told me earlier, was spending the night with a friend after their ball practice.

"I see the local grapevine is in working order. I'm happy to say I took care of the problem and everything's fine between Charlie and me now." Fern seemed reluctant to elaborate on the issue. She did an abrupt pivot to change the topic and it was to my benefit that she did. "It's Buster I'm worried about. He hasn't been the same since Henry died."

"Were they close?" I asked. "I thought Henry broke up Buster's marriage by having an affair with his wife. And I heard that afterward, Henry dumped Clara for another woman whose divorce he was handling in court."

"Yes. That's all true." Fern took a long swallow of coffee as if to bolster her courage to broach a difficult subject. "That's why Buster's altered personality seems so odd. I almost have to wonder if he had something to do with Henry's death and it's his guilt that's got him acting so strangely."

"What kind of unusual behavior has he been exhibiting?"

"For one thing, he doesn't joke anymore. He used to be quite the cut-up, but not now. I don't believe I've heard him laugh once in all these weeks since we lost Henry."

"I heard Buster laugh once. It was after Janet told him her Hyundai Veloster that he was preparing to yank out of a ditch might be a four-banger, but it could really scoot because it was turbo-charged. It was a sarcastic laugh, but a laugh nonetheless. And let me tell you, it truly can scoot down the highway with Janet behind the wheel."

"I'm not sure that counts," Fern replied with a smile. "Buster has also developed a nervous tic on the side of his left eye. It seems to be triggered by the mention of Henry's name or any talk about the night he died."

"I'd like to think the timing of the nervous tic's development was a coincidence, but it sounds like that's not the case if it's triggered by any discussion that involves Henry. And I don't particularly believe in coincidences anyway." I thought for a moment before asking, "Is there anything else he's been doing recently that concerns you?"

"A friend who works as a waitress at the Daily Grind coffee shop told me Buster has started coming in every morning and doesn't leave until he gets called out on a towing job. He drinks four or five cups of coffee while reading through the entire Del Norte Triplicate on his laptop computer. It's the main newspaper in this area. She said it's like he's searching for something. Once, she overheard him ask another customer if he was aware of any leads the homicide detectives might have on who killed Henry Harpodingle. She said at that point, the side of Buster's left eye was vibrating like he was being zapped with a taser."

"That's a little suspicious. What'd the guy say in response to his question?"

"He said he wasn't aware of any leads, but was pretty sure they didn't have any yet, or his good buddy who works for the police department would've mentioned it to him. Buster's nervous tic stopped instantly." Fern studied my face for a few seconds, took a sip of coffee, and added, "The reason I'm bringing this all to your attention is because, like I said before, Rip had told Charlie at one of their practices you had a bad habit of butting into murder cases."

I thought if I heard Fern say "butting into murder cases" one more time I was going to have no choice but to slap the coffee cup out of her hand. She saved herself from that fate, though, and redeemed my husband somewhat with her next remark.

"Rip also said you were surprisingly successful at solving those cases. And when we've talked about Henry at previous quartet practices, you've seemed interested in what was behind his death. I recall you said you didn't believe it was an accident, and I didn't either. And that was long before the police department changed his cause of death to homicide."

At this point, only Janet and Amie knew for certain I was involved in investigating the case. I felt keeping Rip in the dark kept his spirits high and his blood pressure low. However, if more than one person knows a secret, the chances of it remaining a secret are slim. With two other people in the loop, I was already pushing my luck without adding Fern to the mix.

"Actually, although I find the mystery behind Henry's death intriguing, I had promised Rip I wouldn't get us involved in another murder case. But that's not to say I don't want you to share any juicy gossip you hear about it with me. I'm still interested in seeing that Henry's case gets solved, even though I'm not actually involved in it."

Fern appeared to be relieved at my remarks. I'm sure Rip had told Charlie that nearly every case I'd investigated had ended in a life-or-death situation for me, if not me and one or two other people. It appeared as though she was concerned for my well-being, and that didn't surprise me. The way she had stepped in to assist me after the choking incident proved she was a caring, thoughtful individual.

Fern took both of our empty cups inside and returned a few minutes later with full ones. Even though I knew I probably wouldn't fall asleep again until next Thursday, I emptied it and then a third cup while we talked about a myriad of subjects that had nothing to do with Buster or Henry. Just as Rip stuck his head out the door to check in on us chatting on the back porch, Fern said, "Oh, before I forget, I have a delicious cookie recipe I want to share with you."

Rip winked at me and shut the door. Through the window I watched him snatch another doughnut off the pastries platter and return to the living room to resume practicing the Max Q song, *You Can Fly*. It was the tune chosen by the Del Norte barbershop quartet to sing in the upcoming competition. I'd heard it sung so many times since we'd arrived in California that it promised to be an earworm I couldn't shake until at least Thanksgiving. I had to wonder if the song was going through Henry's head as he'd plunged to the pavement from his hotel room's thirteenth-story balcony.

SEVENTEEN

The next morning around ten-thirty, Rip and Jack went to the local hardware store. I never see Rip actually fixing or building anything, but yet he seems to make a daily trip to the nearest Home Depot no matter where in the country we happen to be. Janet said Jack was the same way. It must be a "man thing." It's as if they can absorb testosterone through their nostrils by standing in the middle of a hardware store and breathing in the aroma of lumber, screws, and power tools. It must be an osmosis kind of phenomenon. At least this trip appeared to be for something specific: materials to build a ramp down to Dolly's private privy.

While the men were away, Janet and I sat out at the picnic table on our cement patio. First, Janet told me about her visit to Boeing Towing. She said she'd arrived at Buster's shop around ten-thirty and the office girl told her he hadn't showed up at the shop yet.

"He was at the Daily Grind drinking coffee and reading the Del Norte Triplicate on his laptop," I said.

She looked at me as if I'd suddenly morphed into Sylvia Browne, the famous late psychic. I said, "I'll explain later. Go on with your story."

"I had planned to talk directly with Buster so was thrown for a loop when he wasn't there. I told the office girl I was a volunteer for the U.S. Census Bureau and needed to know how many people resided in the business owner's home. She replied, "One," and I jotted the number down on a pad of paper I'd taken inside with me. I was trying to look official."

"Good thinking. How could she doubt your authenticity if you have a pad of paper with you?" My sarcasm flew over Janet's head like that golf ball had flown past my ear. "Did you ask the office girl for the owner's address?"

"No, it never occurred to me."

"And yet she bought your Census Bureau story?" I asked in amazement.

"She's clearly not the sharpest tack on the bulletin board, you know."

"Is that the clever idea Lexie gave you when you called her last night?"

"No," Janet said with a hint of defensiveness in her tone. "She told me to say I had a nephew who was looking for a job and I was stopping in to ask if he had any positions available."

I'm sure I was wearing a baffled expression when I asked, "And of those two ideas, you chose the Census Bureau option? You do realize, don't you, that if Buster had walked into his office, he would've recognized you from towing your Veloster out of the ditch?"

"What can I say?" Janet said with a grin. "I'm obviously not the sharpest tack on the bulletin board either. This crafty cunningness comes naturally to you and Lexie, but not so much to me."

"That's okay. I *do* admire creativity and thinking outside the box. I'm not sure I wouldn't have put that idea back into the box and gone with Lexie's plan, but hey, it got the job done."

"Seriously, Rapella? That's giving me a little more credit than I deserve," Janet said. "I'm sorry I wasn't able to get any useful information from Buster this time."

"That's okay. You did the best you could. I was able to find out a little more about him from Fern last night, and what I learned is troubling."

I told her about my evening at the Shorts' house and my conversation with Fern about Buster. Even though she tried to restrain her amusement, she laughed hysterically at my account of choking on a rum ball.

"I'm sorry," she said between belly laughs. "I know it was a dreadful thing to have happen to you and you're lucky Rip was able to dislodge it, but I just can't help myself when I visualize Buster asking you if you wanted another rum ball to replace the one Rip had to extricate from your windpipe."

"I understand. If our roles were reversed, I guarantee I'd be laughing at you. If Lexie hears the story, she won't even try to keep herself from cracking up."

"Oh, you can be certain Lexie will hear the story," Janet promised me. "I'll be calling her tonight when Jack's not around just to make sure she does."

"Traitor," I said with a laugh. I went on to tell her about the odd behavior Buster had been exhibiting lately and that Fern had thought I might want to know about it in the event I was doing a personal investigation into Henry's death. "The last thing I wanted is for Fern to talk to Charlie and then Charlie to talk to Rip about my involvement in the case. So I told Fern I had promised Rip I wouldn't get 'us' in the middle of any more murder cases, which technically was the truth. I really do hate to lie to people."

"But you **are** in the middle of another murder case," Janet pointed out.

"Yes," I agreed. "I am. But 'us,' as in Rip and I, aren't. I'm being evasive, not dishonest."

"Is evasiveness better than dishonesty?"

"Probably not, but evasiveness is definitely better for Rip's blood pressure."

Janet smiled impishly. "Whatever helps you sleep at night, my friend."

"You know something?" I said jokingly. "I'm starting to think I don't like you as much as I used to."

"And I'm starting to think you're as crazy as Lexie, which makes me adore you even more than I used to."

Our playful banter continued over another cup of coffee. Janet said, "In other news, Barkus responded so well to the antibiotics and intravenous fluids that he was able to come home first thing this morning. Other than being a little fatigued, he appears to be back to normal."

"I'm so glad to hear that. Rip and I were worried about him."

"I was worried, too. As you know, I was frantic after the vet told me he needed to be kept in the pet hospital under observation."

"I know the feeling. I'm always upset when we have to take Dolly to the vet. Unfortunately, our pets tend to have shorter life spans than humans. I'm always concerned her time has come every time she coughs. Normally, it's just a hairball she's hacking up, but it sounds like she's trying to expel a lung."

"I can imagine. She's so adorable. Dolly kind of makes me want to get a cat to keep Barkus company."

"But you're allergic to cats," I reminded her.

"I know," she said. "And that's the only reason I don't get one. Our motorhome's not big enough for another dog like Barkus, so I guess Jack and I will be all the company Barkus is apt to get. While the men are away, do you have any thoughts on what we should do next as far as our suspects are concerned?"

"Do you have any raisins on hand?" I asked.

"No."

"Don't you think you should?"

"What do raisins have to do with anything?"

"I think we need to make a trip to Wal-Mart and wanting to pick up a box of raisins is as good of an excuse as any. I already used raisins as a justification for a shopping trip, but I don't believe I have any curry in the pantry."

"Do you use a lot of curry?" Janet asked.

"I've never used curry," I replied. "But that doesn't mean I won't need it someday for an Indian recipe I want to try, and it'd be nice to have it on hand if that happens."

"You really are a nut, Rapella."

"Thank you."

———

"What's the sudden fascination with raisins?" Rip asked me Thursday morning after I told him the reason for the trip to Wal-Mart. "Isn't that what you needed the last time I went to the store with you?"

"Yes, but it's just an ironic coincidence that Janet needs raisins now, too," said the lady who always claimed not to believe in coincidences.

"Can't you just loan her your box of raisins? To my knowledge, you haven't used them yet, and probably won't in the next decade or two."

"I offered them to her, but she wants a specific brand. Besides, I decided I should go with her because I need to pick up some curry."

"When have you ever cooked anything with curry in it?" is the question Rip should've asked. Instead, he said, "I'm glad you're accompanying her. You sure don't want to run out of any critical spices. When are you two leaving?"

"Janet's picking me up at nine," I told Rip, who suddenly

seemed very anxious for me to go to the store, and I was curious to know why. "So where have you and Jack got planned to go while we're gone? A gambling parlor? A strip joint? Perhaps a local restaurant that prides itself on its thirty-two-ounce porterhouse steaks?"

"None of those," Rip said with a sheepish grin. He looked like a ten-year old boy who'd gotten caught pouring through his dad's Playboy magazine. "We've hired a guide service to take us salmon fishing on the Mad River. I meant to tell you yesterday and forgot. Ever since that waitress at Annie Creek Café mentioned it was one of the best steelhead trout rivers in the country, I've been dying to try it. You don't mind, do you?"

"Not one bit, honey!" I exclaimed. "I'm glad you two are getting out to do something fun and adventuresome. Maybe if you guys have any luck, the four of us can have a fish fry one night this week."

"Don't jinx us! Planning a fish fry before you've even cast a line is almost as bad as taking a banana on the boat." Rip had explained to me years ago that bananas bringing misfortune if taken onto a boat is a superstition that originated in the 1700s when many ill-fated ships were said to have been carrying bananas to their destination. Nowadays, serious anglers won't allow any bananas on their fishing boats for fear it'll cause the fish not to bite. I'm certain most of those anglers think the superstition is as ludicrous as I do, but few are willing to roll the dice on it.

"Sorry, honey," I said. "Hopefully, you'll still catch a boatload of steelheads."

"Hopefully. And if we do, I'll suggest a fish fry." He kissed me and went outside to collect his fishing gear from underneath the fifth wheel.

"Dolly loves her new personal latrine, Rip. Clean out her kitty litter box while you're at it," I told him. The box was in the undercarriage compartment next to the one he kept his fishing gear stored in.

"Why do I have to do it?" Rip asked. "You're the one who brought Dolly home from the pound."

"That was twelve years ago," I replied. "And ever since that day, you're the one who's been over-feeding her and making her poop so much."

"Yes, ma'am." Rip saluted me. "I'll get right on it."

"Do I really have to buy raisins?" Janet asked me as I crawled into her passenger seat. "I really dislike those dried-up goobers. If I ever decide I want to eat a raisin, I'll clean out under my refrigerator, where at least a dozen grapes have rolled in the past year or so."

"What if the raisins are covered in chocolate?"

"Well, now that's a whole different ball of yummy. Can I just buy a box of Raisinets?" Janet asked with a chuckle.

"Does Jack scour through your grocery bags when you get back from the store?" I asked.

"Of course not."

"Then you can buy fourteen boxes of Raisinets, a bag of hamster food, and a dozen turkey necks if you want."

"It's a hard pass on the hamster food and turkey necks, but I'm not taking the fourteen boxes of Raisinets off the table quite yet."

It was this kind of repartee that I'd always enjoyed so much with Lexie, and now I found myself enjoying it with Janet just as much. I hoped we'd remain lifelong friends when we had to part ways, even if it was a long-distance friendship.

Wal-Mart was packed. We had to drive around for ten minutes to find a parking spot. We walked the entire store at least twice because, by the time we got to the last aisle, we remembered items we'd forgotten to pick up in aisles two, three, and nine. When Janet selected the smallest box of raisins on the shelf in aisle nine, just in case Jack inquired about them, I remembered I'd told Rip I needed a jar of curry, and the spices were located in aisle two. The chances of him asking about it were slim, but in the event he decided to test me, I needed to have a jar of curry to show him.

I looked at Janet and asked, "Are you beginning to feel like a three-year-old in a corn maze as much as I am?"

"Oh, crap!" She exclaimed in response.

"What's wrong?" I was afraid something was physically wrong with her, one of those shopping injuries like a pulled shoulder muscle or eye strain from reading the fine print on the back of unhealthy snack items.

"Your last remark reminded me that Jack asked me to pick up a few ears of corn. He wants to grill them along with rib eyes tonight."

"No problem."

"The produce department is on the opposite side of the store."

"There's nothing wrong with getting every one of your recommended ten thousand daily steps in the grocery store." As I spoke, I wheeled my cart around 180 degrees.

"I know. But my right calf is beginning to cramp."

Uh-oh! Shopping injury, I thought. *Who knew shopping was so physically challenging?*

When we finally got to the self-checkout stands, Amie was nowhere to be seen. Hoping to have another chat with her, we were disappointed at her absence.

"Where's Amie this morning?" I asked the employee working in her place.

"She clocks in at ten, which means I clock out in nine minutes and don't have to report to duty again until Monday. Hooray for me!"

"Yes, hooray for you," I returned with a faked bright smile. "Who doesn't love a three-day weekend?"

I knew Janet's mindset was the exact same as mine when she said, "You know what, Rapella? I don't have any curry on hand, either. I probably should go back and pick up a jar."

"You do know that's on the far end of the store, don't you?" the cashier asked.

"Don't worry," I said. "We are still about forty shy of our daily recommended steps."

The clerk shrugged, Janet nodded, and I whirled my cart around 180 degrees again.

Amie was just reporting for duty when we returned to the self-checkout stands. We loitered in the men's underwear section while she got settled into her clerking duties. Janet was giggling and I asked what had tickled her funny bone.

"I'm trying to imagine Jack wearing these pink and green boxers."

"You should buy him a pair. Rip has a pair with SpongeBob SquarePants on them and another pair with a skunk on the back holding his nose and saying, 'It wasn't me!'"

"Does he actually wear them?"

"Yes, he does. Proudly, in fact."

Janet grinned and asked, "Doesn't that kind of kill the mood when things turn romantic?"

"Not as much as you'd think. But I'll tell you what does kill the mood. The other night, after a dinner of pork chops, broccoli, and lentils, Rip was so gassed up he turned the air quality in the bedroom to that of a water treatment plant. I'm surprised our bed didn't strip the bedclothes off itself. Then he turns to me and asks how I feel about him taking one of his blue 'magic' pills."

"I love spending time with you, Rapella," Janet said when she finally stopped cracking up. "No one has made me laugh this much in a long time. I used to laugh at Jack's jokes, but I've heard the same ones so many times they only make me groan now."

"Since I'm sure you know it by heart now, tell me Jack's favorite joke." We were stalling for time. Amie was currently conversing with another store employee and we didn't want to be a nuisance to her.

"All right." Janet thought for a moment, and then said, "A man named Bob runs across a homeless guy who looks like he hasn't bathed in months. The guy asks Bob if he can spare twenty dollars. Bob tells him, 'Only if you swear you won't spend it on booze or bait.' The homeless man claims he hasn't touched alcohol or a fishing pole since he'd started living on the streets five years earlier. So Bob offers to take him home with him and have his wife fix him a warm meal. Then Bob would bring him back and give him the twenty bucks. The homeless guy asks, 'But what if your wife doesn't want to fix a warm meal for me?' And to that, Bob replied, 'It doesn't matter. I just want her to see what happens to a man when he quits drinking and fishing.'"

I told Janet I thought Jack's favorite joke was hilarious. "If I can remember it, I know Rip will love that joke too."

"Don't tell it to him," Janet warned. "I laughed at it the first time Jack told it, and most likely the second time. But it's not nearly as funny the tenth time you hear it."

"You make a good point, Janet," I replied. "Thanks for the excellent advice."

I glanced up to see Amie leaning against the cash register at her post in what looked like pure boredom. Not one customer was checking out at any of the self-checkout stands. "This looks like it might be the perfect time to go talk to Amie."

We greeted the haggard-looking cashier warmly. She appeared not to have slept in days. I asked her how she was feeling and wasn't surprised to hear her respond, "I feel like a cement truck ran over me."

Feeling like a cement truck ran over her was probably an understatement, but I responded to her by saying, "You look a little tired, sweetie, but still as beautiful as ever. I wish I looked like you on my best days."

"You are sweet, Rapella. You're a dreadful liar, but so sweet." She hugged me and then Janet in turn. "I'm afraid my days here are coming to an end."

"I hate to hear that," I replied. "But no one would fault you for quitting this job and taking it easy."

"Thanks," Amie said. "But I was referring to my life, not my job, when I said my days here are coming to an end. I really should not be working in the condition I'm in, but being at home alone is too depressing for me."

All three of us teared up as Janet and I offered whatever solace we could muster under the sad conditions. I said, "Rip and I ate at the café again, and Amanda told me she is going to be able to take you to Trinidad tomorrow."

"Yes. And I am very thankful for that. Can I run something by you two?"

"Of course," Janet and I said simultaneously.

"In my original will I had split my estate equally among my two sons." She paused, and we both urged her to continue. "As a personal injury attorney, Wilson makes more than enough money to live lavishly. But I've recently noticed he's become more and more obnoxious the wealthier he gets. He no longer has time for his sick mother. Thank goodness Amanda treats me like the daughter I never had. It occurred to me if I left the bulk of my estate to Wilson, he'd become a complete—"

"Jackass?" I offered when Amie appeared to be looking for the proper word.

She laughed so hard the bamboo cap she wore to conceal her baldness fell off her head and landed in my shopping cart. "I was thinking 'jerk,' but 'jackass' works just as well."

"I'm sorry if I sounded insensitive," I told Amie as I handed her the cap.

"If I can offer you a word of wisdom before I pass, it's to never apologize for being honest. If people are castigated for their honesty, then what kind of world are we living in?"

"Amen!" Janet exclaimed. I nodded in consensus.

"Thank you, Amie." I squeezed her hand, not only out of compassion, but also to try to quell her trembling fingers. "How is Wilson going to react tomorrow when he finds out he's been cut out of your will? He's going to go with you and Amanda to Trinidad, isn't he?"

"Oh, hell no!" Amie spat out, as though my question had left a nasty taste in her mouth. "Even if he wasn't home recovering from a trimalleolar fracture of his right ankle, he'd told me he was too busy to take me when I asked him a couple of weeks ago."

"How'd he break his ankle?" Janet asked.

"He broke the three bones that support his ankle on a pickleball date with his fiancée, Lu Ann, which I was glad to hear. It's a severe fracture that always requires surgery, with multiple plates and screws, and then no weight can be put on that ankle for two or three months."

"You were glad he severely broke his ankle playing pickleball?" Janet asked. I knew what Amie had meant and it tickled me that Janet had misinterpreted her response.

Amie was laughing so hard I had to explain it to Janet. "She's not happy her son broke his ankle, but she's happy if he did have to break it, it was while playing pickleball with Lu Ann. My guess is

Amie's hoping the two go ahead with their wedding plans soon because she likes Wilson's fiancée."

"That's it exactly," Amie said. "They had kind of disconnected after Henry's passing. So I'm glad to see them rekindling their relationship. I think Lu Ann would be good for him. And I know she will fawn over him while he's recuperating and make him realize how much he needs her in his life. Hopefully, she'll humble him a little bit too and make him see money isn't everything. The love of family is much more valuable than a huge house and a fast, flashy car."

"Well said, Amie." Amanda had said much the same thing about Wilson to Rip and me, I realized. "And to think, pickleball is supposed to be a relatively safe sport."

"Thanks. But to be clear," Amie began, "Wilson didn't exactly break his ankle 'playing' pickleball. He tripped over a curb in the parking lot and suffered the fracture before they even got on the pickleball court. It's a source of embarrassment for a proud man like my son."

"I can imagine. Where does Wilson live in Somes Bar?" I knew she wouldn't offer an actual address but hoped she'd give us enough information we could find his residence if we wanted to. I wasn't disappointed in her response.

"His ten-acre estate overlooks the Salmon River. He calls his house a 'log cabin.' I call the nine-thousand foot high-falutin' mansion constructed out of cypress logs, with a red metal roof and an Olympic-sized status symbol in the backyard, a monstrosity. Who builds a pool when they can't even swim and never intend to learn?"

"Wow!" Janet and I simply replied.

"Exactly!" Amie said. "In my opinion, if he's too busy to help his ailing mother, he's also too busy to cash a big fat inheritance check he receives from her estate once she's gone. I guarantee you Amanda won't be too busy. She'll quit her waitressing job between taking a customer's drink order and taking their meal order."

We all laughed, even though the circumstances were so grim. I knew Amanda was too responsible to leave her boss in the lurch by quitting her job mid-shift. "It would be nice if she could build the dream home she's wanted."

"Since she was a teenager," Amie added.

"She told Rip and me she wants to build it overlooking the Mad River. I'm very happy for her."

We all looked up as three grocery carts rolled into the self-checkout area all at once. Amie said, "I better get busy."

As Amie pushed away from the cashier stand she was leaning against, her knees buckled and she fell to the floor. Janet and I swiftly crouched down to make sure she was all right. She assured us she was but had just straightened up too quickly. We tried to convince her she should take the rest of the day off to get some rest, but she refused.

She's a kind woman, but a mighty stubborn one, I thought. *And I find that very inspiring.*

Walking out of the store, something Janet had said the previous day was wafting through my mind like a balloon on a string. *There's no telling how far a man might go to save his own skin,* she'd said. Something told me Janet's remark had been prophetic. If it turned out to be an accurate prognostication, and I'd ignored it, I wouldn't be able to forgive myself.

As we loaded our bags in the hatchback of Janet's Veloster, I asked her if she wanted to drive to Somes Bar and hand-deliver a 'Get Well Soon' message. "Nothing we bought is perishable but the milk, and although it's a two-and-a-half hour drive, the men don't expect to be home for another six or seven hours. If we arrive home after they do, they'll just assume we didn't leave the campground for Wal-Mart until mid-afternoon. I just have this sudden hunch it's important we drop in on Wilson."

"I'm game if you are. If we went home right now, I'd probably just spend the rest of the day dusting, vacuuming, mopping, and scouring. What fun is there in doing all that?"

"None at all. But I can't promise you this will be any more enjoyable than housecleaning. Sometimes my best-laid plans go up the spout when I least expect it."

I'm not going so far as to say I'm clairvoyant or anything like that, but that's exactly what happened that afternoon.

EIGHTEEN

We made it to Somes Bar in record time. Janet drove the ninety-eight miles as though she was trying to outrun a tornado that was hot on our tail. Twice, I reached down to make sure my seatbelt was securely fastened. At one point, I said, "You weren't kidding when you told Buster this sporty little car could scoot."

"I never lie about Jassa."

"You named your car Jassa?" I asked, and Janet nodded. "Any particular reason you gave her that name?"

"Jack and I were living in Fayetteville, North Carolina, when I bought this car. Jack had been offered a job in upper management with Miller Lite and that's when we moved away from Shawnee, Kansas. Lexie had moved to Rockdale, Missouri, a month earlier. Jack ended up retiring a couple of years later, and that's when we became full-time RVers like you and Rip."

"Rip told me all that after discussing it with Jack. But that doesn't explain why you named this car Jassa."

"I named her after the Carolina Jessamine Vine, which has bright yellow blossoms that have a heavenly scent. We had a bunch of it in our yard there in Fayetteville." She removed a scented wax cross hanging from her rearview mirror and handed it to me. "This is what Carolina Jessamine Vine smells like."

I was about to say the scent truly was heavenly when Janet swerved Jassa into oncoming traffic. A delivery van swerved the opposite direction and missed us by no more than seven hairs, and fine hairs at that. The Amazon employee driving the van would undoubtedly have to stop at a gas station and change his skivvies after the close call. I was glad I'd just used the restroom at Wal-Mart before we left the store. Janet, on the other hand, looked as cool as a cave in August. *Near-death experiences behind the wheel must be the norm for her*, I thought. *Note to self: offer to drive on the return trip to Klamath.*

"Whoa! That was close!" I exclaimed as soon as I could speak again. "Why'd you swerve so suddenly?"

"Didn't you see that Monarch butterfly about to commit hara-kiri on our windshield? Butterflies are so critical to the survival of our planet."

"Not having a head-on collision with a delivery van is pretty important too. Is it critical enough to save a single Monarch to warrant possibly killing three people? A Monarch's life span is typically no more than a couple of months to begin with." I hadn't wanted to show disapproval, but I hated to see Janet kill herself and maybe numerous others in order to grant a butterfly a few extra weeks of life.

"You're right, Rapella. I hadn't thought of it that way. I promise I won't ever do that again."

"I'll hold you to that promise. I adore you, girl. I don't want to lose you in such an unnecessary way. I have noticed you never touch your phone while driving, even if it's 'blowing up,' as they say. Kudos for that, my friend." I wanted to lighten the tense atmosphere that was now permeating inside Jassa, so I added a humorous anecdote. "I recall the first time someone said something about the possibility of Rip's phone blowing up. He snatched the Samsung Galaxy out of his back pocket and quickly set it down on a table. He'd thought they meant it might have a defect that would make 'blowing up' a literal term rather than a figurative one."

My story worked. Janet found it amusing, and harmony was restored inside the Veloster. I noticed Janet knocked about ten miles an hour off her speed for the remainder of our journey.

It wasn't difficult to spot Wilson's home once we arrived in Somes Bar. It stood out like a bright red hat in a black-and-white portrait. Not because of the color, mind you, but because of its vulgar size compared to all the other homes in the area. I was afraid being able to talk to Wilson would be like getting an audience with the Pope. But it turned out to be much easier than I thought.

We pushed the doorbell at least a dozen times. Dejected, we finally turned to walk back to the car. In retrospect, it would've been a lot less traumatic had we just rang the doorbell and left when no one responded to it. But that's just not the way I roll.

We took no more than three steps toward the car when we heard a scream for help coming from inside the house. Without hesitating, I tried the doorknob and found it unlocked. Janet looked at me in terror. "You can wait in the car, Janet, but I'm going inside. I just can't ignore a scream for help, no matter whom it is that needs it. I'm nearly positive that scream belongs to Wilson, and that it sounds like he needs rescuing. With that trimalleolar ankle fracture, there's no way he can get around under his own power."

She shrugged her shoulders and sighed in a resigned fashion. She then followed me into the house. "I wish we had a weapon. Someone could be threatening Wilson."

"That's actually what I'm hoping for."

Now Janet looked at me as if I'd just told her I wouldn't be happy unless a dozen gun-wielding maniacs were inside looking for an excuse to open fire. "At least we'd have a pretty clear idea who killed Henry, if he or she was now threatening to harm his older brother. Relax. Janet, I have a weapon in my front pocket."

She glanced at my pockets as if expecting to see a Bushmaster machine gun sticking out of one of them, or a flamethrower at the very least. I yanked out the pink Jolt Mini stun gun I often carried in my front pocket and showed it to her.

"That's it? That's your weapon? A taser?" Janet asked in disbelief. She shrugged her shoulders and sighed again. Being a Catholic, I'm sure she was throwing up a slew of Hail Marys too. "Whatever. Let's keep going."

We could hear a commotion going on in the adjacent room. We snuck up to the arched log opening into the living room. Wilson was sitting on a padded chair with his splinted leg resting on an ottoman in front of him. Stan Ledge was pointing a nine-millimeter Glock at him. With Janet tailing me closely, like a shadow, I walked into the room, stunned to see the slightly-built man and asked, "Stan, what are you doing? You know you don't want to do this. Please put down your gun before you do something you'll regret for the rest of your life."

"She's right, Stan," Wilson said in a ragged voice. "Listen to her. Even if she's just a woman, she's right about you regretting it if you shoot me."

Even with Stan pointing a gun at an innocent man, I liked him more than Wilson. I was tempted to shoot Wilson with my stun gun just to shut him up. And, I'll admit, just for the pure joy of it. Instead, I turned to the injured man and said, "You stay out of this and let me handle it."

I heard Janet gasp as both men's eyes opened wide like hoot owls that had just heard lizards scurry past them. Stan now appeared to consider me a bigger threat than the man he'd come to kill. He turned his Glock my way. His hand was shaking like aspen leaves in a breeze as he tried to keep the gun trained on me. "You're the one who needs to stay out of this, Rapella. You don't realize how desperately I need the Del Norte team to win the competition on Saturday. I don't want to have to kill anyone, but if I don't get that money, it'll be me who gets executed. Without Wilson on the Siskiyou County team, our team would be a shoo-in."

"I guess you think since you've already killed Wilson's brother, killing Wilson too won't make much difference. After all, what's one more life sentence? Or, actually, three more because then you'd have to murder me and Janet, as well, because we'd be witnesses to your crime. At that point, the judge would probably just opt to give you the needle."

Wilson started to show off his knowledge of California's capital punishment laws by saying, "Not in California. They halted executions in 2019 because—"

"You're not helping matters," I said, interrupting the lawyer. Without taking my eyes off Stan, I asked Wilson, "Could you kindly zip it for now while I try to convince Stan not to shoot your ass?"

Wilson's lips stopped flapping instantly. I resumed my plea to Stan to spare the man's life. "Besides, I doubt the bookie's goon will kill you, Stan. At least, it's not likely when you owe him a bunch of dough. You can't get money out of a dead guy any easier than you can get a hot cocoa stain out of white linen."

"I didn't kill Henry!" Stan said adamantly. "I had nothing to do with his death."

"Considering you had a gun pointed at the only other threat to our Del Norte quartet three-peating this year when Janet and I walked in the room, I find that difficult to believe," I said.

Wilson was now as quiet as a mime and Janet was doing her damnedest to maintain a low profile behind me. She stood so motionlessly a person would have to look twice to realize she wasn't part of the room's décor. I heard her whisper, "Do you think it's wise to provoke him?"

I could tell Stan's hand was trembling even more than it had been previously. I wasn't sure if it was because I was having an effect on him, the emaciated fellow's arm was getting weak from holding the heavy pistol for so long, or he was scared out of his skull.

"I swear to you I had nothing to do with Henry's death." Stan's declaration was said so passionately I was tempted to believe him. That temptation vanished like an apparition when Stan's Glock went off and shattered an abhorrent blue vase on the table beside me. The vase was so outdated I had to wonder if it was an old family heirloom Wilson had inherited from his grandmother. *I'm thankful you sing much better than you shoot,* I wanted to say, but knew Janet had been right about not antagonizing him. Even though he was too far away for me to hit, I reached for my taser and pointed it at Stan just as he shouted, "I'm sorry, Rapella. My hand was shaking so bad the gun went off by accident. I never meant to pull the trigger. I swear I didn't. And I swear to you I didn't kill Henry. Despite the fact I'm diabetic, I got so drunk that night I couldn't have done anything to him if I'd wanted to."

It was clear Stan was appalled at his own actions. His reaction told me all I needed to know. He could not have intentionally shot me any more than he could've shot Wilson, or even killed Henry, for that matter. Nor did I believe he had the size and strength to maneuver a man like Henry over a balcony railing. Stan hadn't even had the strength to hold the handgun steady. I was convinced despite how desperate he was to pay off his gambling debt, he was not a killer. "Stan, could you please lower your gun before you actually *do* hurt someone?"

"Yes, ma'am." Stan lowered the Glock to his side.

In turn, I lowered my stun gun. To be clear, I'd never once attempted to employ the Jolt Mini stun gun, so had absolutely zero practice with it. When I'd purchased it at a gun show, Rip had told me the only person I was ever apt to stun with my new weapon was me. I'd soon prove him wrong. "So, Stan, if you didn't kill Henry, who did?"

"I did!" Those two words echoed throughout the expansive room as Amanda Castonova walked into the room brandishing a knife. It was large and scary looking, like the kind you'd gut a Tule elk with before you field-dressed it. My first thought was to ask her if she'd heard the saying about taking a knife to a gunfight. My second thought was that her Bowie knife would kill me a lot faster than my taser could have any effect whatsoever on her from the distance we currently were from each other. The only exit was behind Amanda. The chances of getting past her unscathed were slim to none. And the remaining four of us in the room taking her down in a gang tackle was not going to happen either. Wilson couldn't support his own weight with the broken ankle, Stan was clearly incapable of firing the Glock that hung down beside his left hip in a trembling hand, and Janet had turned into a pillar of salt behind me. So I remained quiet and listened to Amanda's ranting instead.

I had hoped Stan would make Amanda back down by pointing his Glock at her. I wasn't surprised when he didn't. Stan appeared to be as frozen in place as my petrified sidekick, Janet. The Glock was still in his left hand, hanging by his side. It was hidden from Amanda's view, and I was afraid if I said anything to him, she'd race over and slice him from ear to ear to keep him from utilizing it. It'd be like carving a block of ice because Stan still seemed unable to move a single muscle.

Knowing I was too far away from Amanda for my taser to stop her. I kept the stun gun next to my side, out of the knife-wielding woman's sight, just in case I got the opportunity to use it. Stan, Wilson, Janet, and I all remained quiet while Amanda raged. "And now I'm going to take out all of you too and stage it to look like a mass murder, followed by a suicide. I deserve Aunt Amie's money a lot more than her two sons ever did. You, Wilson, even claimed to be too busy to take her to Trinidad. With you gone, I'm sure she'll leave her entire estate to me."

"Did you kill your cousin Henry?" I asked her, trying to sound as compliable as possible. I was trying to stall for time, in no hurry for Amanda to turn Wilson's living room into a blood bath.

"I already told you I did. I may seem like an airhead to you, but I'm smart enough to know I was never going to build my dream home on a waitress's salary. With Aunt Amie's two sons gone, I'd stand to be her sole heir. And I deserve to be!"

"How'd you get hold of the Flunitrazepam you used to kill Henry?" I asked.

"You'd be surprised what people leave behind in restaurants."

"Were you in Sacramento the night of Wilson's bachelor party?" I was slowly creeping toward Stan as Amanda and I conversed. Stan had yet to flinch. He was literally scared stiff and appeared to have forgotten he was even carrying a gun.

"Duh," Amanda replied rudely. "I disguised myself as a barmaid, and when Henry got up to dance on a table, I spiked his drink and quickly left the nightclub. I'd booked the hotel room next to his and Devin Tubbs and waited there for them to return from the club. It was just a stroke of luck that Devin went down to the front desk shortly after they got back to their hotel room."

"I suppose you would've killed Devin too if he hadn't gone down to report the clogged-up toilet. He'd have just been collateral damage as a result of your greed." When Amanda refused to respond, I asked, "Was Henry dead from the combination of alcohol and the date rape drug when you found him in his room?"

As I was speaking, I was inching my way closer to Stan. He was still frozen in time. Wilson's mouth had not become unzipped, and Janet might as well have been a coat rack in the corner of the room.

"No, but like a hypnotist who'd put Henry in a trance, I had total control over him. I got him to walk with me out to the balcony. Then, when he leaned over the railing to barf, I grabbed him from behind and hoisted him up over the railing." The self-satisfaction in her voice was nauseating. It made me realize my ability to judge people was so pathetic it was almost non-existent. I couldn't have judged this woman any more erroneously than I had.

"You seemed like such a sweet gal. I can't believe you'd do such a thing, Amanda." She was the last person I could've ever imagined would do something so heinous. I doubted my own instincts all of a sudden, which was something I almost never did. *My judge of character was so off-base; I could've easily been one of Ted Bundy's victims had he ever approached me during the serial killer's reign of terror,* I thought, as I took another small step forward. Because I was closing in on Stan instead of her, Amanda did not seem threatened by my movement.

"Remember when your husband asked me how I planned to pay for my dream home overlooking Mad River and I said, 'Where there's a will, there's a way?'" Amanda asked. "Well, I just explained the 'way' to you and it was to try and manipulate Aunt Amie's will by eliminating her undeserving sons."

She then began to tear Wilson a new one with her tongue lashing, pointing out all the ways she'd treated his mother better than he ever had. I knew that with her distracted, this was likely the only chance I was going to get to do something proactive. Amanda was still too far away to stun with my taser. An attempt to take her down in that way was more apt to make her rip her gnarly knife across my throat than for me to thwart her deadly plans. Then, with me dead, she'd quickly eliminate the other three people in the room. I had devised another option and sent up a quick prayer that it was successful.

I'd been inching closer to Stan the entire time Amanda and I had been conversing. I knew I'd have to react quickly, so I steeled myself for my grand attempt to eliminate the present threat. Not wanting a bullet meant for me to strike Janet, who was still standing behind me, I then whispered to her to duck. I simultaneously aimed my taser at Stan and fired. He fell to the ground like that gut-shot deer I'd mentioned earlier. Like I'd hoped would happen, his Glock fell to the floor as he crumpled down beside it. I dove on the handgun like Derek Jeter diving for a ground ball. As I came up with the Glock, I aimed it at Amanda. "Drop that knife right now, or I'll drop you faster than I just dropped Stan."

When she hesitated, I fired a shot above her head and took out a chandelier that looked as out of place in a log home as a rodeo clown would look at a bridal shower. I heard Wilson gasp in alarm as though the gaudy light fixture had been his pride and joy. I ignored him and warned Amanda, "The next bullet has your name on it."

The stunned waitress quickly set the knife down by her feet. I insisted she shove it toward me. I didn't want it anywhere near her in the event chaos erupted, even more than it just had. "Janet, call 9-1-1 and tell them we're holding Henry Harpodingle's killer at gunpoint until they arrive, and then make sure Stan is all right."

"I'm on it, partner," she replied with a long-winded sigh of relief.

I then glanced at Stan for a second and said, "Sorry, Stan. It was the only plan I could come up with to take control over Amanda. If you promise never to aim a gun at anyone again, and leave Wilson alone, I promise I won't tell the police officers what you threatened to do to him. Nor will I mention your misfired shot that took out Wilson's archaic vase. It needed to be removed, anyway."

I turned to Wilson and said, "You don't need to thank me for saving you, but I would appreciate it if you didn't mention any of this to the police officers who should be arriving any moment. Amanda will undoubtedly be claiming innocence so I doubt she says anything about what went on in here. It would be to her advantage to take the fifth and refuse to speak at all."

Amanda gazed at me with terror in her eyes and nodded. Wilson looked at me as if he was Moses and I was the Pharaoh's daughter, Exodus, who'd rescued him from the Nile River. I felt confident he'd do whatever I asked of him after saving his life. Stan looked at me with heartfelt gratitude. And Janet looked at me as if just realizing her new friend was nuttier than a Snickers bar.

Stan walked over and hugged me while I kept his Glock trained on Amanda. "Thank you, Rapella, for everything, including stunning me with your taser in order to save all of our lives. I don't know what came over me. I'm just so terrified about not being able to pay off my bookie."

"I'm betting the Del Norte barbershop quartet team is going to win on Saturday and your problems will be all behind you. Until next year, at least. You beat Wilson's team two years in a row with Henry singing tenor. Now you have Rip on your team, making Del Norte's barbershop quartet even stronger."

"I never thought about it that way. You're absolutely right, Rapella." Stan spoke as he struggled to get to his feet. He looked relieved and a bit unsteady from having been tagged by a stun gun. "And, believe me, after this, I'm never placing another bet again. I've definitely learned my lesson this time."

"For your sake, Stan, I sure hope so."

"Listen, Rapella." Stan was speaking softly so no one else in the room could hear him but me. He looked nervous, as if he was preparing to ask me something important, such as whether or not I'd mind donating a kidney to him. "Is there any way we can keep what happened today just between the two of us? It would be hard to face the rest of the quartet members if they found out what I did."

"I'd have it no other way, Stan. I don't particularly want Rip to know I was here, either. So if you promise you won't mention it to anyone, I promise I won't either. And Wilson's probably too proud to tell anyone he had to be rescued by someone who's 'just a woman.'"

As we waited for the cops to arrive, I spoke directly to Amanda. I'd made her sit cross-legged on the floor. "Fun fact: Janet and I spoke to your Aunt Amie at Wal-Mart earlier today, and she told us she planned to change her will tomorrow and make you her sole beneficiary. This little stunt you pulled today was totally unnecessary."

Amanda's expression was priceless. If not for the circumstances, I would've snapped a photo of her with my phone.

"She did what?" Wilson asked, speaking for the first time since I'd told him to zip it.

"As Amanda said as she was rattling your cage, your mom told Janet and me Amanda did more for her than you or Henry ever had. She feared leaving all of her money to you would just cause you to become more of a jackass than you already are."

"Mom called me a jackass?" Wilson looked as if I'd thrown the hideous vase out his window before Stan could blow it to bits with his gun. "Actually, it was me who called you a jackass. Your mom called you a jerk but agreed jackass was an apt description too."

"But, but, but…." Wilson was so surprised he couldn't form a full sentence. He was almost as speechless as Amanda, who'd just learned she'd crapped in her own Easter basket. Now, instead of living in her dream house overlooking the Mad River, she'd be going up a totally different kind of river, and her living quarters would be more like a nightmare than a dream.

"You do realize your mother is most likely dying, don't you, Wilson?" I asked the attorney. "It wouldn't hurt you to treat her with a little compassion and love. Pamper her, do whatever she asks you to do. After all, you have the rest of your life to chase ambulances. The woman who birthed and raised you has maybe a week or two left to do whatever she chooses to do. I think it'd mean a lot to her to spend that time with her only remaining child."

I glared at Amanda and added, "Thanks to you!"

Amanda had the decency to look ashamed. Wilson then explained that a construction crew would be working at his log home for the next couple of weeks and he didn't want to leave them alone in his house. A broken pipe in an upstairs bathroom had recently flooded out the entire top floor and caused a lot of damage on the main floor as well, he said. His broken ankle was going to make it even harder for him to attend to his mother's wishes. As opposed to Amanda, Wilson looked completely shameless as he spoke. His callous remarks and attitude certainly didn't endear me to him, but it did explain where he'd gotten the huge insurance payout he'd used to buy his expensive new sports car. The idea that he would now likely be his mother's sole heir made me sick to my stomach.

Two police officers arrived within minutes, as if they'd been waiting in the building's parking lot, hoping for a call from dispatch to go inside and arrest a murderer. I made certain to tell the officers Janet and I did not want our names listed in the paper, or even the police report, if at all possible. We preferred to remain anonymous for our own safety. They told us it went against their policy, but they'd do what they could to keep us out of it. The two rookies admitted they'd been joking and laughing when the gunshots went off, failing to recognize them for what they were. They seemed happy to leave big parts of the story omitted from their report. I had left most of the details of what had occurred out of the statement I'd provided them with to begin with.

Janet and I agreed to never tell another living soul about our involvement in Henry's murder case. Our snooping had not exactly "solved" the case, but it had put us in the right place at the right time. I didn't need accolades or awards. The contentment I felt for being instrumental in discovering who was behind Henry's death and helping prevent the murder of several other people was reward enough. I wished I'd discovered the killer was anyone but Amanda, but if unfulfilled wishes were golden nuggets, we'd all be zillionaires.

Once the policemen had Amanda cuffed, Stan told me he was glad I didn't have to take another shot with his Glock after I'd shattered the chandelier. I asked for a clarification.

"The gun only had two bullets in it when I arrived. Those two bullets killed a vase and a light fixture. There was no firepower left to kill Amanda had she attacked you with her knife."

I smiled and replied, "I'm glad to just be finding this out now. Had I known I was pointing an empty gun at Amanda, I might not have been able to come up with as much bravado, or balls, as my husband would say."

"Something tells me you would've found a way, despite having no bullets in the gun," Stan said. "Again, I appreciate your kindness more than I can say."

"And I appreciate you, Stan, for promising to never mention any of this to Rip. Or at least never mention my name, or Janet's, when you discuss it around him."

"You've got a deal, Rapella," Stan said, with a touch of relief in his voice.

Janet put her arm around me then and said, "Good work, buddy. You knew Wilson's life was also in danger when we left Wal-Mart, didn't you?"

"I couldn't be certain, of course, but I began thinking about a few of the things Amanda had said and had a feeling she was more apt to kill someone for monetary gain than anyone on our suspect list. She'd even assured me that when there's a will, there's a way. So when I walked into the room and saw Stan pointing his Glock at Wilson, I was beyond shocked. I was truly gob-smacked. He was the last person I expected to see threatening Wilson's life.

"Me too," Janet agreed. "All this time I felt sure the killer would turn out to be either Buster or his wife, Clara."

By the time the cops had arrested Amanda and hauled her off to the station, we were running late. I encouraged Janet to push the limit driving home.

"Before, you wanted me to slow down, and now you're asking me to drive as fast as I reasonably can?"

"Yes. That pretty much sums it up."

"Okie-dokie, Pokie. Buckle up and hang on!"

We got home about ten minutes before Rip and Jack. They had no clue we'd been gone all day. Although they hadn't managed to get any fish in the boat, they both had stories about a whopper that got away. The huge king salmon Jack had hooked broke all the tackle off his line about halfway to the boat. I wanted to ask him if he'd snuck a banana into his lunch bag, but I knew the pain of losing a huge fish was still fresh, so I refrained. According to Rip's fish story, his steelhead trout was almost in the net when the fish spit the hook out and sped away. It was enough to make both men determined to return for another shot at the trophy trout. They had booked another fishing trip for Sunday, the day after the singing competition. Rip said, "We're going to have a fish fry if it takes Jack and me a dozen fishing trips to accomplish it."

Janet whispered to me that while they were fishing, she actually would like to take me to the cute little shop in Eureka she had discovered. I agreed wholeheartedly.

Later that evening, as Rip and I relaxed in lawn chairs outside our trailer, Rip remarked, "This stay in Mystic River RV Park has been so relaxing and peaceful, hasn't it, Rapella?"

It depends on how you describe relaxing and peaceful, I thought. *I can't believe I was able to pull off this entire investigation without you ever having a clue I'd "butted into" another murder case I had no business being involved in.* To Rip, I replied, "Yes, it's been almost unbelievable."

No lie there! I was determined that the rest of our stay in northern California was peaceful and relaxing, even if I had to wear blinders and earplugs every time I left the fifth wheel.

NINETEEN

The next day, Saturday, May 14th, the Del Norte Barbershop quartet team walked away with trophies and large checks. We'd arrived just in time for the competition to begin because Rip had forgotten to set the alarm clock and we'd both overslept. Wilson Harpodingle sang with the Siskiyou County team in a wheelchair and helped his team win second-place trophies and five-hundred-dollar gift cards to the local grocery store chain that sponsored the annual contest. I was amused when the injured man refused to make eye contact with me until I walked up behind him and asked him how he was doing.

"Hello, Rapella," he replied. "My ankle is doing well but I'm embarrassed by the way I spoke to you. Thank you for coming to my rescue. I want you to know I will be staying with my mom until the work on my home is finished. I realized that time spent with her was way more valuable than anything a person could steal out of my house."

"I'm glad to hear that, Wilson. And, after all, that is why God created insurance, isn't it?"

The lawyer laughed and I joined in. I patted his shoulder and said, "I hope you recover quickly. I just saw your mom watching the competition from a lawn chair near the stage. I want to go give her a hug as we will be heading east soon."

"She would love that," he replied warmly. "Thanks again Rapella. I promise I will never say anything to anyone that'll expose your involvement in my brother's death. I do miss him terribly. I've tried to look tough about losing him, but now with my mom likely to pass soon, I will be the last remaining member of my immediate family. It's starting to hit me hard."

"What about Lu Ann?" I asked. "Do you see a future with her? I know your mom adores her."

"As do I. I asked her to marry me just as soon as my ankle heals and I can walk her down the aisle with my own two feet."

"Congratulations, Wilson," I said sincerely. "I wish you nothing but the best with your new bride."

"Thanks again. For everything."

After chatting with Amie, I noticed Wilson and Stan exchange a few words and then shake hands. That led me to believe the two had mended fences and come to a mutual understanding about what had occurred the previous day. I'd hoped Wilson would not have Stan charged with threatening to kill him. I'm sure he realized Stan could've never pulled the trigger, just as I'd realized it at the time the situation was occurring.

Stan was so relieved he'd be able to pay off his gambling debt he was almost giddy. I watched him roll the dice on a diabetic coma and polish off a massive cinnamon roll with great abandon. I was happy for him and prayed the harrowing experience had truly made him see the light and that he'd never gamble again.

Rip's share of the purse would be deposited in our savings account. We both felt content knowing we'd begun to build up our nest egg again. Charlie would book a romantic cruise for him and Fern to take as a second honeymoon of sorts. Buster said he was going to buy a new cable for his tow truck and a dozen roses for the waitress who refilled his coffee cup numerous times every morning. *No wonder he was spending so much time at the Daily Grind*, I thought with amusement. *I hope it works out for him and his new flame.*

"Did you hear they arrested Henry's killer?" I asked Rip later. I was testing the waters, unsure of how much Rip knew about my part in the arrest.

"Stan mentioned to me that the murderer had been arrested. Charlie had told me a while back that Henry was a womanizer, but his affairs only lasted a short while before he moved onto another woman. When Stan mentioned something today about a young woman pushing Henry off the balcony, I assumed it was one of the women he'd had a fling with, only to dump her shortly afterward."

"I'm sure you're right, which comes as no big surprise," I said.

"Stan was pretty vague about the details of the arrest, but I was just glad to hear the truth behind Henry's death had been determined," Rip said. "Stan also said he'd heard on the news that two anonymous women were involved in the takedown. I'm just relieved one of them wasn't you."

"Yes, well, I'm surprised you all didn't discuss the arrest in more detail." I couldn't believe he was not more curious about who the murderer had been. Rip's lack of curiosity stunned me at times. And I was shocked the quartet didn't discuss the news of an arrest in Henry's death in more depth. I guess their determination to pocket a nice check had them laser-focused on the singing contest.

"We didn't have time to discuss it before the contest because I arrived late, and then you and I left as soon as the awards were given out. I thanked the other three for including me on their barbershop quartet team and told them we needed to get packed up and ready to head east soon. The other quartet members probably discussed the arrest in great length before I arrived. But that's fine with me. I'm just glad the case was solved. I don't care all that much about the details."

We'd be leaving town in a few days, and I prayed Rip would

never crave any details about the killer, or how her identity had been discovered.

Rip decided to attend the Ripple family reunion in mid-June. It was held annually in Fort Kent, Maine, the state's most northern town. The coast-to-coast drive was over 3,400 miles in length and we planned to make a few stops along the way, including the RV dealership in Denver where we'd purchased our new fifth wheel.

Before Rip and I left the campground on May thirty-first to head east, we walked over to Jack and Janet's motorhome. Hugs were exchanged by all. Rip and I told them we hoped to meet up with them one day soon at the Alexandria Inn in Rockdale, Missouri. Janet said she was eager to meet up with her old friend, Lexie, and her new friend, Rapella, at the inn. The bed and breakfast was owned and operated by Lexie Starr and her husband, Stone Van Patten, and at Rip's suggestion, they'd added a number of RV sites on their property. It'd been a wise decision on Stone's part, as the full-hookup sites had been booked frequently ever since.

"Thanks for being my sidekick, Janet," I whispered into my new friend's ear. "I couldn't have done it without you."

"I loved every moment of it," she whispered back. "Except for those moments I thought I was about to be shot or sliced up like a honey-baked ham because you were antagonizing the two people threatening to kill us."

"I'm sorry, but there was a method to my madness. And, lucky for us, that method was successful."

"It sure was, Rapella. It worked out perfectly and we're still here to talk about it." Janet took note of my expression and added, "But only to each other, of course. I'll never mention a word about it to another living soul, including Jack. He would be livid I'd gotten involved in the dangerous situation with you. To be honest, I'm not sure amateur sleuthing is something I want to make a habit of anyway. I think I'll leave solving murder cases to you and Lexie. I've learned it requires a certain degree of craziness I don't possess. But I do hope we'll remain friends forever."

"We will," I said. "It's a promise. We'll be in touch and arrange a get-together at Alexandria Inn this coming fall. Does that sound like a plan to you?"

"Absolutely, my friend! You two take care of yourselves, and each other, in the meantime."

"You and Jack do the same."

After I gave Janet another long hug, Rip and I returned to our campsite. We packed up the fifth wheel trailer and unattached the sewer and water hoses, along with the electrical cord. The only thing left was to pull out onto Highway 101 and begin the long journey to Fort Kent.

Discovering small issues with a new RV was normal, and ours was no exception. We had a kitchen drawer that was nearly impossible to open or close, a window that was leaking due to a missing seal, and an awning that would only extend about half as far as it should have, along with a few other minor issues covered by the manufacturer's warranty. We planned to stay in a hotel for a couple of nights while the repairs were completed at the RV dealership in Denver where we'd purchased the fifth wheel.

As we pulled up to the large RV lot, I saw the Chartreuse Caboose parked on a platform next to the entrance gate. I was excited and said, "Look Rip! They're using the Caboose to bring in new business."

"They certainly are, Rapella. Now read the big sign next to the Caboose."

DON'T BE EMBARRASSED TO BE SEEN DRIVING AN UGLY RV AROUND THE COUNTRY. STOP IN NOW AND CHECK OUT THE LOW PRICES ON OUR AMAZING INVENTORY OF NEW AND GENTLY-USED UNITS, the sign read.

Although I still had sentimental feelings for the Chartreuse Caboose, I was enjoying all of the fancy-schmancy amenities our new rig had that the Caboose didn't. Rip was chuckling at the sign, so I joined in. "I guess the Caboose is kind of an eyesore, as Regina always called it."

"Kind of?" Rip asked. "Take another look, Rapella."

Searching the internet a few months later, while parked in an RV park in Conway, New Hampshire, I read that Amanda had received a life sentence for first-degree murder and would spend the remainder of her days as a guest of the California Department of Corrections. She was housed at the women's facility in Chowchilla, California, where all of the female death row prisoners were held, even though, as Wilson had said, executions in the state had been halted several years prior. I'd found the information in an issue of the Del Norte Triplicate, which I'd taken up reading on a regular basis. Like Buster, I read it while drinking coffee every morning.

In one edition of the Triplicate, I'd discovered Amie had passed away with liver cancer two weeks after we left California. The article stated she had left half of her estate to her son Wilson, and the rest to the pet rescue charity she'd donated all of her paychecks to the last few years of her life. Now one of the wealthiest pet rescue charities in the country, it was renamed the Harpodingle Pet Adoption Center. The ten cats she left behind inhabited their very own wing in the center. They were extremely well cared for and would be for the remainder of their lives. When other unadoptable cats showed up at the center in future years, they would be welcomed into that wing and given forever homes there, just as Amie would've done if she were still alive.

I found myself happy for Wilson. He was already wealthy and should just be thankful he was still alive. If not for me, he probably wouldn't be. But I'd seen the wounded look in his eyes when I'd told him his mother had called him a jerk and then agreed with me that jackass was an appropriate description as well. My mind drifted back to that Thursday. *Talk about a bad day*, I thought. *How many people have had two individuals show up at their home at the same time with the intention of killing them?*

Another edition of the Triplicate had a front-page article with the headline, "Local winery owner busted in South Carolina sting operation." The reporter wrote that an Anthony Crossing from Klamath had been arrested in Myrtle Beach, South Carolina, for selling bootleg liquor. In this case, it was red wine mixed equally with 190-proof pure grain alcohol, or rectified spirit, which has been making memories and erasing memories since 1950. The potentially lethal result was illegally packaged as Moose Crossing Chardonnay. From the article, I learned a 750-milliliter bottle of the Chardonnay sells for sixty dollars. Moose was able to pick up ten thousand dollars worth of the grain alcohol for seven bucks a bottle. He quickly figured out he could significantly increase his profit margin by mixing wine with the clear, tasteless grain alcohol, which is now banned in California and ten other states because of its potency.

When Moose discovered the Del Norte sheriff's office was on to him, he'd listed the winery and vineyard with David L. Colmer, the Remax realtor, and returned to his original hometown, taking his booze with him. He was selling the "Chardonnay" through high-end bars in Myrtle Beach when he was arrested and extradited back to California to face charges. That explained why Amie's friend Sammi found men loading the bottles up in a truck when she stopped by the winery after he'd fled the state. It also explained why, after two large glasses of Moose's powerful concoction, I'd fallen over like a fainting goat in front of all the mourners at Henry's celebration of life. I felt fortunate now I hadn't died of alcohol poisoning that night, because explaining that to Rip would've been a real bitch.

A couple of years later, while we were eating brisket sandwiches and very tasty French fries at a small café, Rip would say, "I wonder if that waitress at the café in Crater Lake National Park ever found a way to build her dream home on the Mad River."

"I bet she did," I would reply. "Like she told us, where there's a will, there's a way." I didn't tell Rip I'd used that same philosophy to ensure Amanda's dream home turned out to be an eight-by-ten concrete cell.

ABOUT THE AUTHOR

Jeanne Glidewell lives with her husband, Bob, in the small coastal town of Rockport, Texas, on Salt Lake, just off Copano Bay.

Besides writing, Jeanne enjoys fishing, wildlife photography, and traveling both here and abroad. She and Bob recently enjoyed an East Coast vacation with friends, Barb and Rusty Harrison. Among other things, they rode on four historic railroads, took a cruise on Lake Winnipesaukee aboard the M/S Mt. Washington, and marveled at the vivid fall foliage in Massachusetts, New Hampshire, and Maine. It was on this trip Jeanne suffered a trimalleolar fracture of the right ankle, an injury she elaborates on later in her *Rip Chord* tale.

As a 2006 pancreas and kidney transplant recipient, Jeanne is an avid advocate for organ and tissue donation. Please consider the possibility of giving the gift of life by opting to be an organ donor when you no longer need them.

Jeanne is the author of a romance/suspense novel, Soul Survivor, seven novels and one novella in her NY Times best-selling Lexie Starr cozy mystery series, and nine novels in her Ripple Effect cozy mystery series. She's currently writing Ripple Effect book ten titled *Letter Rip* and expects to have it released in the spring of 2025.

www.JeanneGlidewell.com